Tweet Revenge

A Dawn Johnson Mystery

Rickard B DeMille

MacDonald, Barclay & Co., Little Elm, TX

Chapter 1

Sunday Night
Denton County, Texas

The killer, known simply as Justice, slowed the faded blue
Ford and checked his rearview mirrors. Alone, he turned off the
headlights and pulled onto a deserted dirt road. He didn't want to
get ahead of himself, but he couldn't help smiling. He had been
looking forward to this night for quite a while.

The low, scrub oak trees hid his car from curious eyes, but
allowed an almost full moon to light the narrow track ahead. At
barely more than a crawl, he rolled silently forward to where a
foot path crossed in front of him and led off to his right.

Justice stopped and turned off the car. He picked up the
disposable burner phone he would use for tonight and turned it
on. Moments later, the phone's screen blinked reluctantly to life.
He tapped the email icon and waited for new messages to
download.

He swore to himself as he scanned his list of new followers.
Idiots!

He had almost three-dozen new fans, but not one who mattered. He would check them all out later, but he didn't recognize any of the names or profiles.

They really need to hurry. I'm running out of people to kill.

So, Plan B would begin tonight. Since the cops hadn't bothered to look for him, he would start looking for them. If that didn't work, maybe he'd just give the relevant law enforcement agency a call and invite them personally to attend his next murder. He could pull that off, if he had to.

Justice opened the door and got out. No lights came on; all of his interior bulbs had been removed. He slid the phone into his pocket, and then reached back inside and retrieved a small black backpack. He closed the door and turned to face the path toward victim number three.

Before his first execution, he'd worried about getting caught – but not anymore. He'd also worried about the morality of his mission, that purging his list of scumbags from the gene pool might make create an ethical dilemma for him. Fortunately, bringing justice to those who'd escaped it in court became very easy, very fast.

Social media, he realized, would always be his biggest problem, but one he was learning to deal with.

Oh, well! A man has to do what a man has to do.

He raised his left wrist and clicked the stopwatch feature into life. Twenty minutes to do the deed, in and out. Smiling, Justice disappeared silently into the trees and entered the city limits of Denton, Texas.

The requirements of Justice were simple tonight. He had to walk through the woods, break into an apartment, and cross another name off his "To Die List."

Chapter 2

Sunday Night
South Dallas

Dawn Johnson exited I-35 South, and turned left on MLK Boulevard. At the traffic light, her worn-out old car swayed to a reluctant stop. This wasn't the shortest way to Fair Park, or the fastest, but it had been *their* way. Now it was just her way, and that broke her heart. She cranked up the stereo and cranked down the window, venting exhaust fumes and Randy Travis from her junker. The stoplight overhead turned green, and she coaxed her ancient Ford Escort precariously forward into the night.

She'd left North Texas when she turned sixteen, and much of Dallas had changed in almost a decade. South Dallas, however, seemed the same. The fresh spring air felt cool against her face. Street lights revealed the old, but well-kept buildings along both sides of the tree-lined road. New foliage shrouded the aged structures in shadow. To her right flashed a little white restaurant, a fried-chicken place they'd always talked about visiting.

Ahead, shadows shrouded a one-story, red-brick church. She had talked her father into visiting there once. Once was incredible. Once was fascinating. Once was enough. She'd been fourteen, a committed YIT (Yuppie in Training), living in the upscale Dallas suburb of Plano with her dad. She had been amazed by the singing, delighted by the swaying and dancing, and captivated by the basso profundo of the silver-haired preacher. It was there that she finally understood that being an African American didn't make her black.

Her memories of those long past days were fading, aided now by the fact that she was trying to forget. This didn't help.

Dawn watched the church slip past and then looked ahead. She could now make out the impressive silhouette of the Texas Star, the giant Ferris wheel that had become a State Fair of Texas landmark. She noted the sliver of moon hiding behind it. This made the wheel look like a black spider-web of steel, holding an orange caterpillar trapped in its delicate strands.

That's how she felt -- trapped. Just because the restraints existed only in her mind, didn't make them any less real.

She shook her head and concentrated on her driving. Live in the present or die in the past.

At the fairgrounds, she turned right onto Cullum. Even in the wee hours of the morning, she found traffic here. This surprised her. But she'd never been in this part of town so late.

Dawn continued on. More blocks rolled past, and Robert B. Cullen Boulevard became Scyene Road. At that same instant, museums and exhibits became food pantries and liquor stores; "old and historic" became "rundown and dangerous."

Dawn stopped for a red light at a well-lit intersection. She picked up the large manila envelope on the passenger's seat and read the address, written in heavy black marker. She made a right and drove two blocks down the poorly lit street. Finally, she turned left into a small, rutted parking lot. An obscenely large neon sign declared that she'd reached the *Class of Dallas Club*, in brilliant red and yellow. The building itself shouted *class dismissed*, in faded grey and green.

Two old men sat on the curb by the parking lot. They stood and smiled as they watched her shudder to a stop, displaying less than seven yellowed teeth between them. The short one took a drink and passed a bottle of something green, to his not-quite-vertical friend. Both stared at Dawn, leering, hoping she would get out.

They pointed at her bumper, and both laughed. She got that a lot. Her "My Other Car Is a Ferrari" bumper sticker looked almost desperate on her once blue Escort.

Dawn waited, hoping they'd get bored and go back to neutralizing brain cells. While she delayed her exit, she pulled a handful of papers from the envelope. The top pages were copies of licensing documents and permits for her destination, going back over a decade. After scanning those, she examined a large, color picture. The broad black face was bisected by a spectacular white smile. Above the smile sparkled deep black eyes. Below the smile, hands held a sign from the Dallas County Jail, showing an impressive string of letters and numbers. She looked at Jamal Haddad, real name James Hastings, who she understood to be the manager of this fine establishment.

Dawn needed to talk with Jamal. However, she also realized that she probably shouldn't. On the other hand, she knew for certain that if she didn't keep going, her life would never be the same.

Or maybe it would be better. Could she live a lie? There was no avoiding that, she realized, it was only a question of which lie to live. Maybe it would be best to start her car back up and choose the easy way, move on with her life.

Again, live in the present or die in the past.

She was dying already, inside, every day. She looked at her worn and faded keychain, where the dingy white unicorn once frolicked happily on its faded blue background. No frolicking now. Now it stomped in frustration, like her.

Dawn opened her tiny bag and dropped the keys inside. They jingled merrily as they bounced off her wallet and the cute little 380-caliber automatic she carried tonight. She opened her door, stooped painfully, and slowly got out. Though normally five-foot-seven, her Afro tonight put her at almost six-feet. Standing stiffly, she stretched and grimaced from the ache in her leg. She hadn't fully recovered from a "job-related incident" that had required weeks of hospital time and months of recuperation. That event, which had actually put her on life support, also meant she had to pull down the hem of her tiny red dress to cover the scar on her thigh. She walked, awkwardly at first, toward the front of the building. Both of her admirers began to shout, but since they were speaking *Cuervo,* she had no idea what they were saying. They apparently thought she was a hooker, which was good.

She reached the entrance, slouched, dropped one shoulder just a little, and sauntered inside. She wrinkled her nose and choked as she crossed the threshold. It was smoky, but not unbearable. She hadn't been in town long enough to know the current smoking ordinances, but it was obvious there were none here. It reminded her of a place in North Las Vegas she'd visited while attending UNLV, only quieter.

Dawn scanned the room with a glance. A long, almost vacant wood bar stood along the wall to her left. It looked old but well-polished. To her right, a couple of loners occupied two of the tables. Also, a dark-skinned waitress in a tight blue mini-skirt took brown bottles to a young couple seated at a third round table. Against the back wall, two rows of three booths fanned out on either side of a wide, doorless hall.

As her eyes adjusted fully, she made out men in two of the booths on the right, neither of them Jamal.

Dawn walked toward a stool at the far end of the bar. She remembered her cover and attempted a strut. It worked. Half way there a skinny, over-served man in his mid-thirties turned away from the bar, sloshing his fresh beer on the counter. He leaned his stool forward and blocked her path by putting a scuffed work boot on the chair in front of her. He gave her a less-than-perfect smile, and then gave her a much less than perfect pickup line.

"Hey, baby, did it hurt?"

She hated that one. She gave him a *you-can't-be-serious* look.

He was at least three beers past picking up on her contempt and continued being a fool.

"You know, when you fell from heaven."

She kicked the nearest leg of his stool. He flew awkwardly into the air, seemed to defy gravity by hovering there, then crashed painfully into the stool to his right. The drunk, the drink, and the two stools landed in a tangled pile behind her. She looked back at him and smirked. "It felt about like *that*."

She watched him carefully to see if he would object to being humiliated by a girl and get up. Instead, he just laid there, head lolling back and forth. He was out, so Dawn continued toward the rear of the bar.

At the next-to-last stool she stopped, and discovered a logistical complication. Her short skirt, plus the tall stool, equaled not worth the effort. She leaned against the bar and scanned the offerings on tap.

She nodded to the slender, bald-headed man behind the bar. "Corona."

She examined the room again. The brief hall in the back led to another narrow, poorly lit hallway running perpendicular to it. An arrow pointing right said "Restrooms." That meant the office and storage must be to the left. A mirror embedded in the wall near the left corner indicated the office would be there. The two-way mirror would let the manager watch the bar in private.

She found nothing else of note, just a typical neighborhood bar. The furnishings appeared to be from the popular "cheap and tasteless" movement of design and décor. She hated it.

What am I doing here?

This was a mistake. There must be other ways of getting the information she needed. Not as fast, but probably safer. She noticed the bartender glaring at her. She looked around again.

And probably more productive.

So, what she needed to do now was to finish her drink, get out of here and start the search somewhere else.

Dawn heard the muffled sound of a glass being set down and turned to look at the bar. A relatively clean glass rested in front of her on a generic white napkin. Behind it, the bar-keep continued to glare. She opened her wallet and pulled out a credit card, which she held out to him. Without a word or change of expression he turned, took a few steps, and then leaned over the bar to look at her sprawling suitor, who had managed to struggle to his stomach.

Dawn put the card away, when the waitress walked over. She snatched up Dawn's drink and napkin, pivoted nimbly, and walked toward the back. The woman went directly to a booth in the left corner, where Jamal had miraculously appeared. Neat trick.

Dawn followed the waitress to the booth and slid in across from Jamal. The waitress set the drink in front of her, snickered, and left. Jamal smiled, and then came right to the point.

"You'll need to finish your drink and leave." He actually sounded polite. "We're very selective in who works this place."

Dawn leaned back. "Maybe I'm not working. Maybe I'm here looking for someone specific. Possibly someone named Bubba? Someone that might have been regular here about five years ago."

Five years ago was when the calls she'd uncovered had been made. Dawn didn't know anyone named Bubba, and hoped Jamal didn't either. Her actual goal was simply to find out who worked at the club when the calls had been made to this fine establishment. The best place to start was with the manager. If Jamal hadn't taken the calls, Dawn hoped he had the names of the person who did.

Jamal appeared to think this over, but like he was calculating the possibilities, not like he was trying to remember. "No one called Bubba has been a regular here since I took over, four and a half years ago. What did he do?"

"It's what he didn't do. Who might know him? Who ran this place back then?"

She'd had a friend pull the license history for the *Class of Dallas*, but that didn't give her what she needed. It had been owned by the same Nevada Corporation, Entertainment Associates, for sixteen years. A quick background of

Entertainment Associates revealed that this holding company had a "home office" in some place called Nevis. She hadn't been sure that Nevis was even a real place, much less where it was. She'd checked. It was real, located in an informational black hole near the West Indies. Bottom line, she had no way of knowing for sure who owned this dump, or actually ran the place at the time in question, without discovering it for herself.

Her host leaned back. "Who's asking?"

"My cousin. He sent me and our friend Ben to ask around." She pulled a hundred-dollar bill from her purse and set it on the table. "If I leave with Bubba's address, or some other way to find him, Ben stays."

Jamal looked at the bill, considering. "What's your cousin's name?"

"Perry"

Jamal thought a second, and then shook his head. "Last name?"

"Bollick. I'm Anna."

He put his elbows on the table and leaned forward. "Does Ben have any brothers? I may have two names for you."

Dawn pulled another bill from her purse and set it next to the first.

Jamal reached for the Bens, but Dawn drew them back.

Her now greedy source rubbed his fingers together, as if he were already counting the money. "Two guys ran this place before me. Both of them disappeared, five years ago, along with 300 K of the club's money. "

"Full, legal names?"

"Hell, girl, I don't even remember my own legal name most of the time. Look, I got two names, probably real. They are what they are. No guarantees."

Dawn felt just a little disappointed, but realized that this was the best she could do and nodded.

Jamal pulled a pen from his pocket. He took the napkin from under Dawn's drink and wrote two names. He folded the napkin in half and rested his hands on top of it.

"Are they in trouble?"

Dawn shrugged.

"I hope so. If you find them, bust them up a little for us, too."

Again, Dawn just shrugged.

Jamal slid the napkin across the table, and pulled the bills back with his forefinger.

Dawn looked at the napkin. Two names, both legible, but one almost useless. It wasn't what she wanted, but it was a next step. She folded the napkin and slid it into her purse. She stood, pulled down her dress, and turned to leave.

"If you want to work here, I'm sure we can arrange something."

Dawn ignored him and made for the door. Outside, she noticed that her two admirers were gone, but she was long past caring. Her mind was busy elsewhere as she unlocked her car and slid behind the wheel. She knew what needed to happen next. How to make that happen without getting fired, or arrested, would be the problem.

Chapter 3

Sunday Night
Denton, Texas

Justice slipped around the corner of the brick, three-story apartment building. He halted in the shadows, just outside a ground-floor apartment, and turned to examine the black-and-white world around him. No lights, no movement, no noise – so no problems.

He took off his backpack and pulled out the latex gloves he'd lifted from a small, rural hospital. He next retrieved the electric lock pick he'd purchased especially for tonight. It was fast, quiet, easily rechargeable with powerful lithium-ion batteries, and completely tax deductible for a man in his profession. Perfect. Much better than the thin metal needles he'd learned on. Maybe he'd post a five-star review on Amazon.

But tonight, his electric crime-toy ended up being a waste of money. He glanced at the door and found it ajar. Either his guest victim for the night was expecting him, or the POS had come home drunk again from the "320 Club" and forgot to close the door. It wouldn't matter; it would end the same either way.

Justice slipped inside and closed the door behind him. Maybe fat boy didn't mind visitors, but Justice wanted privacy for what was about to happen. He moved quietly to the back of the apartment and stopped.

Outside the bedroom door, he checked the charge on his Taser. It wasn't as powerful as the cop models; he knew from personal experience that police-issue were the best. This one was good; however, and he didn't think that Jimmy Ray would notice the difference.

The killer scowled as he pulled out his top of the line burner phone and struggled to type. Killing was so much easier than tweeting.

Justice_4_theInnocent @mytweetrevenge
Outside his door, payback in minutes for
#kennemanmurder. YW Denton.

Justice sent his message off into cyberspace, then slowly opened the bedroom door and peered inside. A disgusting lump of lard lay on the bed, naked from the waist up. It would be impossible not to recognize Jimmy Ray Oltman. For months after this toad ran over and killed Suri Kenneman, his picture appeared almost daily in every Dallas area paper or newscast. When his high-powered lawyer got him off because an unexplained "lab accident" contaminated the evidence, he got more face time than anybody in North Texas except the owner of the Dallas Cowboys.

Almost a year later, Jimmy Ray Oltman was still a hated man, but a free one. Very soon, however, his freedom would come to a shocking end.

Shocking end. Justice liked that.

Justice slipped his Taser through the barely open door, aimed carefully, and fired.

A puff of nitrogen gas propelled two electrode darts forward.

They connected and penetrated pasty flesh, which prompted a grunt from the human dartboard. A series of clicking sounds meant that a disabling electric current flowed painfully through the pig's highly conductive human flesh.

Justice pulled the handheld stun gun from his belt and turned it on as he entered the room. Justice knew it was his imagination, but he could almost detect the smell of fresh bacon.

He hurried to the bed. The red light on the stun gun glowed ready, so he hit the fat man with a one-second jolt of electricity. He didn't want his victim dead – yet – but he had to make sure that Oltman was disabled and quiet. Justice secured the arms and legs with duct tape from his backpack as the disgusting blob started to recover. The stun gun wasn't fully recharged, so he checked his watch. He'd been on the hunt for eight minutes and thirty-seven seconds now. He needed to pick up the pace.

The red light of the stun gun winked green, "ready." Justice winked back. "More than ready," and hit the child killer with another jolt, two seconds this time. Justice looked around, and then bent to retrieve a pair of filthy underwear from a clothes pile on the floor. He stuffed the disgusting cloth into his victim's just as disgusting mouth. The yellow skivvies were filthy and brown, another good reason for the latex gloves.

He went to the computer in the corner and found it on. He loaded Twitter, logged in, and began to type. It was time to acquire a better class of follower.

Chapter 4

Sunday Night
Jacksboro County, Texas

Nick DaSalvo was tired, but soon to be more relaxed. He'd finish his chores at home by Saturday afternoon, which left the rest of the weekend for a visit to his "hunting lease."

In fact, he was on his "lease" right now. Her name was Barbara, or maybe Beatrice – something with a "B." She was new, young, and very cute - though not as exciting as the last "lease" he'd worked on. She was probably too new, so before he would have time to actually learn her name, she would have been replaced. Lady Maria always had options.

This "B" girl needed to "B" more active. He looked down at the obviously genuine pleasure on her stunningly girlish face. She was a looker, but she had expected him to do some of the work. If he'd wanted to work, he would have stayed home.

Well, maybe not at home.

Definitely not at home.

That thought made Nick DaSalvo shudder as he continued

with his part of the effort. Then shudder again. It wasn't his thoughts. It was his phone on vibrate. He glanced at the screen. It wasn't a call, so it had to be a message or email.

As an Assistant District Attorney for the County of Denton, he had to be available at all times – 24/7 – in case of emergency. This could be an emergency.

Or, this could be an email from another beautiful Russian woman whose heartfelt expressions of love and devotion had slipped through his spam filter. So, no.

Or yes, it could still be an emergency.

DaSalvo stopped "working" and leaned on one arm toward the nightstand. The phone indicated he had one new email. What to do? His phone could hold danger, or new offers of love for him alone.

His hand floated tentatively toward the phone. He knew it wasn't his wife. She would have sent a text. She knew better than to call. He'd made sure his real hunting lease had no cell service. This always gave him an excuse as to why she couldn't reach him.

His office might email. But if it's really important, they would call. Then his caller ID would tell him who it was.

The "B" girl, Bianca! Her name was Bianca.

Bianca suggested, a little too eagerly, "You no answer? Maybe important."

"No, me no answer," he said roughly and flipped her over onto her stomach.

He was going to get his money's worth.

Chapter 5

Sunday Night
Denton, TX

Justice finished the 98 character message and hit enter. What Nick DaSalvo, and the seven other members of the city, county, and state law enforcement community he'd just followed should have seen, became almost instantly available to the 826 other people that did follow the serial killer.

Justice_4_theInnocent @mytweetrevenge
Tased Fatboy, alive but in a medium-rare stupor. Now the fun part. #kennemanmurder almost avenged.

Justice watched the screen to see if he had any new followers, and then returned to his backpack in disgust. He knew it was possible that one of the 'good guys' was lurking – lurking was the term, right? Keeping track of him but not actually following him. He had to assume now that he was being "followed." That's why he needed to keep to his schedule.

He pulled out a snack sized zip-close plastic bag and a pair of swimmer's nose plugs. He knew that Oltman had become a heavy drinker, and quickly found a half-full bottle of vodka on the floor beside the nightstand. This would work out splendidly. He rolled Oltman onto his back, set the items on the edge of the bed, and then returned to the computer.

> **Justice_4_theInnocent** @mytweetrevenge
> Have plastic bag, nose plugs, and booze. What will I do to Jimmy Ray now? Who can figure it out?

Justice didn't know with complete certainty how much time he had, but a sense of urgency had begun to form in the pit of his stomach.

It was exciting, too, which surprised him just a little. Ignoring this new feeling and concentrating on his plan, he quickly clipped the nose plugs over Oltman's nostrils.

No fair breathing through your nose, Jimmy! We need to keep that mouth open.

Justice reached for the vodka - half-full for Justice, half-empty for Jimmy. Soon to be completely empty for the baby killer. He unscrewed the lid from the bottle, and pushed the briefs as far down the mouth of this soon-to-be corpse as possible. Justice fingered the stun gun in case his victim began to struggle. Jimmy Ray did have to work a little harder to breathe, but was still too out of it to realize his situation.

Justice returned to the computer. He needed to share this with the world. When he first decided on a path of revenge, he only had one victim in mind. But once the decision had been made for the seeker of justice to become Justice himself, the number of people who deserved Justice had become truly evident. It had been harder to limit the number of victims than to find them.

At the computer, Justice typed the next planned message. He hoped this brought closure to that poor little girl's family and friends.

Justice_4_the Innocent @mytweetrevenge
Jimmy Ray Oltman drank too much alcohol and killed
Suri Kenneman.

Back at the bed, Justice carefully poured alcohol into Jimmy Ray's mouth. Oltman had been drunk when he ran a red light and killed that wonderful little girl. His second drunk-driving arrest. Suri, a smart, beautiful, and loving daughter, had died a slow death, trapped in a crumpled car. Jimmy Ray tried to flee the scene, but actually crashed into the back of a truck before he got far. Then the child killer claimed he wasn't leaving the scene of the accident, just pulling over so he could go back and help. What a cold, lying, SOB.

Then, a mysterious lab accident had contaminated the blood sample. No one knew how it had happened, but most suspected sabotage orchestrated by the crook Oltman hired as a lawyer. Finally, the slick lawyer managed to confuse the jury and Oltman got off.

Justice wasn't confused. Justice was sometimes blind, but confused? Not tonight.

The thrashing and heaving began again, though weakly. Justice held Oltman's head steady and resumed pouring alcohol into the gaping mouth. There soon followed the involuntary choking, gagging and heaving of a dying man. Justice kept the liquid streaming onto the gag and down the throat. There was another shudder, the last wisps of air bubbled away. The body seemed to relax, but Justice kept the mouth full of the liquid.

You can never be too careful.

Finally, Suri Kenneman's killer stopped moving and stared blankly at the ceiling. His mouth stayed full of vodka for several minutes before Justice set the bottle down and went back to the computer.

Justice_4_the Innocent @mytweetrevenge
Now he's drunk himself to death. Justice 4
#kennemanmurder. Again, YW Denton.

Justice pulled his backpack completely open. He next retrieved the clips from Jimmy's nose and dropped them into the bag. Everything would go into the backpack, along with his gloves, shoes and clothing when he got home.

Fatboy's undies could stay where they were, as a "clue." Justice was getting a little frustrated with the local cops. These BVDs wouldn't help them, but maybe it would motivate them - make them feel like they had a chance. This was his third execution, and no one had a clue yet that a serial killer was involved. He would reward them with a small, if useless one. All they had to do next time was follow his tweets. Fortunately for the cause of Justice, they would be too late then, as well.

He started toward the door, stopped, and hurried back to stand over the bed. He picked up the small bag he'd left there, unzipped the top, and removed a shiny new keychain. He set the keychain on his victim's forehead, and then dumped the microscopic contents of the bag around the room. He looked around at his handiwork and smiled, admiring his efforts. His eyes finally came to rest on the keychain, which showed a little blue bird tweeting "Follow Me." He wasn't really into symbolism, but this made a perfect signature for his work.

He'd forgotten to sign his first murder, but that wouldn't matter. No one could have found the keychain at that execution scene – they never found most of the body.

Justice hurried down the stairs and hunched as he walked calmly around the building. He crossed the playground and retraced his path through the woods. Breathing heavily, he plopped wearily into the driver's seat of the beat-up blue Ford. He pulled out the cell phone and entered his final message for this mission.

Justice_4_theInnocent @mytweetrevenge
Oltman makes 3, 2 more awaiting Justice. Cops are
f****** idiots. This is Justice, so follow this.

He pulled another zip-close from his pocket. He removed the battery from the phone and dropped the battery, phone and battery cover into the baggie. He then dropped the bag into his backpack on the seat next to him.

Almost everything in the backpack, including the backpack itself, would be incinerated completely with a blowtorch in a small steel drum. He would then scatter the ashes as he drove up Interstate 35 through Oklahoma to Ardmore. There were no guarantees that he wouldn't be caught, there were never any guarantees, but this should make it nearly impossible to tie him physically to the crime. This method had worked so far, at least.

He again marveled at his lack of remorse. In fact, Justice realized that he actually looked forward to checking the final two names off his list.

Then things would really get interesting.

Chapter 6

Monday Morning
Lewisville, TX

Dawn silently opened the apartment door, slid inside, and eased it noiselessly closed. She set her shoes and purse gently on a side table near the door and tiptoed toward her bed on the couch.

With an impatient click, the table lamp behind a worn, brown leather recliner blazed to life. Dawn could barely make out the shadowy figure seated there. However, the reflection off the top of his head identified the shadow as male and heroically bald. The black matte finish of the .40 caliber Glock pistol in his right hand, gave off no reflection at all. Still, it was very easy to identify.

"You're in trouble." A tired, angry baritone voice filled the room.

Dawn froze, then reached back and flipped on the overhead light. She turned to face the man in the recliner. He was a very large white man, forty-three years old, wearing black sweat pants and a blue t-shirt in desperate need of incineration, a Dallas Mavericks logo barely recognizable on the front. His shaved head still seemed to glow in the light. His eyes, which Dawn knew were almost as brown as hers, were slits trying to adjust to the blinding brilliance.

Dawn shrugged. "Sorry Uncle Danny, I didn't mean to wake you."

"Uncle Danny" was an honorific title. Danny Balzac was not her uncle by some mere coincidence of biology. She had a *real* uncle back in Miami, somewhere near Miami anyway, that she'd never met. Danny was much closer than blood. He had been her father's partner, and then best friend, from the time she was eight. From right after her mother died. He'd kept her dad, and her, from falling apart when it happened.

"You didn't wake me," he growled.

She walked over and placed a kiss on the top of his head, careful to make sure the lipstick marks couldn't be seen when he looked in the mirror. She'd been doing that since she started wearing makeup, and he started failing to notice at the same time. She set her unicorn keychain on the side table.

He frowned and held up the gun, along with a state-of-the-art smart phone in his left hand. "You're supposed to have these at all times."

She stepped back and held her arms out. "Where was I supposed to carry them?"

Balzac seemed to notice the tiny red dress for the first time and scowled. "Where did you get that?"

She shook her head. "You helped me pick it out. Senior prom, remember?"

"And it was too small then, but we can talk about that later. Right now, let's talk about why I'm up at three in the morning." He held out the phone. "You have several missed calls."

She frowned in confusion, then took the phone and looked at the screen. It showed three calls from a local phone number that looked familiar, with a name below it that she definitely recognized.

"Pratt called, starting at . . ." She studied the screen. "At 2:13 a.m.? Why?"

"Gee, I guess I forgot to ask him when he called me at 2:34 a.m. to ask where you were." He waited for her to respond, but she simply stared back. "So, where were you?"

"Out with friends." She turned away so he couldn't see her face. She walked to his couch, moved the blankets she'd been sleeping on for the last six days, and sat. She sank into the worn blue fabric and crossed her legs.

He shot back, "You don't have any friends." His eyes went wide when he saw the scar on her thigh. It had been covered and wrapped all the times he'd visited her in the hospital. She tried to show him when the bandages came off, but as soon as she'd started to lift her dress; he turned bright red, turned to face away, and muttered, "Later."

He didn't look away now, but did mutter again. "Geez. You'll be a real hit at the pool this summer, won't you?"

The scars were ancient history to Dawn. Well, not too ancient. They still hurt like hell at times, like most of the time. She just shrugged and forced a smile. "That's the pretty one. The others will keep me in one-piece bathing suits forever."

That was something she found ironic. The assault rifle wounds looked better than the pistol scars. The smaller diameter of the high speed, metal jacketed AR15 rounds made neat little holes. The expanding, nine millimeter hollow points made a mess.

Balzac blinked, and then looked her in the eye. "Not a very good way to start your career, at least to Pratt."

She looked at the phone. No voicemail. She looked at Balzac. "What did he want?"

"Don't know."

Dawn got suddenly excited. "Am I cleared for duty?"

"Don't know! He wants to talk to you. I really don't know what about. He asked where you were, and I told him you were looking up old friends." Balzac continued sarcastically, "I assume that's why you wanted me to do a search on Hastings. Old friend, right?"

Dawn sighed, angry with herself. She shouldn't have gone through Danny for her-off-the-books investigation. She didn't want him involved, but she didn't have a choice. Until the doctors cleared her for duty, she had no computer access of her own.

"Be in his office at 10:00 a.m."

Dawn felt the blood rising in her face. Special Agent in Charge Robert Pratt had assiduously avoided her since she'd arrived from Quantico. Danny had claimed that he didn't know what Pratt was upset about, just that he didn't want to see her.

She asked hesitantly, "Am I in trouble?"

"Dawn, you've been in trouble since the second Pratt found out you were coming. For some reason, so have I."

Dawn felt a chill at the revelation. This may be a problem. "Why?"

"I get the impression he doesn't want you here, us here."

Dawn opened her mouth to speak, but he cut her off.

"Don't ask why. I don't know why. There are times when he just seems to know things, things he doesn't share."

Dawn laughed, "You make it sound like he's psychic or something?"

Balzac didn't laugh. "At times I wonder. I don't wonder, however, whether we need to watch our step. Especially you. If you're cleared for duty, he'll probably just have you run Background Investigations for a while. Make sure you're all healed up and up to speed."

She should be so lucky. BI's would be perfect. Lots of records searches with little supervision. She wouldn't have to find someone else to check up on her two new leads.

Balzac yawned, stretched and stood. "I'm going back to bed, where I can worry in private. You should get some sleep, too."

"I will," she lied. She didn't sleep much anymore. What she would do is start on the new names she'd gotten from Jamal.

Chapter 7

Monday Morning
Montague County, Texas

For the first time on this mission to make the world a better place he felt nervous, as well as frustrated.

Not afraid, not even worried, just nervous. Justice still didn't know which, if any, of the pertinent law enforcement types were aware of his field trips into their jurisdictions. Plus, he needed to make sure the information he wanted to reveal got out to the public, without making it look like he knew too much. And finally, he wanted to make the authorities, starting with the Denton PD, accountable for their lack of vigilance.

He thought about how to get the word out, and then it had hit him – The Media. He hated those idiotic, talking heads in the media. However, in this case he could make them useful idiots. He pulled onto a tiny county road and reassembled his death phone for tonight. It took a while, but contacted them all - except NBC of course. When they canned Jay Leno, they became dead to him.

Then he'd sent follow requests directly to all the radio, TV, and newspaper news departments he could find. He'd also asked for more information about the Oltman murder on a couple of the social media sites, and dropped a message about suspicious activity on an anonymous tip line in Denton.

One of those nosey fools would take the bait, and that would start a media feeding frenzy.

And speaking of feeding frenzy, that is how he'd get rid of every trace of his latest crime.

He'd bought a jar of peanut butter from the dollar store. He would still use a torch to turn the backpack and its contents into ashes and slag. Unfortunately, duty called and he no longer had time to scatter the ashes along the highway to Oklahoma.

Instead, he would simply put the ashes in a brown paper bag. He would then mix in a generous portion of the peanut butter, and then drop the bag into Nocona Lake. The fish would take care of the evidence, and the cycle of life would go on. What could be better than an ecologically responsible approach to serial executions?

He checked his watch and threw his car into gear. He did have to hurry if he was going to really mess with the investigation.

Chapter 8

Monday Morning
Frisco, Texas

Careening down the freeway, sandwiched behind a massive pickup truck and in front of some new little import that looked like a jewelry box on wheels, Dawn took the off-ramp from Highway 121. The ribbon of concrete seemed to rise a hundred feet into the air. It then curved tightly to the left as it ushered her toward the Dallas North Tollway. Everything about North Dallas seemed new to her now, although an innocuous sign informed her that she had just entered The City of Frisco.

She remembered Frisco. It had excellent shopping, so her old friends made regular pilgrimages to worship at these shrines to consumerism. Now, to her right, she saw a huge shopping mall. Even as a materialistic teenager, she would never, ever, have traveled this far north to go shopping. Now she noticed a huge, blue and yellow building that she recognized as the IKEA furniture store. Those friends from high school had drooled over that place. She glanced right again and noticed the "acres of free parking."

I'll pass. Dawn avoided any place which might harbor that many bargain crazed women.

Frisco had something that she would definitely not avoid, what claimed to be the world's largest indoor shooting range. Everything was bigger in Texas, right? She couldn't wait to check it out, no matter how big the parking lot.

The ramp straightened out and began to descend. Ahead and to her left, she saw a cluster of seven or eight-story buildings. One of them housed the FBI's Frisco Resident Agency, a satellite office from the main building at One Federal Way in Dallas. She had visited the Dallas Field Office hundreds of times during the ten years her dad had been posted there, but the Frisco office was new.

She'd been away from the Dallas–Fort Worth "Metroplex" for nine years. Her father had been transferred; transplanting his eager daughter to the wilds of Sin City. Las Vegas, however, proved only as interesting as Dawn made it, which meant boring. She was her daddy's girl, and her daddy had been committed to making the world a better and safer place. Dawn grew up wanting the same.

The ramp reached the main freeway, and Dawn hit the gas. She muscled her beat up Ford Escort into the heavy morning traffic, and continued to accelerate until she moved along at top speed - meaning five miles per hour under the actual posted speed limit.

Dawn took the first exit on her right, and at the stoplight she made a U-turn. The faded blue disaster cruised down the frontage road, and then turned right onto Warren. A left at the first stop light, and the building she wanted appeared on her right. Dawn drove past the parking garage and headed toward the main entrance. She found an open handicapped spot near the door, turned in and shuddered to a stop. She'd earned her handicapped status. She no longer limped, but the residual effect of several brutally hot projectiles could still be felt. More importantly, her permit was good for another two months. She had every intention of using it until it expired.

A quick elevator ride and she was on the 7th floor. From here the north Texas counties of Collin, Denton, Hurst and Rockwall were kept safe and secure. From here, she would discover the truth.

Dawn Johnson had arrived – armed, dangerous and on the job. At last.

She gathered herself and strode confidently through the wood and glass door and into a sparse, but neatly furnished reception area. In front of her, the FBI logo seemed to obscure the wall. Below it in brass letters she read "Frisco Resident Agency." This place seemed small, definitely not the main Field Office in Dallas. Still, she couldn't ignore the feeling of warmth and belonging. She was a Bureau Brat - this was home.

Dawn looked around the stern, empty room. She had no idea where to go next. Mere seconds later, an even sterner female voice boomed from overhead speakers.

"Door to your left."

The heavy steel door to her left clicked and then buzzed, like it was being electrocuted. Dawn straightened the jacket of her dark-blue pantsuit, strode to the door, and pulled it open. Beyond she found familiar, sterile grey hallways heading left, right, and straight ahead. She oriented herself and headed right, toward where the corner office should be. As a highly trained investigator, it took less than a minute for Dawn to discern which office belonged to Pratt. It turned out to be straight ahead, with a sign that read "Special Agent in Charge Robert Pratt" next to the door.

The door itself was open. Dawn scanned the empty hall, then turned and went inside. As she entered Pratt's office, Dawn looked around, disgusted.

How can anyone work in a place like this?

The office was spotless. Knickknacks, on a glistening glass table, stood neatly arranged and dusted. The desk was clear except for a functional blotter in the center, and a small stack of folders on the right front corner. The wall behind the desk was adorned with two flags, one a tattered Stars and Stripes – a battlefield flag she guessed. The other she also recognized, a brilliant field of red cloth with a golden Eagle, Globe and Anchor sparkling in the center.

Oh, geez! He was a Marine.

That explained a lot, and foreshadowed even more. She didn't know if she could deal with another spit-and-polish Marine so soon after the Academy. After her time in Quantico, she was sick of Jarheads. One of her best friends had even gone over to the dark side and become an "Officer of Marines."

Not everyone knows that the FBI Academy is located on the Marine Corps base at Quantico, Virginia. That same base housed the Marine Corps Basic School, which stamped out the gung-ho little officer droids that kept America safe from an evil world.

Sherri Kraft, a close friend from the South Texas School Of Law, became a Marine after law school. Sherri received her brainwashing there in Quantico, at the same time that Dawn was becoming the consummate Law Enforcement Professional. They'd met a couple of times for drinks, and Dawn was amazed, then frightened, by how quickly her easy-going friend had been transformed from slacker to stud.

Sherri was going to be a military lawyer, which Dawn admired. However, all Sherri could talk about was calling in airstrikes and firing from a defilade position – whatever that meant. Every Marine, even all of the officers, went through infantry training – pilots, lawyers, cooks – everyone. This makes perfect sense. How can anyone be expected to practice law if they can't run sixteen miles in boots? Sherri really bought into the Marine Corps hype. Dawn eventually got tired of hearing about the best ways of disabling a tank and avoided her friend. Dawn did console Sherri when her application to change specialties from lawyer to Combat Engineering was denied. It seems that grunts are easier to find than lawyers.

It appeared that Pratt had done the same, embraced the Marine Corps "mantle of macho" from the safety of a courtroom in North Carolina. The only thing worse than working WITH someone who's trying hard to be macho, is working FOR them.

Dawn looked back at the door. The Special Agent-in-Charge, SAC Pratt, was still missing in action, so Dawn decided to continue her reconnoiter. Opposite the flag wall was the "I Love Me" wall, covered with diplomas, certificates and pictures. Closest to her were the diplomas, the first ones being a B.S. and a Juris Doctorate awarded to Rajabu Pratt from Brigham Young University.

Rajabu? His real name is Rajabu? What kind of name is that?

She next found certificates of graduation from The Marine Corps Basic School and the FBI Academy. In the center, she stared at a proudly framed certificate, done in crayon, proclaiming him "The World's Greatest Daddy."

Weird.

Next came the military crap. He had apparently been awarded a bronze star and a purple heart — no, two purple hearts. Maybe Dawn should take back some of the petty things she had been thinking. She figured that the Marine Corps didn't give out purple hearts for a chaffed butt-cheeks or paper cuts.

She looked around, still no Pratt.

Dawn walked further down the wall where she found other awards. The gaudiest of which was a mounted—something. It looked a little like a belt buckle, but it was as big as her dinner plates. Under it was a certificate from the Texas High School Rodeo Association. Pratt had placed first, in the whole state of Texas, in Tie-Down Roping.

What's a tie-down? Not a big, ugly animal I hope. And why would someone feel the need to rope one?

Dawn never wanted to find out. She had this thing about animals, especially big ones. Rodeos scared the hell out of her. She'd only been to the rodeo a couple of times, and then always with her father.

Rodeo? Of course!

Her father had taken her to the Cowboys of Color Rodeo here in Dallas one year. They went because some new FBI agent would be participating – bronc and bull riding, she remembered. There probably weren't a lot of black FBI Agent cowboys, so

Pratt must have been the one they went to see. So, she had seen Pratt once before. She'd seen him land face first in the dirt, and then be carried off by a bunch of clowns.

Dawn grinned broadly. She would try to keep that memory from popping up at the wrong time.

Dawn moved on, past the cowboy stuff. She stopped at a large family portrait, which occupied a center position in the personal section. Two adults, a large black man who looked vaguely familiar, and a smiling white woman, sat flanked by one darling black boy and a girl who looked Chinese.

If that didn't make sense, the next photo confused her even more. It looked almost like a school picture, which had been taken in front of a corn field. It showed an older white couple surrounded by a gaggle of kids from all races. Dawn looked carefully, and recognized one of the kids as a teenage Pratt. He stood toward the center, next to the couple, surrounded by a horde of kids from around the world. Dawn saw brown kids, yellow kids, white kids, and another black one besides Pratt. He must have attended some kind of United Nations school or something.

"Where is that?" She mumbled to herself as she leaned closer to the photo, trying to figure out where it had been taken.

A powerful baritone voice stopped her in mid inspection. "It's West Texas. That's my family."

Dawn spun to look at the open door. It was still open, and still empty. She swiveled to scan the room, then the desk, where a very large black man stood holding the folders. She hadn't heard or sensed a thing.

Did he just beam in here, like in Star Trek?

"All but one of us were adopted." Pratt spoke again as he moved to stand next to her, not quite frowning but definitely not smiling. With a glance at the photo and the faintest hint of a smile, he spun and walked out. "With me."

Chapter 9

Monday Morning
Denton, Texas

Detective Arturo Guzman, of the Denton Police Department, watched keenly from the open doorway of James K. Oltman's apartment. Guzman sported brown hair, brown eyes, a light-brown complexion, and a truly black sense of humor. Only on his best days would someone think of him as insensitive.

The detective had examined the crime upon arriving, about two hours ago. Now, however, the CSI unit had kicked him out while they scoured the apartment for evidence. Guzman always enjoyed watching the shrink-wrapped little nerds. In their blue tyvek suits, they looked like giant Smurfs on a scavenger hunt.

They are on a scavenger hunt, of death, and all the stuff they find will soon be mine, he mused.

"Detective Guzman," a voice called from the parking lot. He turned as Nick DaSalvo, a short, slim man wearing a tailored gray suit that probably cost more than the detective's car, staggered toward the crime scene. Nick DaSalvo's family was all politicians, all rich, and all basically useless for anything other than speeches and press releases. Nicky-boy had become a prosecutor for one reason only, to make a name for himself, so he could run for office like his daddy.

One word came immediately to Guzman's mind.

Asshole.

Then followed a second word.

Sorry.

Arturo expanded and combined.

What a sorry asshole.

Somehow, the ADA had been the one to report the murder - from home, while sipping some imported, super mocha chino coffee at his breakfast table. Guzman knew that Nick was actually a pretty smart guy, but calling in a murder over Eggs Benedict and a croissant would have put him into the genius category. Nicky DaSalvo was no genius. That's why Guzman insisted that he come down to the crime scene and fill out the paper work. Guzman would probably have some questions.

Dispatch said something about following and tweets, a bunch of that social media crap. Guzman had personally decided to hold off getting himself into the online stuff until they perfected anti-social media. That he could get into.

Mr. DaSalvo stopped, a little short of breath, and extended his hand to Guzman. "I'm glad you caught the case."

Detective Guzman took the offered hand and shook it firmly. He had been the arresting officer on a couple of the cases that DaSalvo had prosecuted. DaSalvo really did appreciate the effort and detail Guzman put into catching criminals, if not the snotty attitude that came with them. Guzman, on the other hand, pretty much despised the ADA. DaSalvo had a reputation for letting most of the scum bags off light, usually with a plea bargain. That way, he had a much better than average conviction rate, while expending a much lower than average level of effort and detail in their prosecution.

Guzman pulled a pen and notepad from his shirt pocket, "Why were you the one to call it in?"

DaSalvo's face beamed with excitement. Nick, apparently, looked forward to being in on the ground floor of a high-profile murder. He nodded eagerly and began to recite from memory, like he was beginning his opening statement in front of a jury.

"As you know, Detective, I always strive to remain on top of things. It was very early this morning, 12:07 a.m. by my call log, when my phone chimed with an incoming message. I thought about opening the message at that time, but I was deep into something that could not be interrupted. However, first thing this morning I did ascertain the nature and content of the message, which was a follow request from the social media site known as . . ."

Detective Guzman waved both hands energetically in front of the ADA's face. "Stop!"

DaSalvo sputtered to a stop, mouth still hanging open.

Guzman jerked his head in the direction of the parking lot, "This way," and the detective strode off.

DaSalvo sputtered. "W-w-why?"

Guzman ignored DaSalvo and started toward the constellation of flashing blue and red lights. "Consider this is *my* follow request. Let's start on the paperwork first."

The detective was in no mood for the ADA's courtroom oratory. He wanted to move straight to the summation, so they marched rapidly toward Guzman's unmarked cruiser. Maybe DaSalvo would keep it short if he had to write it down.

The counselor shuffled up as Guzman pulled a clipboard from his front seat. An incident report form fluttered mockingly under the metal clasp. He shoved it into DaSalvo's hands and smiled.

"You know what this is, and you know what it's for. I need everything that relates to the case, and nothing that doesn't. Bring it to me when you're done."

DaSalvo blinked, owl-like, then examined the paper as Guzman turned to make his escape. The attorney considered the form in confusion, and then shouted.

"I need more forms. This one is for the Oltman murder,

right?"

Guzman stopped in exasperation and spun slowly back toward the whiney ADA. "That's how it works, one murder, one form."

DaSalvo shrugged and held out the clipboard. "Then I'll need two more forms."

Guzman blinked in momentary confusion, and then swore under his breath when he realized what that meant. Two more murders he could deal with. Listening to DaSalvo recite all the additional details of those murders would be unbearable.

Chapter 10

Monday Morning
Frisco, Texas

Pratt exited the office and turned left. He marched briskly down a long hallway as Dawn lengthened her stride to keep up. A subtle, knifing pain reminded her that assault rifles can make nasty playmates. Still, she quickly reached her stride and began to close on Pratt.

Pratt, however, glanced back and then slowed his pace. He must have remembered that Dawn was still in a no-duty status, and why. He held back for her.

And that really pissed her off!

People didn't hold back for her, she held back for them. She'd grown up with the Bureau. She had always been smarter, faster, more focused, and not just a little tougher than the civilian kids she grew up with. She graduated earlier, with better grades, than anyone else - in both high school and college.

She earned what she got. That's how her daddy raised her.

Her competitive streak did almost get her thrown out of med

school, the very first day. Some entitled little rich boy sat behind her during orientation at the Nevada School of Medicine. He'd sneered at her and whispered loudly to his buddies. "Affirmative action at work."

It had actually taken her several seconds to realize he was talking about her, and even longer to decipher what the annoying jerk had implied. It only took two seconds, however, for her to climb over the back of her seat and grab the wimpy bastard by the throat. She didn't recall her exact words, but someone told her she growled, "My first use of affirmative action will be to put you in the hospital."

The Dean made me apologize, but nobody thought I wouldn't do it again.

Dawn followed Pratt at their more moderate pace. If she'd known where they were going, she'd have walked past and let him try to keep up with her.

They reached the end of the hallway, made a left, and then entered a small conference room on their right. Pratt moved around the conference table and took a seat on the far side. In front of him rested a notebook computer. A video cable ran from the computer to a projector. He then pointed at the chair across from him.

"Sit."

She unbuttoned her jacket, sat, and looked around. To her left, she saw a wall-sized screen, which showed the projected desktop from the computer. An icon labeled "Johnson" stood alone in the center of the screen.

That can't be good.

He began. "I've been instructed to welcome you to the Frisco Resident Agency."

"Thank you sir, I'm happy to be here."

"I'm sure we can change that, because, for the moment you're not welcome, no matter what I've been instructed to do."

She hadn't expected a party and a parade, but this seemed a little harsh. She glanced again at the screen and the icon with her name. An introduction video! Dawn realized that he hoped to bore her into submission with some stupid presentation.

Give it your best shot, Agent Pratt.

He examined her carefully, trying to read her face. Finally, he continued, "Let me begin, however, by saying how sorry I am about your father. I knew him, though not well. I respected him."

"Thank you sir, I know he was proud of you also."

Pratt squinted, and then smiled. "The rodeo, I remember. We did meet there, didn't we?"

Dawn nodded and gave a fake smile. *Glad I made such an impression.*

"So, Agent Johnson, how are you feeling?"

He almost sounded sincere; he must be a good actor.

She sat straight. "Great, ready for full duty."

"Unfortunately, your doctor agrees. You have, in fact, been cleared for duty. Despite my best efforts to have you transferred first. You are a difficult person to get rid of."

What was his problem? And what kind of accent was that?

She asked the question that had been bothering her since she first arrived, and he refused to meet with her. "Sir, have I done something to upset you?"

He continued in a maddeningly even tone. "Have you? You would know better than I."

Wow, great comeback. Maybe Uncle Danny was right, and he was psychic. *Yes, I have done something that would upset you. No, I won't tell you what.*

"Agent Pratt, I'm not even on full duty. What could I have done?" Now for a little misdirection. "Has someone said something?"

His eyes narrowed as he studied her face. This guy must be great in interrogation.

"No. Actually, someone has refused to say something. Agent Balzac, and I've already discussed this with him." Pratt leaned forward. "You need to understand that I will continue to do everything in my power to have you transferred."

Dawn could only stare. It seemed like Pratt did have a party planned, a going-away party. This did not seem like professional conduct. She deserved an explanation.

"I know my attitude is unexpected, and certainly unusual. I owe you an explanation."

This is freaky.

"I have specific, and totally justifiable reasons for not wanting you assigned to Dallas." He stared at her, analyzing her reaction.

She stared back, not knowing how to react.

Pratt went on. "I believe it's very likely that you joined the FBI for suspect reasons and ulterior motivations. I believe you managed to get yourself posted here for even worse reasons. I also believe you are impulsive and undisciplined, possibly unsuited for field work all together. I have other reasons, but these are the principal ones. I believe they are enough to justify your transfer."

Definitely, he's psychic. Sculpting the truth would not be enough with him, so she just lied. "I don't know what you mean."

Pratt reach toward the papers he'd brought from his office. He retrieved the large brown envelop on top, opened it, and withdrew a handful of photos. He glanced at them, and then slid one across the desk to Dawn.

Dawn examined the picture.

Wow, is that what I looked like?

She hadn't seen this one before, and it was more than a little shocking. She stared at a grainy, black-and-white print that must have come from the store's surveillance camera. It was her, lying under a pile of potato chips, soaked in her own blood.

There in that conference room in Frisco, her whole body ached once more, physically returning to that night.

"Those three bullet wounds don't jog your memory? Oh wait, you don't remember because you were unconscious then, doing a marvelous imitation of bleeding to death."

Touché.

"Only it wasn't an imitation, was it Agent Johnson?" He reached for the touchpad of the laptop, and pointed to the large screen filling the wall to her left. Pratt maneuvered the cursor over the "Johnson" icon. With a flourish, he clicked the left pad button. A window opened on the screen. A digital video seemed to fill the entire room.

Dawn gazed again at the interior of the liquor store, which she'd visited on the second most painful night of her life.

Pratt bent forward and looked over at her. "Are you sure you're up for this?"

Dawn met his gaze. "Absolutely!" she lied again.

Pratt pressed a key and the surveillance video from a liquor store outside Quantico, Virginia began to flicker chillingly forward.

Her past rolled on, time stamp in the lower-right corner said, "10:22 p.m." She returned to the store.

The clerk, and frail, ancient looking Korean man stacks cigarettes on a counter-top display. Movement at the door catches his attention, and when two men in ski masks rush in he drops an armful of cartons and backs against the wall behind him.

The short robber holds a pistol, the tall robber an assault rifle. The short guy rushes to the counter and shoves his gun toward the clerks face. The tall one jogs through the store to make sure no one else is there. He then joins the smaller one at the counter. Shorty begins to shout silently on the 'video only' recording, gesturing wildly with his handgun.

The tall one joins in, yelling and jabbing the barrel of his AR15 into the cash register. Stretch is focused on the cash.

The clerk moves hesitantly toward the register, cowering in fear but knowing he had no choice but to obey. He taps a sequence of keys and the money drawer jangles noiselessly open.

Stretch lowers his rifle and harvests the cash. Tiny Bandit gestures the clerk back with his pistol. At that moment, a shadow approaches the front door. The shadow becomes a woman, who reaches for the door then hesitates as she peers through the glass portal.

Dawn forced herself not to react. She had gone there to get beer for their FBI Academy graduation party. Her class had just finished its training, and about a dozen of them had reserved rooms at the Marriott to celebrate by getting significantly impaired.

Pratt paused the video, "What were you thinking?"

I didn't think. I reacted.

Dawn cleared her throat, hesitating while she gathered herself. "I've gone over this a dozen times with my supervisors in Quantico."

Pratt was cool and professional. "I'm your supervisor now, so you'll go over it again. Why didn't you call for backup?"

I don't know.

Dawn sat straight, "I did a quick assessment of the situation and determined that the clerk was in imminent danger. I didn't feel there was time for backup to arrive before the assailants would attempt to leave the premises. My being at the door would have also resulted in a confrontation. Entry seemed the best course. I did dial 9-1-1 as I drew my weapon."

Pratt snorted. "I don't see it that way," and presses play. Her past continued to her left.

Without hesitation Dawn quietly opens the door as she pulls her weapon. She slips inside and pulls a phone from her pocket as she moves carefully toward the counter. She glances down, taps the keyboard of her phone, and then sets it on a stack of Twinkies. She crouches into a combat shooting stance, pulls her credentials from her back pocket and flips them open, then yells silently at the gunmen.

The video paused. "You thought they'd just surrender?"

"I thought they'd kill the clerk."

Pratt examined her skeptically, and then resumed playing the video.

Dawn rushes forward, weapon in one hand, credentials in the other. Short robber pivots toward her and fires wildly, shattering the glass in the door behind Dawn. Shards tinkle noiselessly around her.

A finger of fire bursts from the muzzle of Dawn's Glock as a shorter flame erupts from the other's weapon. Dawn spins as a dark hole appears in her shoulder. From behind, the hole in the chest of the smaller assailant can't be seen, but he crumples to the floor.

Dawn dives behind a display of cheap wine as the tall guy opens up with his assault rifle. Booze and broken glass fill the air as Dawn disappears down the aisle and her attacker moves carefully forward, firing blindly after her. With a quick motion, he jumps into the aisle preparing to fire again – preparing to fire, but not quite being able to pull the trigger.

His right shoulder jerks back, and then he doubles over and staggered backward into the ATM machine. Dawn staggers into view again, fragile wisps of smoke wafting from the barrel of her automatic. Blood soaks her left shoulder and arm. A growing red circle also forms on her left side. One of the 223 rounds has connected.

Dawn winces as she kicks the assault rifle away. Her attention is on the tall one who lies in front of her, so she fails to notice the wild mouthing screams and waving arms of the clerk. He gestures wildly at the floor in front of the counter as the small bad guy staggers to his feet. He aims, fires. Dawn is thrown back into the front window of the store.

Dawn doubles over, but manages to raise her pistol. Two lances of fire erupt from the barrel and the short attacker's head jerks back and he slumps to the floor.

Dawn staggers forward as red and blue lights flash outside the store. She staggers again, drops to her knees, then collapses onto the floor as running men in uniform, guns drawn, rush through the now glassless front door.

The video stops.

Dawn and Pratt sit silently for several moments. Pratt finally asks, "What time was that."

Dawn shakes her head, returns to the moment, and then glances at the lower right-hand corner of the screen.

"Ten twenty-nine."

"What time did your graduation end?"

"About nine-thirty."

Pratt leaned forward. "So, within one hour of becoming an FBI Agent, you had been shot three times and almost killed."

Dawn met his eyes. "And within one hour of becoming an FBI agent, I'd saved one man's life and neutralized two serial robbers who'd already murdered two innocent people."

Pratt leaned back. "You were almost killed yourself."

Dawn leaned forward. "I feel worse that it kept me off the job. And that the others had to celebrate without the Heineken I was supposed to pick up."

His eyes narrowed, "And that worries me, Johnson. That there's something about your work with the FBI that you consider more important than your life." He met her eyes. "What? What is so important?"

She held his gaze. Her answer was only part lie. "Everything."

Pratt hesitated briefly, and then smiled begrudgingly. "You are your father's daughter." He grabbed another folder. "The doctors have cleared you for duty, so I have no choice."

Pratt slid more pictures across the table. She didn't want to see them, but couldn't shy away now. The next was of her being rolled to an ambulance by two anxious EMT's. This one had been in the newspaper. Finally, there were pictures of two dead men in the store, a pair of chalk outlines for each of them, then autopsy photos of the same dead guys.

"What do you think of those?" He stared at her intently.

She couldn't think of an appropriate answer, so decided on an inappropriate one. "They're nice. Do they come in wallet size?"

The corners of Pratt's mouth twitched, but she didn't think it was a smile.

He continued unfazed. "You are a doctor, are you not?"

Technically no, but she didn't think Pratt cared about technicalities at the moment.

"I never completed residency but yes, I have worked as a physician."

"And you applied for, and were accepted, for a position at the Johns Hopkins Diagnostic Medical Center. You wanted to specialize in diagnostic medicine." He paused, still gauging her reaction.

Dawn shook her head, confused. "I wasn't accepted at Johns Hopkins."

"Yes, you were Agent Johnson. They didn't bother to send the acceptance letter."

Dawn realized she'd stopped breathing. She felt numb, but not enough to avoid the sting of Pratt's words.

"So you quit, threw away six years of very intensive, very expensive work and study."

Seven years, actually, but the FBI doesn't hire doctors.

"At that time, you turned your back on the medical specialty you desperately wanted, to attend law school. After another three years of specialized study there, you turn your back on that profession and join the FBI. I have to wonder why."

Dawn still couldn't breathe. *This is getting way too personal, way too painful.*

"Agent Johnson, I know this may still be a painful topic, and I apologize for broaching it in this way. I knew your father. I respected your father immensely. His work, and the work of your grandfather, helped make the FBI a better place for all African Americans. His death touched us all deeply."

Pratt stopped, just in time as Dawn fought back the tears. At least she was breathing again. It had been four years since Agent Balzac, Uncle Danny then, showed up at the trauma center of Sienna Hospital in Henderson, just outside Las Vegas. She had never seen him like that, and when he asked her to drop what she was doing and go for a ride, she knew what it meant.

Children of soldiers and cops don't get to mourn like regular people. The first stage of mourning is denial. But when you've lived your whole life in denial, waiting for your still beating heart to be ripped from your chest, normal person denial just wasn't possible. Dawn moved directly to anger and never planned to reach acceptance.

She looked up. Pratt waited, patiently, maybe respectfully–curiously. He wanted to see her reaction, and she hoped he hadn't. She met his eyes.

Pratt's expression hardened slightly. "I suspect that your father's death is the real reason you joined the FBI. The fact that you have been posted to this office, where he was posted when he disappeared, is too coincidental for me."

"When he died."

"Died, of course. At first he was classified as missing, and then declared deceased. To some going missing is a much greater fear."

His accent had changed. It definitely sounded foreign now. African? Jamaican?

Dawn locked the thoughts of her father deep in her heart, and her control reasserted itself.

"Agent Pratt, I am totally reconciled to my father's death. And I suspect my being assigned here has more to do with Agent Balzac than anything else. I'm certain that others share your skepticism about my motives. Agent Balzac has probably been asked to keep an eye on me."

At least, that's what he'd told her when she arrived.

She continued, "I joined the FBI because I . . ." Then she paused.

Because I am the reason my father is dead. Because I have to know what happened to him. Because the people who killed him will pay.

". . . Am absolutely certain he had more to offer the Bureau, more he wanted to accomplish. He can't do it, so I will. He was totally committed to his work and the people of our nation. He died doing the job he loved. It's one of the things that give his death meaning. For me, knowing his work will continue, through me, makes his sacrifice bearable."

As if his death is something I could ever bear.

Pratt stared like he had x-ray vision, like he could study her mind directly. He took a deep, expressionless breath, and then took the green folder from the stack.

"I have a temporary assignment for you." He slid the folder across the desk. "There is a possible serial killer in the Denton area. I'm assigning you to observe the task force that will be formed to pursue them."

What? This was a shock. She had moved instantly from no job in the FBI, to a serial killer investigation in one visit. Maybe she was wrong about Pratt.

"Thank you sir, why me?"

"Because the task force will probably be formed by Sheriff Bubba Scates of Montague County."

"Isn't Montague County handled out of the Wichita Falls office?"

"Yes, but Sheriff Scates is such a bigoted, offensive, and totally intolerable person that no one there wants to work with him. I'm hoping that having to deal with him will convince you to transfer to a job more in keeping with your abilities." He spread his hands and grinned, "Consider this your first orientation exercise."

Pratt took another folder from the stack and slid it across. And, his accent had changed back to West Texas.

"This is a request for your reassignment back to Quantico; all it lacks is your signature." His face softened. "You have a unique skill set and training, Agent Johnson. Your medical expertise would be invaluable to any number of forensic and support units within the Bureau. If you want to carry on your father's work, that is where you can do it best. There will be a very good place for you in the Bureau, but it's not here."

She had been told that someone had tried to have her assigned to the Laboratory Division out of the Academy. She'd had to beg almost all of her father's old friends and associates to block that and get herself assigned here. Her father had a lot of friends in the Bureau. One of them, "Uncle Richard," was Deputy Director. He had finally turned things in her favor. There was no way she could go back now.

"Yes sir, I'll think about that," more lies as she retrieved the folders.

"I'm sure you will," Pratt said sarcastically. He slid a slip of paper toward her. "There was a murder at this location last night. This is where you're to start. Be sure to wear your thickest skin."

"That's it?" She scanned the papers, just a little surprised and frustrated. "Don't I get a desk, business cards, a local phone and beeper, computer login . . . Anything?

She didn't care about a desk. Computer access is what she

needed.

Pratt stood. Dawn stood in response. "Let's see how your orientation exercise goes."

She had no idea what to say or how to react. Pratt extended his hand. "Thank you for coming in. I hope you'll be leaving us soon."

Chapter 11

Monday Afternoon
Denton, Texas

Dawn took the 288 Bypass exit off I-35 North and headed east. Three minutes later, she saw the flashing red and blue lights of mayhem at the old apartment complex on her left. One minute later, she found herself dodging TV news vans and pushy reporters as she made her way toward a cordoned off section of the parking lot.

She stopped next to a harried young Denton PD officer with a clipboard, the crime scene recorder. She rolled down her window to identify herself, but he immediately walked to the rear of her car. In the rear-view mirror, she watched him examine her blue beast with disdain, leaf through a stack of papers, then walk back to her window.

"Sorry, ma'am, your car's not on the list. Residents only."

"No, I'm . . ."

"Residents only! This is a crime scene."

Frustrated, she pulled out her creds and flipped them open

for the PD – Officer Jago, according to his nametag – to examine.

Officer Jago looked at the badge and frowned. He compared Dawn's face to her photo and squinted at her in confusion. Jago then gave a long, horrified examination at her car. Dawn flushed red and lied apologetically, "I've been under cover."

Still skeptical, Jago noted her name and other necessary details on his log paper, and then pointed to the left. "Around that way, Special Agent Johnson. Arturo Guzman is lead detective."

"Thank you, Officer . . ." She realized she had no idea how to pronounce his name. Totally embarrassed on countless and varied levels, Dawn shut her mouth and pulled around the block of buildings on her left. She parked well away from the crime scene, wedging her ride invisibly between two large pickup trucks.

Dawn dismounted and walked over, holding her creds out as she approached the taped off building. She noticed three men in animated discourse in front of a stairwell, and veered in their direction. A tall, good-looking Hispanic man dressed in official black-and-white – meaning a worn white dress shirt on his back and black Glock nine-millimeter automatic on his belt - seemed to drive the conversation. That would be Guzman.

She could hear the conversation now. Guzman stared intently at a small, rich looking, black-haired man who energetically pointed at a sheet of paper in his hand.

"I'm positive, Detective. I tracked all of the tweets back to when the account was set up. Those other two were the killer's first. This is the third."

Guzman frowned, took the paper, and examined its contents. "You mean you had someone else track the . . . the tweets."

The other man looked confused. "Of course, I don't do that sort of thing myself."

The third man, in uniform, was enjoying the obvious tension. They all looked over as she reached them, and she flashed her ID. "Special Agent Dawn Johnson, FBI."

A burly patrol officer in uniform ignored her credentials and

carefully calculated her cup size. *A breast man*, just what she
needed. The mousy little guy in the suit looked at her indulgently,
and then looked over at Guzman. The brown-skinned detective
couldn't suppress the look of exasperation which rippled across
his face, and Dawn didn't need to be a lip reader to figure out
that the detective was even more irritated than before she arrived.
Apparently, nobody wanted her around today.

The detective took a deep breath and extended his hand.
"Detective Arturo Guzman, Denton PD, I'm lead here."

He gestured to Mr. GQ. "This is Nicholas DaSalvo, from the
District Attorney's Office."

DaSalvo folded his arms and scowled, another testament to
her charm.

To make things worse, the uniformed officer stepped
forward. He flashed a gratuitous, *Yes, I am a chick magnet* smile, and
extended a muscular hand. "Sergeant Cassavetes. Pleasure to have
you aboard."

Dawn shook the sweaty paw hesitantly, and then examined
the assemblage again.

What the hell did Pratt get me into?

The group appeared to have reached an uncomfortable
impasse. Everyone exchanged glances, wondering who should
speak next. Everyone except Sergeant Cassavetes, who had
resumed his memorization of Dawn's bodice.

That's enough! Dawn turned to face Guzman and asked. "I
thought Sheriff Scates was heading the task force?"

That got their attention!

Guzman cocked his head and squinted, like he didn't really
believe what he'd heard.

DaSalvo's arms dropped limply to his side. His eyes bulged
and blinked like he had understood perfectly, but couldn't quite
believe what he'd heard.

Cassavetes almost ducked, like he'd just heard a gunshot and
was trying to figure out where it came from.

After looking around and discovering the world had not
ended, they relaxed slightly and exchanged glances. In unison,

they turned to Dawn in obvious hostility. Guzman spoke for the group.

"There is no task force here; this is a Denton only case. And if there was, I assure you that Bubba Scates, Sheriff of MONTAGUE County, would not be involved."

A low voice, with a down-home Texas accent rumbled behind them. "Son, I think your mouth's writin' a check that your narrow, wet-back ass can't cash."

The others stared past Dawn in horror, fixing their attention toward the parking lot. Dawn turned to find a short, caricature of a man ambling toward them. The blinding glare from mirrored, aviator style sunglasses couldn't completely obscure a perfectly formed white cowboy hat resting on waves of whiter hair.

A small, powerful, wraith-like figure emerged from the brilliance.

"I am Sheriff Bubba Scates, and did I just hear my name taken in vain?"

Dawn stared and tried not to laugh.

Chapter 12

Monday Afternoon
Denton, Texas

"I said, did I hear y'all takin' my name in vain?"

It sounded like a cartoon voice, one she'd heard as a child.

Yosemite Sam! That Saturday morning caricature of a cowboy, with a deep, over-effected accent and features too large to fit on a real face. She stared closely at the person behind the voice.

In front of her stood, not Yosemite Sam, but his grandfather. The figure laboring toward them was short and slightly stooped. Below the oversized Stetson, he sported a matched set of silver chinchillas, sleeping where the brows should have been. Those hung wearily over the sunglasses. All of these perched above a droopy white avalanche of a moustache, which seemed to stop just below his shoulders.

The khaki uniform shirt hung loosely off his shoulders, and the duty belt at his waist seemed way too large for his skinny frame. It was obvious from the trail of worn belt holes that he had recently lost a lot of weight. In the tooled brown holster, he carried a chrome plated revolver. Dawn recognized the Ruger .44 magnum. She liked that weapon. The khaki uniform pants puffed where he had tucked them into the finely tooled, silver-tinted cowboy boots.

Dawn blinked, stifled a laugh, and wondered if she had time to run and get the camera from her car.

The others reacted differently. The Sergeant grabbed the cell phone from his belt, even though it hadn't rung. In a deep voice he barked, "Cassavetes!" He then disappeared in full retreat toward his patrol car.

DaSalvo turned white, swore under his breath, and wordlessly followed the Sergeant.

Guzman mumbled several words in Spanish that Dawn recognized, but was not creative enough to translate in their current context. She and Guzman, alone now, waited to see what would happen next.

Sheriff Bubba Scates walked directly to Detective Guzman and extended his hand.

"Detective."

"Sheriff."

They greeted each other with the warmth of an arctic storm. Dawn almost expected Scates to take out his six-shooter and growl, "Take that you varmint!"

Scates hitched his thumbs in his belt and rocked back and forth on his heels. "I hear you got yourself a murder."

Guzman remained impassive. "Where did you hear that?"

The Sheriff winked. "Tweet, tweet. A little birdie told me. Tweeted something about revenge, I believe."

"We're still investigating. I'll be happy to call when I have something concrete."

Scates took control, and asked. "Why don't you be a good little Pedro and tell me where we stand right now?"

Guzman didn't bite and held his ground. "There is no 'we.' I'm working up leads and will conduct *my* investigation accordingly. You can stand in the corner and watch, if you'd like."

The sheriff chuckled, "Son, I'm not sure you have all the facts about our situation here. You know, of course, this is not our killer's first victim."

"Of course," Guzman continued professionally. "The first was at the Red River Refuge, the second in Oklahoma."

Scates nodded approvingly. "Good boy, you might actually be of help."

Dawn waited for the sheriff to reward the young detective with a lollypop, but instead he pulled a notepad from his back pocket and flipped through the pages.

"Our vigilante calls himself Justice, and apparently likes the attention a robust social media presence offers. That, or he just likes to rub shit in our faces."

Scates smiled at his audience and flipped to the next page. "His first victim was Kerwin Munch, 57, killed by wild animals on the Red River Wildlife Refuge west a' Gainesville. Initially ruled an accident, death by stupid, after several large chunks of his body showed up in the African Painted Dog enclosure. Second victim was Paul Clearwater, an Indian, whose body was found next to an oil well, wood pole stuck up his ass and propped up like one of them giant gummy bears on a stick. The Sheriff out of Ada, Oklahoma hasn't quite decided what to make of that one."

Scates looked up from his notes, making sure he had their full attention. "Bottom line, son, is that victim one was in Montague County, my jurisdiction. When we lump that in with the fact that the Sheriff out of Oklahoma, and the Denton County Sheriff – where a mess a' your most important evidence has been found – have asked the Montague County Sheriff's Department to lead the investigation, that kinda puts me in charge, now don't it?"

Dawn could see Guzman's mind at work, trying to find a way to maintain control. He played his final card.

"I'm not aware of what decisions these other agencies might have made, and I will be happy to work with the detective you put in charge of your investigation. As of right now, we are collecting forensic evidence, interviewing the neighbors, and shutting down our killer's Twitter account."

Scates shook his head in frustration. "Damn, boy, if dumb was dirt you could fill the Grand Canyon. You need to leave that Twitter account alone."

Guzman scowled, confused, then looked from Scates to Dawn.

Dawn nodded. "The Twitter account is your only direct link to the killer. You will want to keep it active."

Scates took a step forward. "Understand now why we need adult supervision on these executions?"

"I'll have to clear any change of jurisdiction with my department."

"I guess I forgot to mention that I had a nice chat with your Chief Anderson on the way over. He volunteered the use of an interrogation room in your headquarters for *my* task force to use. Nice man, your Chief. We've been friends a long time."

Guzman responded by turning red and scowling. Dawn could see that he wouldn't lose to Bubba Scates without a fight.

The sheriff recognized this and smirked. He glanced at Dawn briefly, and then looked back at the detective. "I missed my lunch hurryin' on over from Montague. Could you have your girl here run on to McDonald's and pick me up a number three meal, super-sized, with sweet tea? Then we can move inside so can you fill me in. Y'all get something for yourselves, too. It'll be on Montague County's tab."

Dawn stared briefly, and then laughed. It was a big laugh, not some lady-like chuckle. She laughed so hard that her side exploded in pain, where a nearly fatal round had broken a rib and punctured her lung. It hurt like hell, and finally forced her to stop.

Sheriff Scates raised his snowy eyebrows in shock, and then glared at Guzman. Guzman grinned broadly.

"This is Special Agent Johnson, out of the FBI's Dallas office."

Scates looked at Johnson, in surprise if not shock.

"Frisco office." Dawn corrected. She stared back at the sheriff. "And I eat at Whataburger."

Guzman added coldly, "So, if you're hungry, you should head on out and get your own lunch. Now would be good."

Scates recovered slightly, glancing warily between Dawn and Guzman.

"Hungry and angry," he recited. "Did you know that those are the only two words in the English language that end in ...gry?"

Now Dawn and Guzman exchanged confused glances.

Scates smiled. This brief delay had allowed him to adjust to the change in dynamics. He next moved to regain control. He asked Dawn accusingly. "What's the FBI's involvement in all this?"

Dawn responded in her most professional, *I'm the FBI and you're not!* voice. "I've been assigned to observe your task force. I'll be happy to provide any assistance or support that I can."

"You're here to keep an eye on my investigation?"

"No sir, I'm here to keep an eye on you." Dawn knew that wasn't the reason, but she hoped that her answer would be more irritating than the truth.

Sheriff Bubba Scates was at a momentary, but total, loss for words. This new development seemed to bother him a great deal.

For some reason, seeing his discomfort lifted her spirits.

"I don't think I want the FBI involved in *my* task force."

Dawn's face grew more serious, and her mood brightened even more. "Fact is, Sheriff, this will probably turn out to be a serial killer, who's crossed state lines. This may not be *your* task force long enough to have a meeting."

Dawn heard Guzman chuckle, but she continued to stare at Scates.

Finally, Scates looked at Guzman and growled, "Nine a.m. tomorrow, Denton PD offices. Don't be late."

He turned toward his vehicle and took a step, but stopped and turned back. He walked to Guzman, pulled a business card from his shirt pocket, and thrust it in the detective's hand. "Have your nerds call my nerd. We made an inquiry with the Twitter people 'bout an hour ago. We've dealt with them before. Let's see what they can tell us about our psychopath."

Guzman examined the dog-eared paper; Dawn leaned over to look at it as well. The card was from Radio Shack. The name scrawled in pen said Kenny Fox. It had a hand printed phone number under the typeset store information on the card.

Scates continued, "The hand-written number's his cell. He gets out of school at two and goes to work at four. Don't call him at work unless you have to. Store manager doesn't like it."

Bubba turned and ambled back toward his Suburban, mumbling about the FBI slowing things down. But, it was a subtly different Sheriff Scates. He seemed older, weaker, slightly more hunched, as he opened the door and climbed behind the wheel.

Detective Guzman suddenly raised his hand and waved at the sheriff. "Wait, who is your detective assigned to this case?"

Scates smiled wickedly back at Guzman. "Now let me see. I got you waiting to take over the investigation."

The sheriff paused, and then glared at Dawn. "I got the FBI waiting to take credit once it's over. I got a victim in my county who was eaten by wild African Dogs. And! I got an Indian's been mounted on a stick like some totem pole. This one's got my name on it, son. I'm gonna' get my schedule cleared up and meet y'all in the morning. You'll have the pleasure of dealing with Bubba Scates directly. Nine. Don't keep me waiting."

He smiled at Dawn. "FBI's not invited. If they show up without an invite, they damn well better have donuts."

He closed the door and raced out of the parking area.

Dawn turned to Detective Guzman. "Wow!"

He nodded. "At least he was in a good mood."

Dawn smiled, "I'm available for a briefing."

Guzman looked back at the crime scene, hesitated, then turned to Dawn. "Look, Agent Johnson, my investigation has just turned to shit and I have to go to my happy place before I kill that redneck SOB. If I'm still on the case tomorrow, we'll talk."

Dawn pulled a card from her pocket and handed it to him. "Here's my contact info. Anything you can give me would be appreciated.'

Guzman glanced at the card. "Says you're in Quantico."

"Takes forever to get new ones. You know, lowest bidder. Email and phone are the same."

Guzman shrugged. "Do what I can." He pulled the cell phone from his belt, dialing as he marched toward Oltman's apartment.

Dawn watched him go, shaking her head.

Pratt sure knows how to make a girl feel welcome!

Chapter 13

Monday Night
Lewisville, Texas

Juggling her phone between her ear and her shoulder, Dawn copied down a list of names. The lead of her mechanical pencil broke. Dawn clicked frantically until more lead snaked itself into view. She finished writing the names of victims, and the agencies and officers investigating their murders.

"I really appreciate this Detective Guzman." She spoke as she finished writing.

"I didn't do this for you. I'm not a fan of the FBI. But, with a serial killer working in two states, this will be your case before long anyway. I'm doing this because Scates ordered me not to give you a thing. I told him I'd already given you a complete briefing and sent you copies of our files. So this happened an hour ago, right?"

Dawn glanced down at her watch. "Right, just after seven. If there's . . . "

Guzman hung up on her.

Dawn pressed the end button, set down the phone, and continued to scribble notes madly onto the legal pad. She wouldn't be able to read everything she'd just written down, but it would get her started. Detective Guzman had briefed her on everything he knew about the Oltman murder. He had given her an overview of the victim's family, work, interests, criminal history. He'd also given him a brief list of known, and suspected, associates.

The CSI people were still processing the scene and wouldn't have a complete report for days.

The coroner was conducting the autopsy and should have a preliminary tomorrow.

He couldn't send any of the official reports or documents by regular email, but he could send crime scene photos by fax. Danny Balzac had a fax machine, which at the moment spit out a stack of color photos of a really fat dead guy.

He had requested copies of the books on the previous two murders, and would let her know when they arrived so she could read through them.

His Cyber Crimes people were examining the Twitter and Email accounts of Justice and were looking for any others he may have. They had requested all of the connection and account history from all of his online presence, and were waiting for it to arrive.

He and two other detectives had conducted family interviews, and would do the same at Oltman's workplace tomorrow. They would write up their reports and try to have them available late tomorrow or Wednesday.

Bottom line, he had worked his butt off, with basically squat to show for it so far. Despite his call, Dawn wasn't completely sure that he'd share everything with her. He'd told her about the Task Force Meeting at seven-thirty instead of nine.

Dawn hadn't decided whether she should go to the meeting or not. She'd been waiting for Danny Balzac to get home, so she could get his opinion and help. He wasn't really late yet, but he hadn't returned any of her calls, either.

She went to her call log on her phone, and redialed Danny Balzac. After just one ring, a voice boomed out of the speaker.

"Good evening, Agent Johnson." Pratt's voice seemed amused.

"Sorry sir, I thought I called Agent Balzac."

"You did call Agent Balzac – for the third time."

"But, how . . ."

"How am I getting his calls? We're the FBI, Johnson; we do sneaky stuff like this all the time. And you needn't bother to call him again. Your *Uncle Danny* left this afternoon for L-E-T-S-S training. Seems a spot came open, and I got him in at the last minute."

Dawn tried to remember, LETSS? Then it came to her, from a lecture in Quantico – Law Enforcement Training for Safety and Survival. This was serious training, like *dumping him in the wilderness with nothing but a safety pin and bad attitude for protection* level training. It was also a young agent's school.

"Sir, isn't he kind of old for that?"

"I worked it out." His voice grew serious. "And you need to work through the next few days on your own, Johnson. No friends to fall back on, no ways around your problems. I need to know who you are and why you are here. I will not put the public's safety, or the lives of the agents under my command, in jeopardy. You need to make me believe in you, because frankly, I don't."

She knew better than to respond. She didn't believe yet, either.

His voice grew lighter again. "You should know that I just got off the phone with Sheriff Scates."

She held her breath. This couldn't be good.

"The Sheriff called to complain. He's very angry with you. He claims that you were rude, insubordinate, and threatened to take over the investigation. He has ordered us to stay away from his investigation, or he will lodge a formal complaint in Washington."

Dawn could only wonder how much trouble she was in.

"Excellent work, keep it up. Be early to the meeting, you

know the actual start time, right?"

"Yes sir, seven-thirty."

"Correct. Tell him I advised you to stay away, but left the final decision to you. Tell him that you really want to keep an eye on things and decided to ignore my suggestion."

Dawn couldn't speak, then managed to sputter, "I . . . what? Sir, that will really put us at each other's throats."

"Exactly, two birds with one stone. Wish I could be there to see it. It also means that he'll probably come to me again before lodging a formal complaint. We can't underestimate Sheriff Scates. He's been a Sheriff forever, and been President of the Sheriffs' Association of Texas three times. He knows everyone, and almost everyone owes him a favor. We need to be careful."

Dawn thought that he was being careful, and throwing her to the wolves at the same time.

"Agent Johnson? You can always request a transfer to Quantico."

"I'll think about that, sir."

"No you won't, not yet anyway."

"Sir, what do you have against me? Have I done something wrong?"

He responded carefully. "I have no doubt that you've done something wrong. I just don't know what."

She hoped he never would.

"Besides, Johnson, this will probably be our case anyway. I'm certain we have a serial killer. Do you know what our suspect first message said?"

"No, sir."

Pratt went on as if reading it, "If people aren't brought to justice, justice will be brought to them."

Chapter 14

Monday Night
St. Joe, Texas

Justice ended the call and smiled. The pieces had begun to move, and the endgame was now being played. He set the death-is-coming phone on the seat next to his real-life one, making sure he couldn't get them confused. That would be a problem.

In the late-night darkness, he leaned over, hefted the duffle bag from the passenger's side floor, and set it on the seat. He took out the stack of sealed plastic bags and arranged them neatly across the bench seat beside him, from largest to smallest.

The first bag contained his executioner's uniform, which didn't fit well anymore. He opened the car door into darkness. He had parked on an isolated, tree-lined country road. The stars and crescent moon cast some light, but the trees kept most of that from reaching him. Without any bulbs in the car, he remained in darkness. He had even had turned down the lights on his dashboard display to their lowest level.

He knew that none of this was really necessary; no one would

be around to see him at any point during the administration of
this evening's death sentence. But one can never be too careful,
he reminded himself as he stepped out of the car.

To begin, he extricated a pair of latex gloves from the box
under the driver's seat and put them on. Next, he changed
clothes, donning the jeans and hooded sweatshirt from the first
bag. He neatly folded the clothes he'd been wearing and laid in
the back seat. On the floorboard of the rear passenger section, he
had the overshoes he wore for each of his exploits. These were
the only items that he kept, the only pieces of physical evidence –
besides his body – that could possibly link the crimes.

He closed the rear door and examined his faint reflection, as
well as possible, in the side window of the car. Justice had
selected and acquired his wardrobe carefully. Dress for success
wasn't just important in the business world. Projecting the desired
impression, and avoiding the real one, would keep him alive. For
now.

He reached inside and pressed the button that would open
the trunk. The loud click from the rear of the car seemed
magnified in the isolated silence of the now dormant cornfields
around him. The trunk lid squeaked slightly as it rose. Justice
walked to the rear and picked up the Taser and stun gun. Each
had a new set of batteries, but he checked them anyway. He
wanted them just as charged up for tonight's gala as he was.

Actually, he didn't anticipate having to use them this evening.
His plan was much simpler tonight. It would require another
stroll through the woods, but he enjoyed that. Next he would
climb up the six wooden steps to his victim's front porch. Finally,
he would knock on the door and simply shoot the man who
opened it – six, maybe seven times in the head and chest. That
should do it. He would then close the door, descend the steps to
the dirt patch that masqueraded as a front lawn, and stroll briskly
back into the woods.

No muss. No fuss. No survivors. No witnesses.

Justice frowned thinking about his victim. The soon to be
bullet stop was old and mean, and sick. His victim-to-be's

sickness was mental. Not even his own family had anything to do with him anymore. The *dead-man-sleeping* had killed an innocent kid from Korea, and the courts had found him "Not Guilty." To be honest, he wasn't guilty – legally. He probably wouldn't have been convicted in most places across the globe.

Morally? Yeah, the scum bag knew exactly what he was doing when he killed the boy. Worse, he enjoyed doing it.

Justice had seen the interrogation tapes from the Denton Police. In fact, the whole world had seen them on one of those reality cop shows. There he was, leering that *Yeah I did it, but you'll never make it stick!* sneer that made Justice's stomach turn.

His victim had gotten off. That didn't make him innocent, just not guilty. The legal technicalities had actually been a problem for Justice, logistically and emotionally. He knew there were a number of people that deserved this impending death-prize more than tonight's contestant. His problem was that punishing the guilty had been his number two priority, right behind not getting caught while doing it.

There were a limited number of people who fit all his requirements, and the next victim just happened to be one of them. That's why Justice would be visiting him in the wee hours of the morning.

He checked his watch, then quickly clipped the devices to his belt, closed the trunk, and hurried back behind the wheel. He had a schedule to keep.

The next bag he picked up held the revolver, an older model of the H&R Sportsman. The Sportsman had been built on a heavy frame, for a .22 caliber. The greater weight meant that he would barely feel the recoil. The tiny .22 caliber sub-sonic round, his choice for the evening, was not a very powerful in any gun. It was a specialized cartridge, and a real favorite for city use. Justice had actually practiced with this combination of weapon and ammo, to make sure everything would be in perfect working order when needed. His target tonight, however, would not be in perfect working order when he finished.

Justice wondered if he had been too cautious in his planning.

He had selected the "sub-sonic" round, which in this case was even less powerful than the standard .22 ammunition. Sub-sonic meant the bullet traveled slower than 1126 feet per second, the speed of sound. Sub-sonic, therefore, meant a lot less noise, because the little piece of metal breaking the sound barrier is what causes much of the noise. Many sub-sonic rounds simply used a heavier projectile. Heavier bullet meant less speed using the same amount of gunpowder, like throwing a huge rock instead of a tiny pebble. Same energy, but less speed and noise.

Justice had gone the other way, using less gunpowder and a normal sized bullet. Sub-sonic in this case meant less energy, less power and less penetration, which was not necessarily a disadvantage. The bullet would have enough energy to penetrate the body, but probably not enough to exit – even from very close range. The bullet would just rattle around in his prey's chest until it got tired and decided to stop. That would happen at about the same time his victim's heart decided to stop, too.

Justice wondered if his caution reflected his paranoia. Why worry? You're going to die no matter what happens. He reached across the seat and retrieved the next bag. It held a burned-out Roman candle from last 4th of July. Into the candle he'd inserted six nylon washers. He had worn latex gloves, as always, when he'd performed these tasks as well. Justice had slid the washers in, like pennies in a coin wrapper but spaced apart. After making sure they were in straight and more or less evenly spaced through the tube, by looking down the tube like a kid's homemade telescope. He slid into his pocket. He wouldn't need this until the very end.

Finally, he picked up the last bag, his signature bag, and slid it into his pocket with the expended fireworks. He wouldn't need it until later, either. He looked around the car. He stared at his duffle bag, and thought about all of the pieces he'd acquired to make tonight possible. He appreciated all of the help that went into making these executions a reality, even if his helpers had no idea what they were doing.

Indeed, it takes a village. And one North Texas village would soon be short its idiot.

Justice started the car, turned around, and drove calmly toward his next rendezvous with retribution. Maybe two wrongs will never make a right, but in this case, the second wrong would make the first one easier to live with.

Chapter 15

Monday Night
Lewisville, Texas

Dawn took another bite of cold pizza, completely lost in her thoughts, as the screen saver app -on her computer flickered to life. The universe returned as she inhaled the powerful aroma of exploding joy which wafted in from the kitchen, where microwave popcorn burst into exquisite sounds and scents. Cold pizza, microwave popcorn and Buffalo wings – which she'd ordered with the pizza – and a large glass of Diet Dr. Pepper.

Almost heaven.

She felt the urge to turn on the TV and watch a few old episodes of Miami Vice on Netflix. She'd done this many times, especially right after he died, disappeared, whatever. It was a time machine.

Almost every Friday night while it was on the air, Dawn and her father would accumulate vast quantities of junk food and diet soda. They would arrange it on the coffee table in front of them, put up their feet, and watch Sonny Crockett as he battled crime with cool. Dad grew up in Miami, but that didn't explain why he loved this show so much.

Dawn looked at the TV, maybe she should. Go sit on the couch and spend an hour with his memory, celebrate her first real day on the job with him. He must be in heaven, because at times she could feel him with her, like he was thinking of her, watching her – praying for her.

If he was watching, she would need to apologize. He tried so hard to give her a better life, away from the crime and danger he dealt with every day. She graduated college and did what he wanted, became a doctor – almost a doctor.

I'm sorry, Daddy. I did all that FOR you, when all I really wanted was to be LIKE you.

She would find out what happened to him. She had no idea if the Bureau was telling her the truth, a lie, or a convenient combination of the two. He disappeared on assignment and was declared dead after a year of no contact. She'd attended the ceremonies, listened to the speeches, received the plaques and the carefully folded flag and the condolences. She had even been brave like he would have wanted.

She'd understood as a child, from the time she first helped her Daddy put on his holster one morning, that he may never come back. It was part of the job, his *calling*. She accepted it. She accepted everything.

Especially the blame for his death.

So, the truth was more than all of that. Much more.

It was her fault. She was why he died. One day, she decided that *her* plans were more important than *their* plans, and she abandoned him. She didn't have time for him, and as a result she would never have time with him again. She paid every day for her part in his death. The person that actually took his life would pay as well. That was her promise to his memory. She would find justice.

She took a deep breath and wiped tears from her eyes. Gentle tears. Progress. She hadn't started bawling this time.

Yes, she would find justice, so Justice would have to wait.

Dawn stood and walked to the kitchen. She took the steaming popcorn out of the microwave and refilled her Dallas Cowboys souvenir cup. She made her way to the desk where her computer screensaver still cycled pictures from her past.

Onscreen beamed a picture of them at her Med School graduation. He was so proud that he had her picked up in a limo, with a two-car police escort, and driven to the ceremony. The next picture was of their first deer hunt together. She was only thirteen, but bagged an eight-point buck with one shot from her .243 caliber Savage. Her father made her field dress the deer, which was supposed to be gross. Instead, she thought it was great. Then and there she decided that if she couldn't be an FBI Agent like her daddy, she would be a surgeon – or taxidermist.

The last picture was of their final vacation to Disney World. They'd scheduled another vacation, to Disney Land this time, one that she'd cancelled. If they'd gone, she would be a doctor, and her father would still be alive.

She told herself to delete that picture, again. Again, she realized that she could never do that.

Dawn blinked away the wetness forming in her eyes, and hit the space bar on her keyboard. The system blinked and whined its way back to life. As the desktop appeared, she patted the little unicorn mounted on the top of the monitor. Uncle Danny had watched her tape it there, but didn't say anything. He knew the story, and he was the only person besides her and Daddy who did.

That was the first unicorn Dad gave her, mounted like that on her very first computer. It was painful. She wanted to take it down but couldn't do that, either.

Stop!

She needed to get on with her work. Other people were dead, too. Dawn would do something about that later.

She was about to have some *me* time.

She minimized the browser, where she had been learning about African Dogs in Texas. She had discovered that Texas and Africa had a number of similarities. Texas had become Africa's home away from home, with hundreds of ranches and preserves for the husbandry, and harvesting, of dozens of different African species. African Painted Dogs, however, were rare – and pretty. They had big, round ears and bigger teeth. Some were colored like they'd just lost a paintball war. The only place she'd found with a population living in the wild was the Red River Wildlife Preserve in Montague County.

Satisfied that she'd done enough follow up on her official obligations, she went to Lexisnexis for what she really wanted to do. She loved Lexisnexis. It wasn't nearly as good as Sentinel, the FBI database, but this was still pretty good. She'd learned about it in law school, for doing legal research, but it offered a lot more than just that.

Dawn reached beside the desk and retrieved a large, metal briefcase. She entered the combination and snapped open the lid. Inside was everything she had on her father's case. It wasn't much, but it was more than enough to get her started, and fired.

She pulled out the napkin she'd brought from the club. Two names were written there: John Jones, which was so common that it would be impossible to track down alone. And Jamais Bousaid, which would be much more productive. She'd never heard that name, how many hits could she get on that.

She adjusted the keyboard and did a search on *John Jones Dallas*. This would take a while, so she pulled a stack of papers and one of her burner phones from the briefcase. The papers were photographs of her father's case file that she'd managed to copy illegally while visiting friends at the Hoover Building.

She'd hated deceiving her father's friends, but she really hated that they wouldn't tell her a thing about what he'd been doing or where he'd gone. It's always a question of priorities, and sometimes priorities clash.

She went back to his phone log. By calling all of the numbers that he had called before disappearing, she was trying to discover some clue as to what he'd been doing. The previous half-dozen numbers were disconnected or had been reassigned by the phone company, but then came the Class of Dallas. And that was a real clue, maybe she'd find another. She called the next number.

It rang twice, and an elderly lady with a strong Texas drawl answered sweetly. "Is that you, honey?"

Dawn hesitated, and then answered. "I'm not sure. This is Cali Stenic, from the Texas Health United's Demographic Survey. Who were you expecting?"

Dawn's new friend cackled with joy. "Why, ain't this just wonderful, my first real phone call. Who'd ya'll say you were with?"

"I'm with THUDS, ma'am, and I'm trying to . . ."

"My grandkids got me this new phone, and . . . do you know Lisa Kaye and Bobby Joe? They got me this new cellular telephone. I only have to press one button to call people. I hold the one for those nice people at the fire station, two for Sarah, that's Lisa Kaye and Bobby Joe's . . . Who'd y'all say you were with?"

"Sorry, wrong number." Dawn disconnected.

That was strange.

Dawn crossed that number off her list and started to dial the next.

The computer dinged as the Lexis search ended. She looked at the results, and as she'd expected, there were well over a million entries.

Useless.

She did a new search on the second name, *Jamais Bousaid,* and resumed dialing the next number on her phone list.

Her FBI cell phone rang. The Caller ID said Denton Police.

"Agent Johnson," she almost shouted into the microphone.

Guzman's voice on the other end almost shouted as back. "He's at it again! Get over here."

"I'm on my way."

She turned off the burner phone, and then threw it and the papers back in her briefcase. She made sure it was locked, and then rested it behind the desk. She opened the desk drawer and punched in the code to Uncle Danny's gun safe. The lid popped open, and she grabbed her .40 caliber Glock and slid it into her belt holster. Then she grabbed her jacket off the back of the chair and threw it on.

I should have showered and changed, she realized.

Finally, she picked up her tablet computer, where she'd started gathering a dossier on Justice, and hurried toward the door. The call meant she had to stop work on her father's death, but she was still kind of looking forward to working a real case. A serial killer, on her first day. Her father worked a lot of serial killer cases. They got him excited, and made him feel good. He loved a challenge; he desperately wanted to stop the killers, and he desperately wanted to save any future victims.

Dawn realized that her breathing now came heavier and faster than her physical exertion demanded. She recognized the excitement. She realized that she now had that desire as well.

I am my Daddy's girl.

Chapter 16

Tuesday Morning
St Joe, Texas

Justice turned off Farm to Market Road 677 and drove slowly down Fielder Lane. He passed a narrow, ill-kept driveway and stopped. After carefully looking around, he stared down his next victim's long winding, tree-lined drive. Everything seemed quiet. Everything looked dark.

The next person on his "To Die List" had recently purchased this old frame house on the outskirts of St Joe, in Montague County, population now more than one thousand souls. This particular house rested in the middle of an acre and a half of trees and brush. It appeared to be a thoroughly uninviting piece of land, which perfectly reflected the personality of its new owner.

The executioner put his car in reverse, turned the wheel to the left, and backed into the drive. He moved his vehicle far enough up the gravel lane so that it would not be noticed by any passersby. Facing toward the road, he could glide straight out the drive and hurry away down the road, making for a neat and efficient getaway. He scouted this location before, and knew exactly where to stop so that he would be invisible to both the house and the road.

You can never be too careful when it comes to recompensing the wicked—or avoiding a lethal injection.

Car and lights off, Justice retrieved his murder phone. A tap brought the screen to life. The second tap opened his twitter app, and he began the laborious task of sending his next message. It was time to beguile the world in general, and the cops in particular.

Justice_4_theInnocent @mytweetrevenge
Justice 4 the people of Korea is moments away. Cops are watching now, like that matters. Clueless sphincters all.

Justice opened his door and got ready to begin. He reached reflexively across the seat to grab the duffle bag, and then stopped. He wouldn't need it here, so there was no point in carrying it along. He got out, and closed and locked the door before setting off up the drive. He was Justice, justice for an unjust world. At this moment, however, his journey would bear him unalterable toward Montana.

Jerry Montana had never been married, and probably never been laid. After unsuccessfully completing one term at Collin County Community College, Jerry became a postal carrier. After thirty-five years of reluctant, resentful service, he retired. Actually, he had been forced into retirement for disciplinary reasons, some fifteen years before tonight's impending encounter.

Throughout his life, Jerry Montana had been a nasty man—unyielding, though efficient and exacting in everything he did. His obsessive dedication to the "letter of the law" had been appreciated by his superiors, and despised by everyone else he came in contact with.

After retirement, Jerry moved back to his home town of

Denton, Texas. Retirement can change a person. Unfortunately, instead of aging gracefully like a fine wine, Jerry Montana fermented like a half-finished glass of grape juice left in the sun. He became a bitter old man who reveled in his acerbic and confrontational existence.

Enter Jin Soon Kim, Korean exchange student at UNT in Denton. Kim majored in Accounting, with a minor in Campus Wildlife. Kim was a party animal who never left a social gathering under his own power. In fact, he often needed help getting to the festivities, since his personal party schedule began when his final class bell rang. Kim had been very well liked, friendly, intelligent, popular, and currently quite dead – this last part thanks to the nasty Mr. Montana.

It happened on Halloween, three years ago. Kim, in a heroic manifestation of self-restraint, stayed sober enough to drive himself to the party thrown by a group of Chinese students. Unfortunately, he hadn't stayed sober enough to make it the whole way there. Kim made a fateful left turn just one block too soon, on Montana's street by mistake. Kim managed to find house number 2317. Instead of a raucous soiree, however, he found a sleeping racist. Kim burst into the non-party and stumbled through the house, yelling in Korean as he looked for the expected revelers. At this point, most believe that Jin passed out. Blood spatter indicated that Kim was laying against the wall when a single round of buckshot closed the ledger on Jin Soon Kim.

There was an international outcry, but Jerry Montana had his story down pat. He claimed, but almost no one believed, that he had been defending himself from an enraged intruder. After all, his very capable lawyer argued, the stranger had broken into his house, dressed in a very realistic ninja costume, and ranted like a mad man. The trespasser had refused to leave as ordered, and Mr. Montana had been forced to defend himself. Actually, almost no one in the jury believed it was self-defense. Forensics suggested that Kim had probably passed out before he had been shot. But, what's strictly legal prevailed over what's probably right, and three members of the jury could not shake their "reasonable doubt."

Hung jury. The Denton PD was still trying to get the case prosecuted. The ADA on the case, one Nicholas DaSalvo, didn't want to risk another blemish on his record.

Still, Jerry Montana soon found himself the object of incessant harassment. He also discovered that the Denton police now found his house very difficult to locate. Jerry's frequent tormentors always seemed to get away before the police could arrive. Finally, Mr. Montana sold his house and moved quietly to St. Joe, where no one knew him at all. Now he lived peacefully in a house without neighbors or tormentors. So far.

Justice, however, cannot be fooled. Even if a jury can. Justice knew the disgruntled former postal worker was there, and that he was a murderer. Justice, therefore, would dispense some tonight.

The executioner retrieved the gun from his pocket. He really liked this gun. It was actually older than him, and in better condition. It had no rust, and very little pitting on the outside of the barrel. Justice actually looked okay, too, but his pitting was mostly on the inside.

Justice felt a small, but sudden pang of loss. This well-made weapon would have lasted for centuries, if he weren't planning on melting it with a cutting torch in the morning. It was a useful weapon. It had a history, though Justice had no clue if it was a good history or bad. He did know that the final chapter of that history would be a good one. He was about to write it.

Justice then recognized another small, but sudden bit of irony. He felt bad that he would have to destroy the gun, but absolutely no remorse for his execution of Jerry Montana. Justice was amazed at how much he had changed after embracing this new sense of right and wrong.

He could see the house ahead through the trees and stopped. He pulled out his two phones and began to get ready. He hummed to himself. People to talk to, messages to send, trash to dispose of, then off to work.

Justice was tired. He would be glad when this was over so he could rest. For eternity.

Chapter 17

Tuesday Morning
Denton, Texas

Dawn followed Sergeant Cassavetes down a hallway, to the door labeled "Computer Crimes Division." The Sergeant bowed slightly and opened the door. He winked as she entered, and she managed not to laugh – or gag.

Inside she found Guzman and a tall man in his late fifties, standing behind a younger officer hunched over a computer terminal. They all stared at a bank of monitors on the wall behind the desk. She examined the eight large monitors, in two horizontal rows of four, and then moved up behind Guzman to see what had them so mesmerized.

Detective Guzman turned and smiled. "Sorry to get you up, but I figured you'd want to be involved."

"No problem, I was doing my own research anyway. Painted Dogs do not make great pets."

Guzman looked at the man standing next to him. Dawn saw he had weathered skin, unique, gray-blue eyes and an easy smile.

"Special Agent Johnson, this is Detective Allen Bird, from the Pontotoc Sheriff's Department. He's working the murder there."

Detective Bird extended his hand, and Dawn took it firmly. Bird had a nice handshake. His hands were rough, and his grip was solid without being overbearing.

Guzman pointed to the man hunched over the keyboard. "This is Officer Walker, one of our Computer Crimes Specialists."

Dawn was about to offer her hand, but Officer Walker just nodded, mumbled, and typed in a string of commands that appeared on the black screen directly in front of him. He leaned forward and squinted at the rows of numbers that flowed in scrolling lines below his entry.

He pointed at the bottom row of numbers. "There, that's the IP Address, he's been using the same one all night."

Dawn was familiar with all of this; the basics had been covered at the FBI Academy. "Can't you just trace it back to its source provider?"

Walker glanced over, annoyed. "Thank you! That's the first thing we did." He looked over at the monitor on the top row to his right. "It's routing through a Dark Internet cloud, located in Moscow as best I can tell. At least, that's where its exit portal is."

Dawn glanced at Guzman and Bird, who seemed to understand what that meant. Guzman glanced at Dawn, and recognized that she didn't. Guzman explained.

"As Walker just explained it, and I really don't understand much, is that the Dark Internet is made up of computer networks that can't be accessed from the regular Internet. A lot of them are actually networks that existed before the current internet address system was established. Some are networks set up to hide from the regular Internet."

Dawn asked again, "Right, but a portal for what? Is he tweeting again?"

Walker responded in his most professional, almost computer-generated voice. "Yes he's tweeting. No, this particular portal is not for that. He actually logged onto the Denton PD Website and posted a tip to our hotline. He's a cocky little nerf herder."

The others exchanged glances and confused shrugs. Dawn wanted a better explanation, but decided to wait like the others.

Walker continued in a mumbled monotone. "So even if we can find out where the Darknet he's using actually interfaces with the real Internet, we have no way of tracing where it enters that unofficial network. Only where it exits. The two infrastructures are totally independent and unrelated." Walker ceased to vocalize. With his voice, that was good. And during the whole monologue, he had been working his keyboard. It was like his brain was a Darknet, and his mouth and hands were totally independent and unrelated portals to the reality of Officer Walker.

Dawn smiled. *Maybe Walker's an android, with a Darknet for a brain.*

At that moment, the police-bot at the keyboard pointed at what looked like a standard Windows desktop on the lower monitor to his right. "The tweets now are different. Before he was working on a computer, now he's on his phone. These are his previous tweets, Twitter entries, from tonight. All but the first from his phone. The IP Address is from a twitter anonymizer he's using, located in Belarus." Walker looked up at Dawn, and she nodded back. She knew what an anonymizer was; it stripped out all of the original sender's information and substituted the anonymizer's instead. It meant they had hit a computer brick wall.

Dawn thought about that, but it didn't make sense. She looked at Walker. "If it's being routed through an anonymizer, how did you get all this information so fast?"

Walker stopped, looked up at her with surprise. "You're smart. Smarter than these two." He gestured at Guzman and Bird. "They never asked and I didn't have time to tell them."

Guzman ignored this, but Detective Bird did not look amused.

Walker went on. "Most of what I know comes from Kenny – that nasty sheriff's nephew, great nephew, some kind of nephew, whatever. He's damn smart for a High School kid. I knew about him, he helped track down an identity thief in Nacona a couple of years ago, and helps track down threats made on Twitter or Facebook in Montague and Grey County. He'd already asked Twitter to trace all of the killer's previous tweets. The people at Twitter do this all the time, and are really, really good at it."

He looked over his shoulder at a large stack of paper. "It's all over there; it's pretty cool how he did it."

"Excellent, let's take a look." Guzman smiled and started toward the printouts.

"Don't bother, it's useless." Walker informed them with a smug little smile.

Dawn massaged her temples and tried to rub away the headache and fatigue from her now weary brain. Things were getting cloudy, but she still remembered why she hated nerds.

Guzman looked over and swiped wearily at his own eyes. He gestured to the door. "This way."

Dawn followed him out of the door, then right down the corridor. He walked past the restrooms and pulled opened the next door on his left. They entered a small room that looked a lot like her room as a freshman in college. Along two walls rose bunk beds, three sets, that appeared clean and freshly made. To her left were the sink, mini-fridge, and counter with coffee maker and accessories.

Guzman ushered her inside. "Our crash house. It's not much, but it's all we got. Okay for a couple hours shut-eye." He pointed at the wall next to the door. "Rules."

Dawn turned and read:

1. Keep all weapons under positive control at all times.
2. No loud noise of any kind.
3. If you didn't bring it, don't eat it.
4. You snore too loud; you're gone.
5. Farting strictly prohibited.

Good rules, she nodded and sat on the bed next to Guzman. She discovered that fatigue had begun to creep into her mind and body. She looked at the counter. Coffee was out of the question, but she considered going back to the task force room for water and cookies.

Guzman started snoring, so much for the rules.

Chapter 18

Tuesday Morning
St Joe, Texas

KISS

Keep It Simple Stupid. Justice would keep it simple, and direct. Walk up, dispense justice, walk away, tweet it.

He looked at his watch, 3:27 am, and hit send after completing his next tweet.

> **Justice_4_theInnocent** @mytweetrevenge
> I can see the house, looks peaceful. The guilty die tonight not the innocent, no matter how drunk or stupid.

Someone was about to kiss their life goodbye.

He resumed walking as he retrieved the spent Roman candle shell from his pocket. He slid the notched end of the tube over the barrel of his pistol, which transformed it from expended noise maker to improvised sound suppressor. The tube, with the nylon washers acting as noise baffles inside, would almost completely eliminate the sound of the weapon. This constituted the next move in his endgame, the white knight was about to claim another piece. But the knight would move more carefully now, because the black queen had entered the game.

The homemade silencer may have been overkill, but underkill could be a real problem. There couldn't be any noise, the neighbors had dogs. Dogs had exceptional hearing and even louder voices.

You can never be too careful.

Justice reached the house, and trudged up the steps. He heard loud, excited barking from inside. He knew Montana had two large dogs, and the killer appreciated the fact that they were kept inside at night. Justice certainly didn't what to hurt any innocent animals in the discharge of his duties.

He reached the door and was about to knock, when an angry voice boomed from inside.

"Who's there, what do you want?"

"Officer Guzman, it's the St. Joe Police. We've received another complaint."

There had been several recent and anonymous complaints that Mr. Montana had been discharging a weapon on his land. The speculation was that he'd been poaching the occasional deer, which still thrive in the semi-rural environs of St. Joe.

Justice had become aware of the complaints, since he was not only the person firing the gun, but also the one who had called in the complaints. Two entries in the local paper had confirmed that Montana had received official visits from the police – among other law enforcement agencies.

Montana's voice seemed to indicate that he did not enjoy these visits. "Damn it to hell. I told you it ain't me! Go away and leave me alone."

"You know I can't do that, sir. Please make sure your dogs, and any weapons you may have on hand, are secured and out of the way. Then I need you to open the door. This is our third visit on the same grievance, so I will have to present you with a formal complaint. I'm sorry."

"This is harassment! I'm going to file my own complaint when I find out who's doing this."

The sounds of a very angry Jerry Montana roared through the heavy front door as he locked his dogs in another room. Heavy, slippered feet stomped back to the front of the house, followed immediately by the sounds of a chain and deadbolt being unlocked.

The door flew open, and a red-faced stick of a man stood framed by the crumbling white wooden frame. He shook his finger, and his agitated voice croaked out. "I'm warning you, if . . ."

Montana stopped in mid-sentence and stared, then squinted at the figure on his porch.

"Wait, you're not the St. Joe Police."

Jerry looked down and saw the red, white and blue label of the fireworks, attached to a dark shape in Justice's hand. He didn't recognize it, and shook his head in confusion.

"What the hell? What's going on?"

Justice raised his gun and fired three times. The H&R revolver was double action, so he didn't have to pull the hammer back manually with each round. He did notice that the trigger pull seemed a little heavier than when he'd test fired the gun. Maybe it was just him getting weaker. Double action revolvers are a little harder to fire, but there's the decided advantage of not having to retrieve any empty cartridges. They stay in the cylinder instead of being ejected, like with an automatic pistol.

Justice again felt startled by the emotionless thoughts which played through his mind, as he watched the tiny red dots appear in the center of Jerry Montana's chest. He thought of trigger pull as the astonish man took two small, staggering steps backwards.

Justice pulled back the hammer, took careful aim, and fired. Montana froze in place, probably a heart shot.

The small, low velocity bullets lacked the power to knock him down, but they would reach his heart – or if necessary, his brain. Justice aimed to fire again, when Jerry's face went slack and his hands dropped limply to his side. Finally, Jerry Montana took a final, halting step forward and collapsed to the floor.

Justice cocked his head and looked, watching long enough to be sure that his victim was indeed gone. He'd seen a photo of Jin Soon Kim's mangled body, and Montana's body was in much better shape – though just as dead. Justice looked at his victim, who stared vacantly at the wall socket next to his head. Justice fired another round, at the head this time.

You can never be too careful.

Justice looked down at his weapon. The silencer had worked better than expected. No one could have heard a whisper of the pistol's report, as he'd planned. They may have heard the frantic barking of the dogs, however, which should have been factored into his plan.

He looked carefully at the body. There was no doubt that Jerry Montana's soul had been dropped into that dead letter box in the sky. However, the bullet grouping was pretty good, maybe too good. He fired one more round into the right shoulder of the body, then his final round into the picture of a little girl holding flowers that hung on the wall. A couple of misses would throw them off.

Justice spun around and marched down the steps and off toward his waiting car. He listened carefully as he moved down the drive, but heard nothing from the neighbors. If anyone had heard anything, they would probably just call the St. Joe's police, and in an hour or so they may really be paying Montana a visit.

Back inside his car, Justice quickly replayed the execution in his mind. This is one he had actually looked forward to. The next one, the final one, he had selected as an unsuspecting favor to someone else. Justice was not looking forward to killing a woman, but the final execution wasn't for him.

As he again remembered the bullets punching neat little holes in Jerry Montana's chest, he also realized his worries about being able to carry out the final murder were unnecessary. He was a committed man. He was a changed man, too, but he could deal with that later.

Justice pulled out his phone and entered the final tweet for this evening's execution. He then drove carefully home.

Chapter 19

Tuesday Morning
Denton, Texas

"I think he's done!"

Dawn looked toward the door. Walker had mysteriously appeared in the room. Guzman still snored, and she decided to get that water before she went to sleep.

Walker walked to Guzman. "I said he's done."

Dawn blinked and focused on the nerd. *So fast?*

Guzman opened one eye. "I will shoot you."

"Come on; get your asses out of bed. I think we've got enough to work with."

Guzman dragged himself to a sitting position. "How long?"

"Couple hours," Walker set a stack of papers on the counter. "I gotta get back."

As Walker left, Dawn sat up.

"Let's get at it." From the third bed Bird sat, and then stood. He slipped into his loafers, stretched once, then grabbed the paper and walked to the door. "Let's go talk to Walker."

Bird seemed fully awake by the time he'd left the room, while Dawn hadn't even known she'd fallen asleep. She hated him right now.

She stood. Guzman stood. Both rubbed their eyes and struggled to reach full wakefulness. Dawn looked for her jacket, which she picked up off the floor, and followed Guzman out. They went directly to the restrooms, and then met in the Computer Crimes bat cave.

As they entered, Bird handed them a copy of the latest reports. Dawn and Guzman sat facing Bird, who'd already read through the information.

Guzman mumbled. "What've we got?"

Bird opened his mouth to answer, but Walker interrupted from his ergonomic black throne. "More tweets." He pointed at the screen, where Justice's Twitter account remained on the display. The first tweet read:

Justice_4_theInnocent @mytweetrevenge
Say good-bye to my little friend. Dim R sum obvious clues I left, but cops and walrus R 2 stupid to figure it out.

The group read the tweet, thought about it, then looked blankly at each other and shrugged. They read the next one.

Justice_4_theInnocent @mytweetrevenge
ROFL at stupid cops. Hurry, only 1 more chance before Justice is fulfilled. BFN

Dawn looked at the time stamp. It had been posted 28 minutes ago. *Why such a long delay?*

Bird shook his head. "What does R-O-F-L stand for?"

Walker answered the question without even thinking. "It means 'rolling on the floor laughing.' He could have used L-O-L, meaning 'laughing out loud,' or L-M-A O, 'laughing my ass off.'

There are lots of others, too."

Walker pushed himself away from the computer desk, held up the fingers on his left hand, and pointed at his pinkie. Dawn realized he was about to recite some painfully boring, dweebishly annoying list. She raised a hand to interrupt, but Guzman beat her to it.

"That's great information, Officer Walker, thank you. Do you think you can locate a complete list of acronyms and print them out for us? I doubt any of us have your expertise with the subject, and will probably need to refer to it in the future as well."

"Sure thing." Walker rolled forward to the desk.

Dawn wanted information about the murder more than a glossary of nerd terms. Again, Guzman moved first. He held up his copy of the papers, "Officer Walker, does this have everything?"

Walker huffed and looked offended. "Of course. All the tweets, from the beginning. All my email and IM's from Kenny and the Twitter people. It has the location and ownership of all of the anonymizer and Darknet sites we've been able to identify. It also has a list of our killer's close friends and favorite flavor of gum."

Guzman's head spun from the papers to Walker. "Really?"

Walker smirked back. "No."

Guzman extended his middle finger until it almost came in contact with Walker's nose. Walker gave a satisfied smile and returned to his keyboard.

Bird hesitated, and then finally asked. "Are we sure he's done?"

Guzman answered before Walker could get started again. "B-F-N is bye for now. He's signing off."

The Cyber Crimes Officer nodded and bent over the keyboard; his fingers began to move in a blur. Seconds later, a massive laser printer in the corner whined to life. Detective Guzman moved around a vacant desk as the printing started, and waited for the stack of papers to stop growing. Finally, he grabbed them and hurried toward the door.

He stopped and turned to Walker. "I need coffee. We're set up in Interrogation Room 3 if anything else comes up." Bird grabbed a briefcase sitting next to the door, and Guzman ushered them out and down the hall. Dawn realized she hadn't remembered to grab her briefcase or laptop from the apartment, just her tablet.

They walked down several hallways, and entered Room 3. Inside they found a large Formica and steel table with half a dozen chairs around it. In the middle, they saw several stacks of papers, note pads, and a forest of coffee cups and sandwich wrappers. It appeared that Guzman hadn't made it home yet. He gestured for them to sit, and he moved to his roost at the head. Dawn and Bird took seats on either side of him.

He rubbed his eyes, suddenly looking worn out and frustrated. "He's out there right now. How the hell do we find him? Who did he just kill?"

Bird folded his arms and rested them on the table. "I'm sure someone will report it before too long." He looked at the cups in front of Guzman. "I actually do need some coffee."

Guzman pointed at a corner of the room, to the left of the door they'd just entered. A small folding table held a large thermos and a stack of white Styrofoam cups. There was a cup holding sweeteners and a plate with a stack individually wrapped chocolate cupcakes. Bird's eyes brightened. His day was looking up and hurried over.

Guzman set a stack of papers in front of Dawn. "These are the final printouts from Walker. Now you have tonight's tweets, and a bunch of meaningless numbers and names. As if that's supposed to help."

Dawn looked at the addresses and routing information on the first page. It may mean something to her, but probably not much. She asked, "Any chance of getting some computers in here, with Internet access?"

Guzman nodded. "Good idea. I'll check on that."

Bird set two cups of coffee and a cupcake on the table. "Anything useful from the asshole's tweets?" He opened his briefcase and retrieved a notepad and pen.

Dawn had a pen in her purse, and turned the last sheet in her stack of papers over to write on. She needed to get herself organized. Just because this was her first case didn't mean she could act like a rookie.

Guzman's phone rang while she chastised herself a little more.

"Detective Guzman." He listened, and a look of anguish distorted his face. He rolled his eyes as he spoke. "Yes, Sheriff, we've been following the . . . yes, this phone has a speaker . . . fine."

Guzman set his phone on the table, pressed a button, and spoke loudly. "I'm here with Detective Bird from Oklahoma, and Special Agent Johnson."

"No need to shout, boy, I can hear just fine. The little FBI lady made it, huh? I'll be sure and bring some croissants and apricot marmalade when I come in. I'm driving back from Bowie. I really didn't think our killer would move so quick, damit. Why don't you read me those tweets, maybe we can get a line on our nutcase or his victim."

"Fine. First, you should know that we haven't been able to get a trace on any of the . . ."

"I got all that," the sheriff sounded impatient. "I just talked with Kenny. He pulled an all-nighter, and man oh man, is his mamma mad at me."

No kidding, Dawn thought. *He's a child, no matter how smart he is.*

"Okay," Guzman read the first page of his printout. "This was posted at 12:07 AM, but no telling when it was actually typed. It says 'Justice for the people of Korea." He looked around "Korea'?"

No one had a comment, so he continued reading. "Cops are watching now, clueless assholes all."

Sheriff Scates chuckled. "I don't think he respects us, which is good. Anything ring a bell?"

Everyone around the table shook their head, so the detective read the next tweet.

"Okay, next one, posted about an hour after the first. 'I can see the house, looks peaceful. The guilty die tonight, not the innocent, no matter how drunk or stupid.'"

Scates spoke first. "He's watching his victim's house, maybe still in his car or driving by."

Bird picked it up from there. "All of these are a type of revenge killing. Someone got away with a crime, and this joker is paying them back. Sounds like his next victim killed someone, someone innocent, maybe from Korea. So, the one he thinks is guilty will die tonight. The victim was stupid, or drunk, or both. Is our killer talking about the victim of that first killing or the perpetrator of it?"

"I'm thinking victim," Guzman thought aloud.

"I agree," Scates' voice came over the phone. Everyone nodded in agreement. "Next?"

Guzman read on. "This one came half an hour later. Just before 2 a.m. 'Say good-bye to my little friend. Dim R Sum obvious clues I left, but cops and walrus R 2 stupid to figure it out.'"

There was a pause. In the room, they stared at each other blankly.

Scates voice scratched out of the tiny speaker. "Anyone?"

Bird asked. "Any place around here with walruses?"

Guzman shook his head, and then asked. "Is that another Korean reference? Dim Sum?"

Scates replied sarcastically. "I thought Dim Sum was Chinese."

Bird nodded. "No, Dim Sum are small, bite-sized things that . . ."

"Save it," Scates interrupted. "We can all sit down together and watch the cooking channel after we solve this. What else, about the case?"

Dawn added. "He probably likes Scarface, the movie."

Guzman nodded. "Say good-bye to my little friend."

Dawn continued "The exact quote is 'Say hello to my little friend.'"

The sheriff concurred. "Yeah, that's right. But Scarface is before your time, sweet thing. Are you an Al Pacino fan or something?"

Dawn shook her head for the benefit of those in the room. "No, my dad was from Miami. He loved Miami, and we watched about every movie about Miami, or that was ever made there, at least a dozen times."

"Miami, right," Scates chuckled, "What was the name of that movie with the fish? A crime movie. What was the name?"

Dawn really didn't care about fish movies. "I'm not sure, but in Scarface, Al Pacino's character, Tony Montana, has an M16 with a grenade launcher. He is about to . . ."

Dawn looked as Guzman stood. He stared at the floor. Then he shook his head slowly, mumbling. "Korea. Montana." Arturo smacked his forehead in frustration. "Remember! What am I missing?"

He stared directly at his phone on the table. "Drunk and innocent. I know who tonight's victim is, but I think he's moved."

Scates sounded excited. "If you got a name, try DMV first. They'll have the latest address. I'll be there in three hours, maybe more. Bad cell on the way, so text when you get an address."

Dawn wasn't sure Detective Guzman heard, as he sprinted for the door.

Chapter 20

Tuesday Morning
St. Joe, Texas

During their drive to the crime scene Dawn had gotten to know, and appreciate, Detective Guzman. While he had been born and raised in Texas, both of his parents were illegals. They snuck into the US just before his birth to ensure that their baby would be born on American soil. The detective himself used the term "anchor baby," and Dawn felt relieved, she didn't have to do any PC tiptoeing around the subject.

Anchor babies are common in Border States with Mexico, though less common now than when little Arturo Guzman entered the world. Then US Immigrants, usually illegal immigrants, would come to the US and have a baby. Any child born in the US qualifies for citizenship. This citizen in Pampers acts as an anchor, helping to keep the parents in the country as well. It's almost always in a child's best interest to keep his parents, and a US citizen can't be deported.

Now they don't bother sneaking in to give birth. Now there

are thousands of kids pouring into the US every day, and nobody does a thing about it. When the child gets older, they can then act as sponsors for their parents. This comes with the advantage of being the immediate family of a US resident.

Daddy Guzman didn't take that route. Instead, he enlisted in the Air Force. Military service is another shortcut to citizenship, and it worked out well for the family. Guzman's father became an airframe technician, a taxpayer, and a Republican. Little Arturo became the first of their family to graduate from college.

Detective Guzman was also a very thoughtful person, and intervened when Sergeant Cassavetes volunteered to assist with the investigation by acting as chauffeur to the task forces' FBI liaison. Simply stated, the Horn-dog Sergeant wanted to get Dawn alone in his car. Guzman took pity and insisted that she ride with him. Maybe he didn't want the Sergeant's car out of service while they cleaned up all of the drool, the stains, and finally the messy blood splatter. Either way, Detective Bird ended up with the jealous and disappointed patrol sergeant, while Dawn and Arturo became friends and fellow fighters of crime as they discussed the case on their drive to Montana.

They had traveled up I-35, and then taken a state Highway east. They'd traveled down a series of farm roads, whose names Dawn never saw, until they saw the flashing blue and red lights ahead. An officer started to wave them past, and then allowed them to enter when Guzman held his badge and ID out the window. Dawn saw that the officer on traffic duty was from the St. Joe's Police Department as they passed.

Dawn sat up and looked ahead. "I'm surprised they're letting us use the driveway."

Guzman stuck his head out the window and examined the road. "It's gravel. They're not going to get anything off it, so why make everyone walk in. It doesn't look like Scates should get that much exercise."

Dawn shrugged. She would have secured the scene differently.

The winding drive seemed about fifty yards long, but she

wasn't sure since the house had been set back from the road and surrounded by trees. About fifteen yards from the house, the drive curved left and the house came into view. She noticed now that only the ambulance, a crime scene van, and Sheriff Scates' Suburban had been allowed to use the driveway before them.

The house was an old frame structure with wooden siding, all of it held together by mold and rot. The front porch had been taped off, and two deputies, a tall man with a clipboard and a petite and attractive female, stood guard on either side of the tiny porch. Beyond the tape, a pair of crime scene technicians in white protective suits knelt working in the open front doorway. Even from that distance they could hear the frantic barking of two, enormous sounding dogs.

As they approached, they saw a body lying on the floor just a few feet inside the threshold. Sheriff Scates stood watching, just outside the tape. He turned as they approached and waved them closer. He smiled at Detective Guzman.

"Damn fine work, detective. He has no family, and fewer friends, so it would have taken a long time to discover the body if you hadn't figured it out."

"Thank you Sheriff, but Jerry Montana's almost as well know as Jimmy Oltman. The clues were pretty obvious; anyone from the Denton PD could have figured it out. Our computer nerds did most of the work after that."

Sheriff Scates' face transformed into a weird, almost goofy facsimile of itself. He half smiled at Guzman.

"Nerd. Interesting word. Know where it comes from?"

Guzman looked at Scates, and then rolled his eyes toward Dawn. His silent plea for mercy told her that he didn't know, didn't care, and definitely didn't want to find out. Scates must not have noticed, since he continued with his explanation.

"Dr. Seuss."

Guzman looked back at Scates and scowled. This only encouraged the Sheriff more.

"That's right. *If I Ran the Zoo*."

This had Dawn shaking her head in confusion. Scates

beamed. For some reason, this seemed to make his morning.

"The Dr. Seuss book. A Nerd was one of the make-believe animals they wanted to stick in the zoo. They were supposed to be unpleasant little critters, so you can see how it stuck."

What Dawn could not see, was why he brought it up or thought they'd care.

Guzman must have felt the same. "That's fascinating. I'll read it to my kids after we've nabbed our killer."

Scates became serious, or at least pretended to. His eyes narrowed, and he stared at the detective. "Son, you need to think about everything, all the time. Keeps the mind sharp, and you never know what relates to a case and what don't."

Guzman didn't respond, and instead just stared back at the sheriff.

"See, I got stuck with this task force comprised of you, this FBI pinup babe, and a detective from Oklahoma that only wants to go home. So it looks like I run the zoo, don't it?"

Dawn stared at the Sheriff, and considered drug use as a possible explanation. He still wore those stupid, polychromatic shades which almost completely hid his eyes. Almost, but since they were in heavy shade, they'd lightened up enough for her to make out his pupils. Pupils which appeared slightly dilated. A feint slurring had always occurred in his speech, so maybe that was normal.

Scates returned her stare, and then sniffed loudly. "Anyone want to examine the body?"

"From there!" The smaller, female criminalist insisted from inside.

The sheriff stepped aside, and the four new arrivals crowded up to the tape. Dawn noticed that Scates kept his eyes on her. He knew this was her first case, but didn't know that it was definitely not her first dead body. She examined it critically, trying to determine if there was anything out of place.

The wounds were small caliber. Three, maybe four neatly grouped bullets had penetrated to the left of the victim's sternum. Fatal, even for low weight bullets. The same rules applied for real estate and for bullet rounds: location, location, location. The fact that she still had a heartbeat attested to the truth of that. For her, a few inches higher and she'd have a piece of real estate right next to her father.

She heard Guzman speaking. "Small caliber, definitely. I'd guess a little pocket pistol."

Scates nodded in agreement. "Sounds right."

Dawn looked around, carefully examining the scene. She then shook her head as she analyzed what she saw. "Revolver, .22 caliber, probably the short rounds, but they were definitely low energy bullets."

"Really, now?" Scates sounded skeptical.

Dawn nodded confidently and pointed toward the victims head. "Look at the side of his skull. One round struck the cranium, below the inferior temporal line. Probably very near the squamosal suture. It failed to penetrate, even though the bone there is very thin and weak. I would expect perforation there from almost any round, though if he used a silencer that would adversely impact the velocity. My guess is that it had to be a revolver firing shorties, with a silencer."

Dawn nodded again to herself, certain she'd gotten it right. She then looked at the others who appeared much less certain, or at least much more confused.

Sheriff Scates finally nodded appreciatively. "I'll buy that, except the suture thing. I don't see any scars."

Dawn didn't want to give a lesson in cranial anatomy, and let it pass.

They were interrupted by the ambulance crew, who wheeled a gurney toward the porch.

A short, stocky female pulling a gurney gently moved Dawn to the side. "Y'all will have to leave; we need to load the body."

Scates glared at the team from the coroner's office. "Let's all sit in my car," and led the way to his Suburban.

Chapter 21

Tuesday Morning
St. Joe, Texas

They moved to the Sheriff's SUV. Scates and Guzman sat in the front seat, Dawn and Detective Bird in the back. Once they'd settled in, Sergeant Cassavetes opened Dawn's door and squeezed inside beside her. Dawn scooted over as far as she could, but still couldn't get away. She really didn't need this.

Scates turned in his seat to look into the back. The lenses of his annoying sunglasses faded from black to almost clear, definitely polychromatic. No wonder he never took them off. They must be prescription. And his eyes were clearly dilated. When Guzman also turned to face the back, Scates spoke to Detective Bird. "We're not all up to speed on all the murders. You start; give us a one paragraph synopsis of your victim and investigation so far."

Bird looked uncertain. "I'll try." He shifted in his seat then looked at everyone in turn as he spoke.

"The 'vic' was Paul Clearwater from Ada, Oklahoma. He was

an oilfield roughneck, working for a drilling company operating in the area. He first came to our attention three years ago, in the rape of Tanya Burke. Sixty-three-year-old Burke, a very devout member of the Pontotoc Missionary Christian Fellowship, was on her way home from church one Wednesday night, when she was assaulted. Her intoxicated assailant was positively identified with the aid of his wallet, which fell out of his pocket during the attack. DNA confirmed it was him."

Bird paused briefly and Dawn saw him look at the others, making sure they had processed this information. When he had everyone's full attention again, except Cassavetes, who seemed to be inspecting the buttons her Dawn's blouse, he continued.

"We couldn't locate Clearwater, but Ms. Burke ID'd him in a photo lineup. We had photos from previous encounters. While we were looking for Clearwater, he visited his victim again, at church. He stopped her before services that next Wednesday night. Our Mr. Clearwater isn't smart, but he's clever. You see, the traumatized Ms. Burke had recited the Lord's Prayer the whole time Paul was having his way with her, helping her make it through the ordeal."

Bird paused briefly to compose himself. "The piece of shit Clearwater convinced the poor old lady that her prayers had touched his heart. He went with her to the services, and right there in her church, he repented. Said he accepted Christ as his Savior and threw himself at the mercy of her and God. They even prayed together, and the wonderful old lady forgave him and promised she wouldn't press charges, or even testify. Lucky thing, too, because we are convinced he would have killed her right there if she hadn't. Not that it helped. A week after the case was dismissed, she died in her sleep. Cause of death unknown, but we suspect she was suffocated."

Dawn found that she had been holding her breath, and let it out with a sigh. She had heard similar stories at the Academy, but this was different, personal. She almost felt happy that Paul Clearwater had met Justice.

Detective Guzman had listened carefully, less affected than

Dawn. He asked. "How was he killed?"

"We think he was hit with a stun gun, then beaten to death with a large crucifix while he was alone, manning the graveyard shift on a drilling rig. His relief found the body mounted on the derrick, arms spread wide apart and a fence post jammed up his ass. That part was postmortem, but it was still pretty brutal. I brought copies of our files, with a full photo workup. They're back at the Denton PD offices."

Sheriff Scates read from a paper on his lap. "Only two tweets that time. First one said 'This isn't the road from Damascus. Justice will finally have retribution.'"

Scates looked around. "In the Bible, the Apostle Paul was converted on the Road from Damascus."

"To Damascus," Dawn interrupted.

Scates turned to stare at her.

She repeated. "He was killed on the road to Damascus not from."

The Sheriff raised his eyebrows quizzically and looked at the others, who shrugged.

He looked back at Dawn. "Who gives a shit?"

Cassavetes saw the opportunity to score some points. "Sheriff, I think it's important to be precise. You never know what details will be . . ."

"Shut the hell up, we know what are "de tails" you're lookin' for. In fact, why don't we take this opportunity to be precise? I want you to get out a' my car and take *exactly* ten steps toward those trees. Then you can stop and try and figure out if there's any way you could be a bigger dumbass than you are now? I'm bettin' you can't."

Cassavetes chuckled, like he was going along with the joke.

Scates stared, like he was going to rip Cassavetes head off.

"I'm serious, boy, get on outta my car."

The sergeant got out and walked toward the woods. No one counted the steps.

Scates sniffed disgustedly, and then looked down to read the final tweet. "The violators will be violated," he looked at Bird.

"Probably a reference to how y'all found him."

Bird nodded solemnly.

Scates winced as he adjusted himself in his seat, obviously uncomfortable from having to twist his body to face them. After a moment, he continued. "My victim, here in Montague County, was Kerwin Munch, a doctor. He moved from Philadelphia, PA, to the lovely little town of Stoneburg in Montague County. Claimed it was for his health. He opened an office downtown, and became acquainted with Madam Graves. Harriett Graves runs the Stoneburg Championship School of Cheer and Gymnastics. They mainly teach little girls to be cheerleaders."

Scates paused briefly to catch his breath, and then continued. "Being new in town, and wanting to fit in, he offered to treat any of the girls from the academy that got injured at a big discount. With little girls and gymnastics, there was always someone getting hurt. He seemed to be a good doctor; people liked and respected him at first. Before too long, though, people started having questions about his therapy methods, especially one he referred to as 'internal muscle manipulation.' There was a trial, but he bought off most of the parents. The little girls couldn't testify to exactly what went on, and his lawyer came up with some bogus study that described 'the therapy' which the doctor employed as "innovative and effective in some cases." Dr. Munch got off and was fixin' to move on, again for pressing needs related to maintaining his health and heartbeat, when he ended up in the African Painted Dog enclosure at the nearby Red River Wild Animal Refuge. The coroner thinks he was dead before he was put there, but there were so few pieces left she couldn't be sure."

"The tweets for this execution were almost identical to the ones from Oklahoma. I have current copies of our files right here. Obviously, they're bein' updated as we look closer at the murder. With our killer pickin' up his pace like this, we may be a little behind the curve."

"We have the same problem," added Bird.

Scates turned to Detective Guzman, "Your turn."

The Detective went through the death of Jimmy Ray Oltman,

in greater detail then either Bird or the sheriff had regarding theirs. He pointed out that they had the benefit of knowing early on it was a serial killer, and had been able to conduct the investigation accordingly. He promised everyone that copies of all Denton PD's current material would be waiting when they got back.

Everyone sat in silence for a moment. Even for experienced law enforcement professionals, these cases were hard to deal with. Dawn had dealt with enough brutality during her Emergency Room work that she'd become hardened against evil. Hardened but not immune, and she had to wipe at the tears clouding her vision.

Scates grinned at Dawn. "And what does the FBI have to contribute?"

Hygiene came to mind first. None of the men seemed to have attended to their personal grooming in the last couple of days. "What kind of assistance are you requesting?"

"Formally? Not a damn thing. Informally, why don't you go over what you were saying about the murder weapon?" The Sheriff grimaced and turned around to face the front of the car.

Dawn gathered her thoughts, and began. "It's not that hard. You're looking for a .22 caliber, seven shot revolver loaded with . . ."

"Seven shot?" Guzman interrupted.

"At least seven. There were five shots in the body, one to the head, and a third in a picture to the left of the victim."

"I didn't see that, did you?" Bird looked at Scates and Guzman, who shook their heads.

"Forensics will find it when they finish with the body and go over the crime scene itself. I suspect the killer was an expert shot. The fatal wounds were tightly grouped around the heart."

"Doesn't sound like he was an expert shot if he missed from that range. I saw one shot in the right arm, and you said he missed entirely and hit the wall."

"Yes, but the shot to the arm was entirely clean, no blood, and therefore postmortem. You would expect at least some blood flow from the wound if the heart were still beating. The others showed significant bleeding. The wound to the head, as I said, failed to penetrate. It was a very weak round, even for a .22."

She stopped and looked around. The others stared back, processing.

Finally, Guzman nodded. "Makes sense, how did you learn so much about guns and gunshots?"

"I've had some medical training. And I've been shooting since I was a little girl. My father was FBI, and besides the formal training, my dad just loved to shoot. It was something we could do together. My grandpa too. He had a small gun collection."

Scates nodded imperceptibly, and then mumbled as he looked out his window, "I remember hearing that."

Everyone looked at him. Dawn had to make sure she'd heard him right, and was about to ask what he meant when Scates opened his door.

"I need some air."

He got out, and everyone followed. Dawn wanted to get around the car to Scates, but she saw Cassavetes make a grinning bee line in her direction. She turned and made her escape toward the house.

At that moment, two women and a large man wearing SPCA t-shirts strode up the drive carrying capture poles. When they tried to enter the front of the house, the crime scene team went into hysterics. The SPCA people were insistent, since the whining and barking of the dogs inside was now constant. The forensic techs were equally insistent that the crime scene not be disturbed.

They finally reached an agreement, and the SPCA team entered by the back door. A few minutes later, the sound of an epic struggle exploded from inside the house. There was growling, barking, then the sound of breaking glass and shattering furniture. A cry for help from inside prompted the male deputy and Sergeant Cassavetes to sprint to the rear of the house to assist.

About five minutes later, the five humans staggered around the house in a violent struggle with . . . Dawn first thought they were two brown horses, horses that barked and growled. Dawn stood petrified as the procession of angry claws and teeth approached.

Even Sheriff Scates was impressed. "Jesus H. Christ! Those are the biggest mastiffs I've ever seen."

The dogs and their barely handlers approached, but Dawn was a statue, frozen in place. Detective Guzman must have seen the fear on her face, and rushed to her aid. He guided her back to the Suburban, and safety, before the animals reached her. Dawn could only stare as the undulating mass of human and canine body parts struggled past and wrestled their way toward the road.

"Are you OK?" Guzman sounded concerned.

Dawn shook her head.

"You don't like dogs?"

"Dogs don't like me. Animals don't like me. Especially big ones."

Scates moved next to them. "We need to pull up tent poles and get this circus back on the road." He looked around. "Where's our Okie boy?"

Scates located Bird, and then called everyone over.

"There's a lot to do, and we need to divide our efforts."

Guzman frowned; he showed no interest in letting Scates order him around. "I need to interview Oltman's family, friends and co-workers. Also, we should . . ."

"Right, that's your assignment," Scates interrupted. "Start with his friends, girl friends if he had any. If he's had problems or threats, he would most likely have told them. Then coworkers, see if there were any incidents at his job. I'm going to set up a conference call for tonight, so we can compare notes and go over any forensic evidence that's come in?"

Cassavetes crept back toward the group, and Scates pointed in his direction. "You!"

Cassavetes stopped in his tracks.

Scates continued. "You drive Detective Bird around. He's going to help work that little gook boy angle in Denton while it's still fresh."

Bird scowled, "Gook boy?"

Scates scowled, "Gook boy. The slant eyed kid that Montana shot."

Dawn snapped, "You mean Jin Soon Kim? He has a name."

Scates waved his hand dismissively. "And it sounds like the noise from an old pin ball machine."

Cassavetes had been staring at Dawn. "Agent Johnson doesn't have transportation. I thought . . ."

Scates wasn't interested. "I'm sure we all know what you were thinking." He turned to Bird. "Start at his school, ask if any of his friends talked about getting even. Then check with the other . . ." he glanced at Dawn, "acquaintances and neighbors of the Asiatic persuasion. See if any of them know anything or act suspicious. Then check in with Guzman, he'll know what y'all need to do after that. Me and my detectives will interview the neighbors here, then try and locate any of our victim's family or friends. I want to talk to the folks up at the refuge, the Wildlife Refuge, about our first murder. I need to look at that place again, in light of the new developments. Now that we know this is a serial killer, I have more questions."

Scates thought for a minute, and then looked around. "Anything else?"

Dawn's face turned red, *damn right there's something else.* "You didn't mention me, so I assume I can pursue my own areas of investigation. The forensic evidence should be looked at, and I'd like to visit with the coroner."

Scates raised a hand, whistled very loudly, and then yelled. "Sharp!"

The female deputy looked up, looked around, then hurried toward the group. She stopped in front of the Sheriff with eager, doe eyes. Dawn was afraid he would pat her head and say, "Good girl, sit!"

Instead, he ordered, "Please take Special Agent Johnson to that coroner, and other places, like we discussed. You are authorized to stay as long as necessary. After that, I'd like her to meet with Kenny and go over the Geek stuff with him. After that she will probably want to go back to her car in Denton."

Scates looked at Dawn. "When you're done at the coroner, you may want to check out the status of our online investigation." He nodded toward Deputy Sharp who now stood next to Dawn. "She'll take you to talk with Kenny if you like. You understand this computer mess better than the rest of us, so you're more likely to understand what he's found."

The sheriff paused, and then smiled mischievously. "Take all the time you need. If there are questions or problems, feel free to work them out on your own and leave us alone."

He looked around the group. "I've got some administrative stuff to get rid of back at the office, and then I'm off to the wildlife park."

He put his hands on his hips, "If there are no more questions, let's meet up tomorrow morning in Denton, at seven. Everyone needs to get some sleep tonight. That's an order. We can compare notes and go over any of the forensic stuff that's ready. I'm going to have poor cell reception most of the night. If you need me send a text, or leave a message with dispatch. If it's absolutely critical, have dispatch patch you through by radio."

Without another word or glance, he turned and walked toward his Suburban. Suddenly he stopped, pivoted on the balls of his feet, and turned to face Dawn.

"I got it." He stated excitedly.

Dawn shook her head. She had no idea what he meant.

"That movie," he grinned broadly, very pleased with himself. "That crime movie, in Miami, about the fish. *Ace Ventura*. Hot damn, that Jim Carrey is one funny fellow."

He chuckled to himself, pivoted again, and strode away.

Dawn thought for a moment, and then called after him. "That was a dolphin." But she suspected he already knew that. Sheriff Bubba Scates had just manipulated two experienced detectives and a cynical young FBI Agent, into following the orders of a backwoods lawman. He'd easily manipulated them all. She would be very careful with good old Bubba in the future.

Chapter 22

Tuesday Afternoon
Montague County, Texas

Dawn slouched in the front seat, with Deputy Eddie Marie Sharp sitting razor straight behind the wheel. The deputy wasn't so much driving, as aiming her Crown Victoria down the road. Her real name was Edna, but threatened to shoot anyone who called her that. The hurtling patrol car was spacious, and meticulously well cared for. Not even one fast food wrapper or empty drink cup blemished the perfect interior. Dawn was impressed, and a little disgusted. This is probably how Pratt's car looked, although he probably drove with all four wheels on the road.

Dawn sniffed, more appalled than before. Somewhere in here, Deputy Sharp had hidden one of those lilac scented air fresheners. Dawn felt herself growing allergic to clean and courteous.

Deputy Sharp ignored the road, looked over and smiled pleasantly. "We've got a pretty full day ahead. How long do you think we'll need with the coroner?"

Dawn didn't think it was that full. "We should play that by ear, why?"

"I was just going to give Kenny's mamma a call, give her some idea when we'd be by. And, I'm not over fond of the dead docs, that's what we call 'em. I'm wondering if I can wait outside; maybe get us some supper while you're in there. That's assumin' you can eat after being around all them dead folk. I can't, but I heard someone say you are a doctor? Is that true? Are you a doctor?"

Dawn absolutely had to change the subject. "Tell me about this Kenny boy, where do we find him?"

"Kenny will be up in Nacona now, but he probably won't be there when we head off to see him. If he's at home, I think we should just head up this little access road to Field Road, then cut back to Highway 388 and on up to . . ."

Blah, blah, blah. Dawn's mind went numb from the meaningless directions and chatter; everything looked the same out here in the country. Her escort may as well have been speaking Spanish. Dawn was so lost, that she didn't even think the GPS map software in her phone would be able to find her a way out of this place.

Dawn simply nodded back. "Whatever you think is best." *Just, keep your eyes on the road!* "How do you find your way around here? I'm completely lost."

Sharp looked casually forward. "I grew up here, and this is my patrol area, so I know just about every house, bump, and dirt road."

Dawn changed the subject. "Did you work the first murder, Munch?"

Sharp looked at Dawn, who smiled back. The deputy chuckled as her cruiser hit a bump in the road and launched itself skyward and onward. She didn't seem to notice as the shocks bottomed out with a thud. "We didn't know it was a murder then, only that he . . ." She chuckled.

Dawn asked, "What's so funny?"

The deputy hesitated slightly, and then shrugged. "Munch.

He was eaten by those wild dogs, you know, so we took to calling it the 'munch on Munch' case. That's a little unprofessional, I know, but it's still kind of funny."

Not funny for him, Dawn thought.

Sharp continued. "I didn't work it, my area's down here. But we all talked about it a lot, so I know most of the facts."

Dawn asked. "Why are there Wild African Dogs around here, anyway?"

Sharp shifted her weight in the seat and sat straight. She glanced over at Dawn as she transitioned from Deputy to official Montague County tour guide. "Texas has a lot of wildlife parks. Texas is big, like Africa, and they are quite similar, in terrain and weather, and such. Animals from Africa seem to like it here, and there are a lot of places in the Lone Star State that breed exotic wildlife. There are probably thousands of places you can hunt African game here."

Sharp swerved slightly to miss the dead carcass of something. Dawn now suspected may be a meerkat or wildebeest, or something.

"Oh!" The narrator's eyes got big and bright. "And did you know, that Texas has more tigers per person than any place else in the world? We have more tigers than India. Isn't that amazing?"

No, Dawn did not know that. And "amazing" isn't really the word she'd use to describe her feelings about Texas being overrun with tigers. She involuntarily scanned the open land around them for predators before returning to her questions about the first murder.

"Why did everyone assume it was an accident?"

"Oh, people here are still a little afraid of those dogs you know."

No again, Dawn didn't know, and shook her head. But this sent up a red flag in the back of her mind. Something about animals, but what?

Sharp continued before Dawn could think about it. "After what happened in Pittsburgh?"

Dawn scowled; she still had no idea what the deputy meant.

"Ya' see, a while back this little boy fell into the African Dog pen at the Pittsburgh Zoo. Well, quick as greased lightening the dogs set upon that poor child and killed it. Dead, before anyone could do a thing. It was sad, and since the Red River Refuge has a large pack of those Painted Dogs, folks around here just got a little concerned. Those beasts are kept pretty secure, and people can't just meander on in, at least if they're sober or in their right mind. Sheriff made us look into it, but our detective and the coroner agreed it had to be an accident."

"Was he drunk?"

"Kerwin Munch didn't spend much of his life sober, as it turns out. Not very professional for a doctor, if you ask me."

Dawn understood, though she would look into it further if she got the chance. Right now, she was more interested in the recent murder. There were a couple of questions she really wanted to ask Scates, but he had managed to get rid of her.

"How long had Jerry Montana lived here?"

Sharp frowned, "I don't rightly know? I remember hearing about him and that poor little Korean boy, but we never realized that this Montana fellow was here. I imagine he went out of his way to keep folks from knowing who he was and where he was living."

Dawn nodded, that made sense.

The deputy went on. "His residence is technically in the city of St. Joe's jurisdiction, but we patrol the rural areas of some cities as well."

Dawn smiled. They had driven through St. Joe, population 977 according to the sign. It was all rural to her.

"Us in the Sheriff's Department didn't receive any notification; neither did the St. Joe Police. Mr. Montana just snuck in, kept to himself, and never gave us any reason to know he was here. If it hadn't been for those tweets, and the murder of course, it's likely that no one would have ever known."

Sharp looked over again, hesitant but clearly excited. "But I've never worked a case with an FBI Special Agent before;

anything special I need to know?"

I've never worked a case with the FBI Special Agent, either, Dawn realized, but neglected to mention this to Sharp.

Instead, Dawn shook her head. "Approach this case like any other. If something changes, I'll let you know."

The deputy nodded, and then glanced over again. "Where are you from, Special Agent Johnson? I've only met one other Agent, and he was from San Francisco, in California."

"Just call me Johnson, or Agent. I was born in Houston, but grew up mostly in Dallas. My father got transferred to the FBI Field Office in Las Vegas when I was sixteen, and I lived there until I went to law school."

Deputy Sharp smiled brightly, "That's really nice, that he's an FBI Agent, too. Do you think you'll ever get to work together?"

Dawn paused; there was no way Sharp could have known.

"No."Dawn looked out at the dormant fields flowing past her window. They were all empty, like her. She needed to decide how to handle the issue of her father. Yes, he was dead, but he would always be an FBI Agent, as long as she was.

Dawn pulled out her phone, "I have to send an update to my boss." Dawn began to type, sending Pratt an Email, updating him on the investigation and outlining what she thought her schedule might be.

Her message to Pratt away, Dawn looked over at Sharp and decided that she wasn't ready to resume their conversation. She went back to work on her phone, and check the New York Times for headlines. Then came the sports pages. Dawn finally got tired of reading about the Yankees and put her phone away.

Deputy Sharp took that as a signal to resume their conversation. "Don't they let people in the FBI work with family?"

Oh, jeez. Dawn realized that she might as well get it over with.

Chapter 23

Tuesday Afternoon
Montague County, Texas

Justice had hurried home "for his lunch break." Actually, he was there to get everything ready for tonight. He hadn't wanted his work to move this fast – things could get out of hand this way – but he had no choice. He was tired, getting only a couple of hours sleep a night. But he would be getting very tired, very soon.

And then he would sleep forever.

Oh, well. A man's got to do what a man's got to do.

He sat down at his computer and placed the headphones over his ears. He found the icon he'd placed on his desktop labeled "Tweetbots," along with all of the other recordings containing the excellent information he'd used to torment the authorities and get away with murder. He clicked on the "Tweetbot" icon and sat back. He'd listened to this before, but needed to go over it again. He still found the last part confusing.

The recording began, and he listened to the instructive young voice once more.

"Tweetbots are programs that people use to automate a portion of their online presence. Tweetbots let you prepare a number of tweets ahead of time, then have the program send them out exactly when you want. Like a business might do for advertising. A spammer can get a whole week's worth of messages ready on Sunday, and then harass their customers all week, while they themselves sit on a beach and count their money."

Justice hit pause and rubbed his eyes. Ah, the voice of youth. At some point soon, this boy will probably have his own pile of money.

The killer hit play and resumed listening.

"The way Skank did it was by logging into a machine at the library, setting up a bogus account with information gotten from an ID spoofing website, then having the Tweetbot send the messages out when he was somewhere in public. That way, a bunch of people could testify that he was with them when the messages were sent, he had a perfect alibi. The basics are pretty easy, but he took it to the next level. He combined that with a plan to hide the identity and location of the originating machine. Unfortunately, he didn't hide it well enough."

Justice had learned to do it better, he had hidden everything completely.

Justice sat there for half an hour, meticulously entering times, web addresses, names and text into his own, custom-made tweetbot. This was the finale, the end game. If things worked out, tonight's labor would eventually kill three people instead of just one. All three may not die tonight, but they would all die just the same.

Justice stood and went to his spare room. He walked slowly to the fire place and lit the starter log that he'd placed there seven months ago. That's how long he'd been working to put his plan into motion. The log had come to represent something else, something more. He now realized that when he destroyed the evidence of his crimes by fire, he will have destroyed his past. All of it, the pain of loss as well as the joy of his successes. He would leave it all behind.

He watched the flames embrace the paper wrapping, flare, and then spread across the log. He could still read "Burns for 4 hours" in red on the flaming mass. In four hours, he would be on his way to the next and final victim. Four hours after that, his victim would be dead. This time would be a little different than the others; it would have to be different. He still felt that what he was doing was right, but that didn't mean he wanted to get caught. That would ruin everything; make all of his work a pathetic waste.

Justice opened the cedar chest and removed the final set of bags. Again, the first bag held a cell phone, but this one was a more expensive, more advanced model. A top of the line smart phone. It would have to be smart. He would have to be smarter.

Next came the clothes, identical to the others he'd used. He knew that wasn't necessary, but he liked uniforms. He'd come to think of this as his "Justice" uniform. The next bag held a metal box. The box had originally contained throat lozenges, the menthol kind that can relieve the pain of a sore throat. Now it held about a dozen round blue pills, each 30 mg of Oxycodone, and a cloth, with a large rock of black tar heroin wrapped inside. It was enough heroin to keep his victim from feeling anything. Ever.

The next bag held his victim's "slamming kit." These were the items she'd once use to prepare and inject the black tar heroin into her arm, and then leg, to get high. This was the kit she'd used to kill her baby. This was the kit Justice would use to kill her.

The bag contained two syringes. These were new; he'd lifted them from a hospital more than a year ago. These were the ones he would use tonight. Next was a large, metal spoon, blacked on the bottom from countless dates with oblivion. There were various cotton balls, pads and swabs. He didn't understand why such a broad assortment was necessary, and never planned to find out. He only had one goal in mind at the moment.

There was also a small baggie with Q-tips inside, more cotton, though he did understand about the Q-tip. Not the best filter, but his target wasn't the most conscientious person – if she had been more careful, she probably wouldn't be the evening's target. She would have her own kit, but he wanted her to use this one.

There was a small tube of hand sanitizer, several toothpicks in paper wrappers from a local restaurant. Apparently, she enjoyed country cooking as much as Justice did. There were two razor blades, still with the cardboard over the cutting edges. Safety first. Finally, there was a small pack of Zig-Zag wrapping papers. His victim must have wanted to keep her party options open.

Justice laughed, picturing what the corpse to be and her friends might do at a party. After smoking a little ganja, slamming a little Chiva – then maybe a line or two – would they finish off the party with a game of Twister? Maybe he would challenge his final prey to a game of Twister before the tar melted the brain cells forever.

Then he remembered that the little girl, the one her victim had killed. She would never get a chance to grow up and play twister with her friends.

Things didn't seem so funny anymore.

He needed this to be over. He had changed since he began his career as the dispenser of righteousness. He was not entirely happy with the changes.

Yes, this needed to be over. This was the last time. He knew there would only be one more murder victim after today, and it would be him.

Strangely at peace with this end, Justice pulled the last plastic bag from the chest. It held only one item, an old, empty one-ounce bottle of generic nasal spray. Ready at last, he loaded the implements of his final night's work into the duffle bag, along with the bottle of vodka he'd purchased earlier. He zipped up the bag and set it by the door. The bag, and any remaining contents, would be incinerated by torch, in the normal fashion. The torch burned a lot hotter than his fire would. There would be nothing left.

The fire, however, would be fine for this room's contents. He'd planned and prepared every part of his campaign of vengeance in this room. Everything he'd made had been constructed in here. So, everything in here would have to be destroyed as well. Starting with the chest he'd stored things in.

He ran his hand across the top of the cedar chest. He'd had this chest for fifty years, though he wouldn't really have much of a chance to miss it. He opened the chest as far as it would go, then put all of his weight on the open lid. After bouncing on it twice, the lid finally broke.

Justice slid the cedar lid into the fireplace sideways. He knew it would fit, barely, because he'd measured. The chest itself he had to break into pieces, stomping on one side at a time until it had collapsed into kindling sized sections. These all went into the fire.

The table was bigger, but not nearly as well built. He easily broke it into pieces, which burned much faster than the cedar. Next the chairs, tools, manuals, books . . . everything. All in all, it made a nice fire, though some of the items didn't smell very good. He wished he could sit here a moment to enjoy it. Unfortunately, someone needed to die. He had plans and couldn't let anything, or anyone, set him back.

Chapter 24

Tuesday Afternoon
Montague County, TX

Dawn looked back at Sharp and attempted to smile. "My father's dead, killed on the job."

Deputy Sharp looked like she would die as well. Her jaw dropped, and her eyes blinked in dismay and regret. "I – am – so - SORRY, I didn't know."

And now Dawn felt sorry for Sharp, who looked like she'd stopped breathing. "Don't worry about it. You couldn't have known."

Dawn smiled reassuringly at the Deputy, who relaxed only slightly.

"Really," Dawn continued. "It's okay."

More importantly, Sharp started breathing again. But she still looked like she could burst into tears at any moment.

And, there was a question – a nagging word – that kept clawing its way back into Dawn's consciousness. A word from Justice's tweets.

Dawn held up a finger. "Deputy, can you give me a minute?"

Sharp nodded and turned back to the road, which allowed Dawn to relax. Dawn pulled out her phone and started searching the Internet. After several minutes of unsuccessful queries, she lowered the phone and rubbed her eyes.

"Deputy Sharp, is there an aquarium around here?"

The Deputy frowned as she thought about the question. She glanced over at Dawn confused. "There's a pet store in Nacona that sells fish. We can stop there if you want."

"No, a big aquarium, public, for big fish and animals. Like a zoo or wildlife park. The killer mentioned a walrus," Dawn went through the killer's tweets in her mind. "He said something about a walrus being too stupid to figure it out."

Sharp thought for a moment then struggled to surpass a giggle. She then shook her head. "I don't think that's it. But, Fort Worth has a really nice zoo, with an aquarium like that. I'm sure Dallas does, too. I can't say for sure about any walruses though." The Deputy smiled. "Penguins, I know they got penguins. It was on the news."

Dawn didn't care about penguins, now she was curious. "Something I said made you laugh."

Sharp smiled again. "Walrus. I worked in the county jail before I moved up to patrol. Walrus is what the inmates call Sheriff Scates, you know, because of the moustache. It's not meant as a compliment, I don't think."

Dawn could see how that fit, actually. "I wonder why he didn't say anything."

The deputy gasped, looking over in horror. "I don't think he knows! No one in the jail is crazy enough to call him that to his face, and none of us are going to tell him."

Dawn didn't think she'd bring it up, either, but it gave her another line of investigation. She turned sideways in her seat, facing Sharp. "So the killer may have once been in the county jail."

The deputy though a moment, then nodded. "That, or knew someone that was in there. But it's definitely something worth looking into."

Dawn agreed, and pointed to her radio. "You should call him."

Sharp shook her head, wide eyed. "Oh, no-o-o-o! I'm not going to tell him, especially over the radio."

Dawn smiled. "Is everyone afraid of the Sheriff?"

"Oh, no, not afraid. I love Sheriff Scates," she caught herself. "Not like that! Not love like in LOVE, but like a father. He takes care of us, watches out for us. None of us would dare hurt his feelings."

Dawn had questions about Sheriff Scates, and this was her chance to get a few of them answered. "What is Sheriff Scates really like?"

"He's a fantastic sheriff. He really cares about the people here in Montague County, and about us, who work for him. That's why he keeps getting re-elected. He doesn't always get along with others in law enforcement, and he can be kind of crude at times, but that's all an act. Sheriff Scates is the smartest man I know. He goes back to give lectures at Texas A&M University in criminal justice all the time, he's even got a law degree. I heard rumors, after his wife got killed, that thought about being a professor there. Her death broke him up real bad, and no wonder, too. We were worried for a while. But he recovered, and decided to stay a sheriff."

That was a lot of information, and it did not match what she knew about the sheriff - not even close. And what had happened with his wife? Deputy Sharp recognized Dawn's uncertainty and continued.

"Like I said, he's been sheriff here forever for a reason. People here like him. He really cares about the people. More important, he keeps Montague a safe county. Take Kenny, for instance. That boy is too smart for his own good, kept getting into trouble. The contrary little snit kept shutting down the school district's computers and changing people's grades. Sheriff caught him, and the school superintendent wanted Kenny locked up forever. Even wanted the court to prohibit him from ever touching a computer again. Sheriff Scates convinced the judge to let him handle it by himself. Probably saved the boy's life."

This didn't sound all that generous to Dawn. "Well, he is the boy's uncle."

"Not by blood or nothing. Kenny's daddy was killed in Iraq, and his momma works two jobs. It was Kenny who got himself into trouble and all, but the Sheriff decided to put him to work instead of putting him in juvie. Sheriff Scates does things like that."

Dawn had again begun to suspect that Sheriff Scates was not the person he seemed to be. She had also just been informed that a juvenile delinquent was an integral part of their investigation.

Dawn asked delicately. "Should Kenny really be involved in official Sheriff's Department business?"

"Oh, yes. He's a good boy. His problem was never honestly; it was authority. Now he is the authority, and he's very conscientious about it. He's actually helped us catch several criminals, online predators and identity thieves and such. He's the one that caught Skank Hernandez."

Dawn looked over and chuckled, just in time to see a truck hauling hay pass to their left as they sped by on the right shoulder. The chuckle was instantly replaced by a gasp.

Once they were safely past, Dawn collected her thoughts and asked. "Skank Hernandez?"

"Oh, he was a bad one, he was. That Skank was a hacker and a criminal, a dang clever one too. Stole over a hundred people's identities, but mostly in Mexico and South America. Never here. He got the name Skank because sometimes he would hack into the computers of pretty girls and look for dirty pictures. But like I said, he was careful, never minors and never in Montague County where he lived. He was a right clever little shit stain."

As the deputy zipped by a farm tractor in the oncoming lane, Dawn's heart rate zipped into a staccato beat.

Sharp went on. "Once Skank had the pictures, he would threaten to put them on the Internet if they didn't go out with him. We knew what he was doing, but we couldn't find anyone willing to press charges. Finally, Kenny tricked him into hacking into the computer of the head of the Dallas Police Department by redirecting addresses or something. Poor ole Skank was surprised as hell when Sheriff Scates showed up with the Dallas Police Chief and a full SWAT team, Dallas folks wanted in on the bust, of course."

Deputy Sharp slammed on her brakes, slowing deftly behind another tractor towing a massive trailer, blocking almost the entire roadway. The tractor was piled high with big round bales of hay, obstructing any view of the road ahead. Sharp slowed, fell back several car lengths, then reached over and hit her lights and siren. The tractor moved slightly to the right and slowed further. Sharp eased her car to the left, checked for oncoming traffic, then hit her afterburner and launched them onto the opposite shoulder.

They flew next to a trailer with lights flashing, siren wailing, and gravel flying around like shrapnel from an artillery attack. As they reached the tractor, the deputy forgot about the road and looked over at Dawn to continue her narration.

"Anyway, Kenny was the only reason we had a case against Skank. He's been a real help to us ever since. He made us a really nice Website, too. Though my picture makes me look kinda fat."

She stopped talking long enough to swerve back into her own lane, then look at the road ahead and turn off the lights and siren. Having returned to the right side of the road, and resumed cruising speed, she went on.

"But what about you? I bet you've been on some really exciting cases?"

"Not really." The only excitement she'd experienced was being shot and almost killed. This was her first case, and she was technically only an observer at that.

Dawn returned to the previous topic instead. "So Skank got caught?"

"Yep! He plea bargained down to misdemeanor identity theft. The international theft charges were almost impossible to prosecute, and none of the girls would press charges. A couple of them even wrote him letters while he was in the county jail—go figure! When he got out he moved to Gainesville, just east of here in Cooke County. Kenny still keeps an eye on him. He appears to be going straight."

Sharp hit the brakes yet again, and stared across the road. A faded green pickup was parked halfway into the trees, right front tire in a ditch. "Damn it, Danny!" Sharp mumbled.

She grabbed her radio mike and pressed the send button. "Control, looks like Danny Fortis tied one on again last night. His truck's in a ditch at mile marker 31 on Nacona Road. You'll need to send a wrecker."

The deputy replaced the mike and accelerated back to light speed. Dawn had had enough. She pulled out her phone, and with her head down, trying to remember again the tiny fact that had flared in her mind.

She remembered and looked over at Sharp. "This thing about Walrus, it's a nickname for Sheriff Scates, right?"

Sharp nodded, "That's right."

At that moment they turned onto a four-lane state road, and ahead they saw the freeway. Dawn couldn't help but notice a sign a massive green sign saying "Dallas," with an arrow pointing right.

That's not right.

Dawn stared as they passed under the freeway and made left, following the directions of a sign saying "Oklahoma City," with an arrow pointing left.

Dawn felt a stone form in the pit of her stomach. "Sharp, where are we going?"

"To see the coroner."

"Which coroner?"

"The one in Ada, Oklahoma. Sheriff said you wanted to start there."

Damn him! Ada would be a five or six-hour trip, costing her most of the day. She'd already lost a couple of hours by coming this far north.

Dawn watched helplessly as they entered the freeway and

Sharp accelerated to 85 miles per hour.

Dawn tried not to sound angry. "Maybe we can skip Ada. In fact, can you take me back to Denton, so I can get my own car?"

Sharp slammed on the brakes and turned left onto a narrow dirt path across the median. She pulled into the southbound lanes of the freeway, cutting off a very large truck and trailer, and accelerated back up to warp 6.5.

The Sheriff had tried to ship her off to Ada, like sending a misbehaving child to her room.

Sharp frowned. "You didn't want to go to Ada, did you?"

Dawn shook her head. Sharp, for all her down-home openness, was smart enough to grasp instantly what had happened.

"Sheriff Scates played a trick on you, didn't he?"

Did Sharp have to keep ending every statement with a question?

"Montague County doesn't have a coroner, so we use the one in Hunt. Do you want to stop in Gainesville?"

No more questions, please!

"I need to use the facilities. Pull over at the next gas station?"

Scates, you will pay.

Chapter 25

Tuesday Afternoon
Montague County, TX

"You jerk. You unprofessional asshole!" Dawn barely kept control of her temper.

Scates snapped back, "Is Deputy Sharp there with you?"

She looked out the window of the gas station to where the Deputy filled up her cruiser. It would take forever; the decrepit pumps here at "Friendly Freddie's Fuel Stop" looked like antiques from when her father had been a kid.

"We're at Friendly Freddy's; she's outside filling her car. I wouldn't do this with an audience."

Scates hesitated, then said almost civilly, "Thank you." Now his voice sounded almost cheery, "You should try the fried chicken there. I understand you people like that. And unprofessional? That's a little harsh, isn't it? I think I've kept you out of my hair in a professional manner. I guess you didn't make it to Ada, then?"

"I had her start back as soon as she hit the freeway toward

Oklahoma. I still lost a few hours, though."

"Very observant, Johnson, I'm glad I had her take the back ways then. I got a couple extra hours without your meddling – I mean monitoring."

"Sheriff Scates. The FBI has considerable resources and experience in these types of crimes. You are ignoring the best interests of the people of your county, and any future victims, when you refuse to avail yourself of those resources."

"Stop right there, little girly, because everything I do is for the best interest of my county. I know what my county needs, and wants, and not a one of them wants some snot-nose in a cheap blue suit comin' up here from Dallas, trying to tell us what we should do or how we should think. I've been . . ."

Scates paused for breath, a little longer than Dawn thought was necessary. When he resumed, however, he hadn't lost a bit of his anger.

"Sheriff for twenty-eight years, in the department for almost forty. I've kept the county safe. People are very happy with the way I do my job, which is why I've stayed sheriff for so long. And almost everyone in Montague County thanks God every night that we're not like Dallas. We are the way we want to be. When I die, I plan on leaving it that way."

What? Dawn thought about what he'd said. Something didn't sound right. "Retire."

"What?" Scates answered.

"Retire. When you retire you want to leave it that way. You said die."

Scates hesitated, almost flustered, and then chuckled. "I have never, ever thought about retiring."

Dawn kept her anger in check. Earlier today, he'd hinted at something else. "Did you know my father?"

"And your grandfather."

Scates waited for her to respond. Dawn waited for him to go on. She wanted him to speak freely, not just answer questions.

Finally, the standoff ended as he continued. "I met your granddaddy just after I first got elected Sheriff. It was civil rights thing; some person of color didn't think they were getting paid enough."

Dawn interrupted, "What's wrong with being paid a fair wage."

Scates chuckled again, "Missy, Montague County is runnin' about thirty years behind the rest of the state – and we're fine with that. What we're not fine with is everyone else tryin' to make us act like we're in Los Angeles or New York. And for your information, nobody in Montague County gets paid a fair wage by Dallas standards, including the Sheriff. And we're fine with that too."

He paused again. Again, a little longer than she though normal.

"Your granddaddy came in treating us like . . . let's just say I thought we deserved a mite more consideration than we received. Everything ended okay . . ."

He chuckled, "But Grandpa Johnson never quite made it onto my Christmas Card list. I met your papa a couple of times. Seemed smart and professional, but we never quite hit it off."

"Funny," he paused, pensively this time. "I'm not quite sure what happened to him."

Dawn replied with a hint of anger. "You'll have to take a number on that one!"

She realized instantly that she shouldn't have said that. Scates was much smarter than he wanted people to believe. She changed the subject.

"Did you ever work with my father?"

"Once, some stupid crackers hijacked a big rig in Gainesville and tried to get away through Montague County. Truck was loaded with military night-vision equipment headed to Fort Hood, down south. FBI had to investigate the terrorist angle. Your father helped us find it, hidden down in a little place called Sunset. An inbred group of rednecks were holed up there, trying to figure out what they had."

Dawn held her breath. She remembered that case. Rednecks. Exactly what Daddy called them. He didn't like being in

Montague County. He called it "Leave it to Beaver" country.

"Are you there, Johnson?"

She came back to the present. "I'm here."

"Good, now go away. We don't want, or need your help."

"Well, until my orders change, you've got it. Are you going to keep trying to get rid of me?"

"Count on it."

The line went dead.

Chapter 26

Tuesday Night
Denton County, Texas

Deputy Sharp turned right into the Denton PD parking lot, and stopped in front of the main entrance. It had been actually a pleasant trip down from Gainesville, and they had arrived almost ten minutes before the conference call was scheduled to start. Sharp had almost driven in a safe and sane manner, part of the time. And, Dawn had grown to enjoy the backwoods charm of Deputy Sharp.

They had waited as long as possible in Gainesville for the autopsy results, but left empty handed. The coroner had barely begun when Dawn had to leave. Dawn had the task force meeting to attend, and Sharp had a PTA meeting. Her two daughters sang in the elementary school choir, and they were performing their spring concert tonight.

Dawn found it surprising how the deputy could shift her mental and emotional perspectives so quickly. One minute they discussed which appendages had been chewed off by wild dogs, the next she worried about whether the other parents would like her recipe for snickerdoodles that she planned on bringing to the concert. Whatever snickerdoodles were.

Dawn tended to focus completely on the task at hand. She did have the ability to shift focus quickly, but when she concentrated on something, it tended to obscure everything else. It had been frustrating for her to leave the hospital in Gainesville, where the autopsy of Jerry Montana had just begun. She hated to admit it, but Pratt had a point about the value of her medical training in situations like this. He had also been right about her having a personal agenda that required her to be in the field. That said, her personal scorecard still read: Personal Agenda - 1, FBI Needs - 0.

Dawn climbed out of Sharp's cruiser, then leaned back in to say good-bye.

"Deputy Sharp, I really appreciate your time. You've been a tremendous help."

"Please call me Eddie, since we're off duty and all. I have totally enjoyed our little time together. I'm off tomorrow, but I'm going to radio the Sheriff and tell him I'll volunteer to drive you around tomorrow, too."

"That's very nice of you." *That will never happen!* "I have my own vehicle, so it won't be necessary."

"Okay, but my offer still stands. I'm sure we'll see you later."

Dawn wasn't sure what to do next. Shake hands? Kiss each other on the cheek? Exchange recipes, or what? Instead, she just waved and closed the door, and Deputy Sharp hurried off.

Dawn did have her own car, and after the meeting she planned to hop into the clunker-mobile and get back to the coroner in Gainesville as fast as she could – which wouldn't fast enough. If she had questions on the autopsy, being right there with the body would allow her to get them answered, and hopefully expand the investigation.

Her first task, however, was to get back to their meeting room and find out what everyone else had learned. She entered the station, made her way to the task force room, and took a seat next to Guzman. Bird sat across the table, and both of them hunched over their new computers, typing up their notes for the day. Dawn left her tablet in her car. It would only take a few minutes to retrieve it, but the meeting was supposed to start in two minutes, and she didn't want to give Scates an excuse to leave her out.

Dawn instead listened to her phone log. She had recorded her notes there, and would use the voice-to-text feature to type them automatically. She had used this feature extensively in the past, and found it to be a real time saver.

She glanced at her watch. One minute before seven, so she played her first recording for the day. Her voice gave the date and time, but the playback stopped when the phone rang. She looked at the Caller ID – Pratt.

She hit answer, "Agent Johnson."

"Pratt. Where are you Agent Johnson?"

"I'm in the task force meeting room in the Denton PD building."

"Are you alone?"

"No, sir."

"Get alone."

She stood and hurried into the hallway, where two other officers stood outside an adjoining interrogation room comparing notes. Dawn hurried into the ladies room, and after making sure it was vacant she raised the phone.

"I'm alone, sir."

"Good. I'm going over your report, and have some questions."

"I'll be happy to answer them."

"Excellent. When will you have a real report for me to look at so I don't have to be a mind reader?"

Busted!

"I'm sorry it's not a more detailed report. I had to prepare it while . . ."

Pratt interrupted. "When?"

"Tonight, before the end of the day."

"That will be fine. How are things going with the investigation, and Scates?"

Dawn hesitated, organizing her thoughts. "The investigation is progressing as well as can be expected. The killer has claimed another victim, and things are moving very rapidly now. I believe Sheriff Scates is trying to avoid and marginalize me. We've only had limited contact. Personally, I think I'm adapting well to the situation and have had a positive impact on the investigation. I like being involved, sir."

A Denton PD officer entered the restroom, and Dawn slipped back into the hall as Pratt continued.

"That's what I was afraid of. I think it's time we take you off this investigation. I have several important, if routine, BI's for you to run."

You can't do that! Dawn fumed to herself.

She forced herself to calm down, and thought about how to convince him to let her stay. She began slowly.

"I'm sure the background investigations are important, but I'm up to speed on the investigation here and believe I can offer meaningful input and support."

"Such as?"

Right, such as . . . what? Think?

Dawn could bring up her medical knowledge, but that would just give Pratt more ammunition for putting shuffling her off to Quantico. And Scates seemed to have things under control on his own.

She remembered her questions about Kenny's participation. The alarm in her head, what had set it off?

"Sir, there are several aspects that I would like to investigate further. One is the involvement of the sheriff's computer expert. I feel that his input and past investigations may be significant."

"Very good, Johnson!" Pratt actually sounded happy, honestly pleased with her assessment. "I agree that the work of Scates' delinquent store clerk merits closer scrutiny. That's why I'm replacing you on this investigation with an agent from our Cyber Crimes Division. All I need you to do is to brief him as fully as possible, and then introduce him to the other members of the team."

Dawn began to pace. This was not at all what she wanted.

"I see your point sir, but I already have a feel for the case." She replayed the events of the day quickly, searching for anything she could use as an excuse to stay. She thought of Deputy Sharp. "And, I've established an effective working relationship with members of all the other agencies that make up the task force. I've been able to work extremely well with Deputies from the Montague County Sheriff's Department and local police."

Pratt paused. "I will take that into consideration as the investigation progresses, but I doubt that Sheriff Scates will allow me to increase the number of FBI resources. I want one of our computer specialists involved, and that means you need to stand down for now."

Dawn would not give up so easily. She turned and started back to the meeting room. "I'm sure our computer experts can work from our offices, using our resources."

"I already have them investigating from here, but they need to get information directly from the people there."

"Yes sir, but I'm sure that . . ." Dawn stopped in her tracks as she looked into their meeting room. Guzman and Bird sat hunched over a phone. Guzman was talking and gesturing while Bird nodded in agreement.

"Sir, they started the meeting without me."

Pratt replied calmly. "Get back inside."

"Yes sir, I'll call you back when . . ."

He interrupted. "No, you'll put your phone on speaker and set it on the table so I can hear."

"Yes, sir."

Dawn hurried inside, putting her phone on speaker as she strode to the chair next to Guzman. She set the phone down and interrupted.

"Sorry I'm late; I was on the phone with my office. What did I miss?"

Scates' voice answered sarcastically from a box on the table.

"The meeting. I think we're pretty much done here. You gentlemen have your assignments. Please call me back as soon as you have something new."

Dawn stammered briefly. "Don't you want to hear what I've found out so far?"

"No need," Scates answered with just a hint of satisfaction. "Deputy Sharp was with you all day, and she's already reported in. The autopsy has just finished, and they will email me their findings. I think we've got it covered, Agent Johnson. You can head on home, now, and get your beauty sleep. We'll call you in the morning if we need more donuts."

"Sheriff Scates." Pratt's voice from her phone sounded amazingly clear.

Everyone hesitated, and finally the sheriff asked, "Who's that?"

"Robert Pratt, Special Agent in Charge for North Texas. We've worked together before. How are you?"

"I'm trying to catch a killer, how am I supposed to be."

Pratt ignored the sarcasm. "Happy to hear that. I hope Agent Johnson has been able to contribute in some small way."

"She's been downright invaluable. In fact, she's got us to the point where we can handle the rest on our own now. Without any FBI assistance at all."

"That's excellent, Sheriff; this is actually her first active investigation."

Scates feigned surprise. "Really? I could not tell. I'll send her a commendation. Leave her forwarding address with my dispatcher."

It was like they were doing some kind of dance. No, it was like they were fencers, keeping up their guard while looking for an opening to attack through.

Pratt parried, and then counter attacked. "I'm sure it will look good in her dossier, but there is something even better you could do for her."

Scates asked warily, "Which is?"

"Agent Johnson has been quite impressed with how you've

handled the investigation so far. She's already learned a great deal by working with you. I think she would benefit significantly by being able to continue her participation, strictly as an observer of course, for a day or two."

Scates was trapped, and he knew it. That didn't stop him from regrouping and deflecting the assault. "Why, I'm pleased to have been of assistance, and am happy to continue my tutelage of the young agent. I already have her address, and Deputy Sharp has volunteered to continue acting as my liaison to the FBI. I'll have her stop by and pick up Agent Johnson in the morning."

"What a gracious offer, Sheriff Scates, but I have already requested a vehicle for Agent Johnson, and approved per diem so that she can get a hotel close by. I will be bringing her the vehicle shortly."

Scates hesitated, but only briefly. "That's excellent. Have her contact me when she's mobile, and we can . . . hold on."

The line went dead for several seconds, and he came back on. "I have an urgent call from my jail supervisor; it will require my attention for a while. Guzman and Bird can get started with what they have. I'll get back with Agent Johnson just as soon as I can. Sorry, have to sign off."

The line went dead.

Guzman and Bird knew what had happened. They gathered their notes, mumbled a hasty farewell, and left.

When they were alone, Pratt spoke again. "You did fine, Johnson."

"Thank you sir, I felt like a ping-pong ball."

"You were. Just sit tight there and wait for my call. It will be a couple of hours. I need to arrange for a car and get your per diem approved. Don't go anywhere, or do anything until you hear from me."

"While I'm here I can sit down with . . ."

"Nowhere, nothing until I get there. Understood?"

"Yes, sir, I'll . . ."

Dawn heard the line go dead. If Pratt had a plan, it meant that she had a problem.

Chapter 27

Tuesday Night
Denton, Texas

Dawn walked impatient circles around her car, in the parking lot of the Denton police station. Pratt had called and told her to wait in her car, but she'd tired of sitting in the Escort's worn, sagging seat. That was an hour ago. So, for the fourth time, she found herself walking very small laps while drinking a very large cup of very weak coffee. She'd stopped carrying the white, plastic trash bag with a red tie top, in which she'd stuffed the few items she wanted from her car. It rested on the passenger's seat.

She wanted everything ready to be transferred into her motor pool vehicle when Pratt arrived. When she got her dad's car out of the shop, she wouldn't bother with official cars. At that point, the quality of her ride would be taking a massive step up.

She took another sip and grimaced. The coffee was terrible, maybe they had just been rinsing out the pot in the interrogation room and left it standing. She looked around. No one had been in or out of the station for quite a while. She considered dumping the coffee into the plants near the entrance, but then she'd want to go inside and get another. The desk sergeant was already giving her a bad time. The last time he'd given her the phone number of a homeless shelter and offered to call her a cab.

She decided to put up with the harassment and get another coffee and started toward the station's entrance. Her phone rang, and she checked the Caller ID, Pratt.

"Good evening sir, Agent Johnson here," she answered confidently.

"Where are you right now?"

She must have missed the *Good evening Agent Johnson,* or, *Sorry to keep you waiting Agent Johnson,* that he had certainly meant to say.

"I'm at the Denton PD's main station."

She'd walked around her car and unlocked the driver's side door.

"I know that, where at the station?"

She grabbed the garbage bag, shut the door. She looked around to see if he was there yet.

"In the parking lot, sir, waiting for you to arrive. Are you almost here?"

"Do you know where their computer crimes division is located?"

"Yes, sir."

"Is it currently manned?"

"Yes sir, they man it 24 /7."

"Good. Go sit with their cyber crimes officer. Sit next to him and look over his shoulder. Sit in his lap, I don't care. Just make sure you stay there until I find you. Got that?"

"Yes sir, but the task force has a room where we've got everything set up, it would be more private."

"Cyber crimes room, Johnson. Now."

She heard nothing else.

"Sir?" The line was dead. He'd hung up. He did that a lot, she realized.

Dawn hefted her white plastic tote bag, and then opened her car door. She set the bag back on the passenger seat, closed the door, and marched back inside. She punched herself back into the main office area, and then made her way back to the Computer Crimes Division room. Inside, she pulled up a chair next to Walker, and watched. He glanced at her impatiently, and then resumed his work.

She examined the screens in front of her. One screen appeared to be a chat session between Walker, someone named *KWiz*, and another person named *Support57*.

The screen to his right displayed lines of data scrolling up on a light-blue display. Dawn recognized web site names and IP addresses. IP addresses are the addresses computers use to identify themselves on a network. Most of it, however, made no sense to her at all. In fact, it looked like someone had accidentally set a book on the keyboard causing random characters to flow endlessly down the screen.

She cleared her throat, "What is this?"

Walker actually hunched closer to the keyboard, ignoring her more intently.

This will be fun.

She looked over at the monitor to his left, which had a local sports Website. One commentator had written a long, scathing diatribe about how Jerry Jones, the owner of the Dallas Cowboys, was the reason for the all of the team's failures. She hadn't lived in Dallas for almost ten years. She felt comforted to realize that some things hadn't changed.

Dawn looked at her watch, and felt a piercing sense of irony as she actually hoped that Pratt would get there soon.

Chapter 28

Tuesday Night
Gainesville, Texas

Justice hadn't been comfortable with the idea of killing a child. Fortunately, the State of Texas allows for minors over the age of fourteen to be considered as adults. Justice didn't feel quite as bad when using that as his guideline.

The idea that evil is ageless made him feel almost good about killing an eighteen-year-old girl; especially an evil one like Suzie Cooper. Suzie was born in Gainesville, Texas, just south of the Oklahoma border. And no one would deny that poor little Suzie had started life with about all the disadvantages you could think of. As she grew, it became obvious that she would be skinny - not thin, but skinny. This got worse as her chemical addictions did also. She had been born a normal baby, but the physical abuse by her mother and stepfather, which started at about the age of one month, resulted in a deformed left foot, slight brain damage, and scars and burns that made parts of her look frightening.

Her mother, Carla Cooper, was killed by Suzie's stepfather

when the girl was ten. Suzie then went to live with her grandmother who tried her best, but managed little control over her granddaughter. Suzie ran away after six months and never went back. No one can say for sure what her exact mental age or physical mileage age was, but it's certain that by age ten she began her addiction to opiates, heroin, crack, even morphine for a while - which ever drug she was able obtain at the moment. She became a prostitute at age eleven, pregnant at age twelve, and a murderer at age thirteen.

Suzie had a tough life, a brutal life, and any vestige of innocence had disappeared long before she saw her thirteenth birthday. The difficulties of her young life were why the State of Texas hadn't tried her as an adult. Juvenile custody meant that at age eighteen she was released, there had even been someone worth releasing her to.

Suzie's grandmother, Gladys, felt guilty. The remorse was made worse by Suzie's constant complaining that her grandmother should have done more for her only grandchild. Gladys wrote letters, and came to visit on special occasions. Gladys even sent money from time to time to make Suzie's stay more bearable. On the day of Suzie's release, her grandmother was there waiting, ready to take her baby home and make sure she got a second chance. Her granddaughter had other plans. Without saying a word of thanks, Suzie Cooper hurried past her only living relative and returned to the street.

Suzie bragged about how she had returned to prostitution less than an hour after being released. That allowed her to resume her addition to opiates before midnight. Over the next month, Suzie "worked" her way south to Dallas, with its amply supply of drugs and Johns.

Suzie, at five feet ten inches had ballooned to an enormous one hundred three pounds during her mandatory time with the state. After eleven months of freedom, she weighed less than ninety pounds - much less. Also during those eleven months she had become pregnant twice, both times resulted in miscarriages because of her frequent and heavy drug use. But then again, that was better than what happened to her first child.

Suzie had been incarcerated for killing her first baby, a beautiful little toddler named Carlie. Carlie split time between her mom and her grandmother. Suzie had gone out shopping for the day with her daughter, but scored a double while she was out – a John with drugs. They got a motel room, but her John objected to a crying kid in the next room, and threatened to take his money and black tar heroin, and find another trick. Suzie solved the problem in the way she knew best, by grinding up a small amount of heroin and blowing it up her little girl's nose with the straw from a local convenience store. It wasn't a small enough amount. Carlie stayed quiet after that, and will remain that way forever.

The maid found the cold little body in the bathroom the next day. Several people identified Suzie as the mother, and fingerprints confirmed that she'd had been in the room. Justice knew that his victims, all of them, had committed horrible crimes. Suzie was about to do it again. She had stolen her grandmother's jewelry, and then beaten Gladys almost to death when she tried to keep her wedding ring.

Of all of the people he'd killed, this would be the hardest for him. And the easiest. There was little question that *little-girl Suzie* had deserved a better life than the one she'd lived, and there was also little question that Suzie was a monster, and deserved to die for what she did to her baby girl. There was certainly no doubt that Suzie would eventually kill again. So, for the first time ever, Justice was about to kill a woman.

The how of it would be easy. Justice became a John, John Smith, and reserved Suzie for an entire night over the Internet. They agreed on price, a hundred dollars and some tar. He thought it better not to ask about her refund policy, but he knew that he'd get his money back when the evening ended early.

Justice drove to Gainesville, and parked behind a closed down restaurant in Suzie's neighborhood. Instead of latex gloves, he wore an expensive pair of black kid leather, which he pulled on tight as he got out of the car. He reached across the driver's seat, grabbed the vodka he'd brought. He stood, and then closed and locked his car. After making sure the hood of his black sweatshirt completely hid his face, he walked two blocks to a dark corner near her apartment. She'd wanted to meet there, public and anonymous, so they could check each other out.

Suzie waited next to the graffiti covered pole of a street light, rocking nervously, swaying to a beat that only she could hear. She turned to face him as he crossed toward her. Justice stopped a few feet away so she could see him. Her head bobbed and swayed slightly, as she tried to make out his face under the hood.

Justice opened the vodka and took a drink, which allowed her a better view of his face as he tilted his head back. He held the bottle out to her; she hesitated.

He asked suspiciously, "We're not going to party?"

Suzie looked around, eyes flitting nervously, and then shrugged. She took the bottle and drank. She took a second, longer drink and wiped her mouth with the back of her hand.

She opened her coat, so he could see what he would be getting. "Don't I look like I know how to party?"

Suzie Cooper may once have been an attractive girl, and it's possible that some men still found that to be true. She had stringy blonde hair with light brown roots. Her pleasing face had high cheekbones and desperate, sunken eyes that disappeared into caverns of too much eye shadow. Her gaunt figure grabbed, and held his attention. Suzie Cooper had a figure that any bulimic would die for. She closed her coat and nodded for him to lower his hood and identify himself.

He left his hood and sweatshirt in place. Instead, he took the metal box from his pocket and opened it, holding it out so that she could see what it contained. Suzie didn't need to see any more. The large black rock inside was the magic door to her heaven on earth. That was ID enough.

She took another drink of vodka, handed him the bottle, then grabbed his arm and led him back to her apartment.

Chapter 29

Tuesday Night
Denton, Texas

Pratt took nearly an hour to get there. Dawn had almost fallen asleep when the door opened and Pratt strode into the room. A tall, slender man in his sixties followed him inside. The second man had thick grey hair, and wore a rumpled grey suit. Dawn wasn't sure if they were together, or if the other man and simply been caught in Pratt's wake and been accidentally sucked along. Pratt stopped behind Dawn, and the other man took up a flanking position to his right. They had obviously done this before.

Dawn stood and turned to face them as Pratt spoke.

"Agent Johnson, this is Agent Tucker." The second man held out his hand to Dawn. His handshake was firm but rigid, no shaking involved. They nodded, muttered to each other, and then both looked back at Pratt.

"Agent Tucker will give me a ride back to the office when we're done."

Tucker nodded, and then looked down at Walker. Tucker then looked back at Dawn, and jerked his head toward the jerk behind the keyboard.

"Oh, right. This is Officer Walker, from the Denton Computer Crimes Division. He's the tech support for our task force."

Walker waved over his shoulder, barely glancing back. "Pleased to meet you."

Dawn continued. "Walker, this is Special Agent in Charge Pratt, and Special Agent Tucker."

Walker waved again without looking, "Still pleased."

They returned his greeting. Tucker then asked Agent Johnson. "What is Officer Walker looking at here?"

Dawn hesitated, then turned to look back at the screen. "Well, he's in a chat session with two other people; it appears they are trying to find out something about where and when something else happened. The middle screen looks like it might be a traceroute, trying to follow a message or other Internet traffic that someone had received . . ."

Walker had heard enough. With a massive, nerdish sigh, he pivoted in his seat. "I'm in a chat session with Kenny Fox, the Montague County computer crimes technician, and Pawan Navashowee, or something like that. He's with the Twitter NOC, their Network Operations Center. We're monitoring some of the sites we think our killer has used to cover his tracks, then tracing back anything that looks suspicious."

Tucker leaned closer. "Cool! I've been studying like crazy, trying to get into our Cyber Division. This stuff fascinates me." He pointed at a string of numbers, and IP Address, and asked. "Isn't that in the Ukraine?"

Walker looked up and smiled. "Yeah, a hacker in Odessa that runs an anonymizer." He shook his head at the blank faces staring back.

In exasperated impatience, he explained. "Anonomizer, it makes email anonymous. It removes all of the sender's incoming traffic identification and replaces it with the anonymizer's own info. We can't track anything coming out of his site, so we're trying to monitor what's coming in. As Pawan identifies any traffic coming from a suspicious source, he forwards it to us. We then try to monitor incoming traffic to that site. It's hit or miss, and we're not getting a TON of data."

Tucker nodded thoughtfully. "Have you tried capturing the incoming traffic and filtering out the non-US sources?"

Walker glanced over like he'd just been insulted. "Of course! Kenny has a program that isolates any traffic from North Texas providers – I need to ask what he wrote that for. But there is a ton of traffic, and we're trapping on about a dozen other sites. And it wouldn't be too hard for our guy to be forwarding through a different site, so the inbound traffic could be coming from anywhere."

Tucker said, "Yeah, I didn't think of that." He gave Pratt a smirk and sat in the chair Dawn had just vacated. He pulled it next to Walker and leaned close. "You guys are pretty good."

Walker smiled. "Kenny's a hacker at heart, and damn smart. But we can only trace so much, and we're falling behind."

Tucker looked innocently up at Walker. "I could help! I can at least run a traceroute and search. I'm not as good as you guys, of course, but it may help speed some things along."

Walker gave Tucker a hesitant, skeptical look, and then glanced back at Dawn.

Dawn realized that Pratt had set this up, and played along. She shrugged. "Couldn't hurt. He is an FBI Agent, so he's cleared for it."

Walker looked suspiciously from Dawn to Tucker, then back at his monitor when a loud chime sounded from his computer. On the chat screen was the message *R U there? New IP to track.*

"Shit," Walker swore under his breath as he replied to the message. Walker pounded the enter key with a flourish and finished his reply. He then slid his chair to the left, pressed the spacebar on another system, and began logging in, causing three new monitors to blink to life.

With efficient mouse and keyboard commands, a chat session

appeared on the right hand monitor of this system also. Walker looked over to Tucker, "See what you can do."

Tucker dragged his chair over and began to work the keyboard. As the sound of fingers dancing across keyboards grew louder and more frenetic, Pratt touched Dawn's shoulder and nodded toward the door. She followed him out.

He closed the door behind them. "Nice work, Johnson. Tucker's head of our cyber group, and I have two more agents back in Frisco ready to jump in. I just needed a foot in the door. We can follow their progress from our office once Tucker gets us in."

That seemed to imply she would be at the office. "But I need to head back to Gainesville and follow up on the autopsy."

"This is a serial killer, Agent Johnson; you need to ease yourself out so we can get a more experienced agent in and up to speed on the investigation."

Dawn realized what was happening, and was not happy about it. "Sir, I'm not an experienced agent, but I'm already up to speed. I think that is more important."

"I'll consider that thoroughly before I say no."

"You lied to me. Sir." It came out before she could stop it. And wasn't sure the *Sir* would help. Fortunately, Pratt did not seem to take offense.

"I reconsidered my options as SAC and modified my plan. That's not lying."

Dawn replied carefully. "Which, of course, is your option. However, I think there are other factors you should consider. I already know the background of all the previous victims and the details of each of the murders. I'm acquainted with all the participants in the investigation, and have established a good working relationship with all of them."

Pratt frowned. "I don't think Sheriff Scates is all that happy to have you involved."

"Sir, Sheriff Scates will not be happy no matter who you assign to the investigation."

Pratt smiled, "Probably not."

Dawn pressed her advantage. "Fact is, sir, that even though he's not happy with me, he has accepted me as part of the investigation," she lied. "There are no guarantees on anyone else you may assign. It will probably be a few days before our killer can get things ready to strike again, so we will be working the evidence we have. One of the more important elements of the investigation will be forensics, including the results of two autopsies."

She needed to be careful here.

"As you pointed out yourself, sir, this is an area where my previous training can be of unique benefit. We both agree completely on that point. It only makes sense to give me a few days to examine what comes to light, and be in a position to follow up on anything that requires further analysis."

Pratt smiled slightly. "The autopsies will be finished tonight. I can give you a day. However, I don't think our Justice will wait long before acting again. He seems to be accelerating his pace. Also, I'm in contact with Dallas and Washington. In twenty-four, seventy-two hours max, this may be our case anyway. You can have one day."

Dawn wanted to smile, but didn't allow herself the luxury. Pratt had compromised, let the negotiations begin.

"I will need time to analyze the results and then at least three or four days to follow up."

"Two days. Unless we take over before then."

"Of course, but if there is something I'm actively pursuing it may take a little . . ."

Pratt cut her off, "Don't push it Johnson, or we can discuss it further on our way back to Frisco."

Dawn took a step back, shaking her head vigorously. "No need, sir, two days should be more than adequate." She backed down the hallway. "I'll check in every night. You won't regret it."

Pratt smiled broadly, shaking his head. "I already regret it. In fact, maybe I'm letting you continue just so I can find out why. But what about you?"

"Yes, sir."

His frowned slightly, now serious. "Aren't you worried you'll regret it?"

She shook her head. "I don't understand."

Pratt continued grimly. "Maybe you should quit while you're ahead, and you are ahead Agent Johnson. You were thrown into a fast-moving murder investigation with no advanced preparation and less support. You have successfully worked in a hostile, multi-jurisdictional environment, and have made a noticeable contribution. More importantly, you have managed to irritate Sheriff Scates so much that he wants you gone, but not so much that he's filed a formal complaint. Any excuses I had for excluding you from full duty as an FBI Agent have been eliminated. I don't know what your goals were in beginning this case, but I suspect you've achieved them."

Dawn paused, considering what Pratt had just said. He was right. She wanted to disappear into the agency. Become another brick in the wall between our citizens and the evil-doers trying to harm them. Most of all, she wanted to do it anonymously, which would eventually allow her to conduct a secret, dangerous, and totally unauthorized investigation into her father's death.

Pratt continued, "I threw you into the deep end, hoping you'd drown. At this point, you're walking on water."

Pratt was still right, but she found that the words would not come when she tried to tell him that. Instead, she heard herself say. "But I still think I can help."

Pratt continued his assault. "And you don't think Agent Tucker, or other more experienced agents can help?"

Dawn looked down; she had no answer to that. Of course they could help. Certainly, they had more experience than she did. The smart thing, the logical thing, would be for her to cash in her chips and celebrate her victory.

She looked up. "You're absolutely correct, sir."

He smiled and nodded.

Dawn continued. "But, I just can't quit while this killer is still out there.'

Pratt shook his head. "Your call, but watch yourself. Don't

get crosswise of Scates. He can make things very difficult for all of us, at which point all of the good will you've accrued will disappear."

Dawn turned to leave; she wasn't going to give Pratt a chance to reconsider.

He called after her. "I'll be here for a little while if you change your mind. Be safe, Johnson, no rushing into things."

Be safe? Why would he think he needed to say that?

The burning in her side and the stretching of scar tissue from a trio of bullet wounds reminded her. She would definitely be careful, and hope that would keep her safe.

Chapter 30

Tuesday Evening
Gainesville, Texas

Instead of walking to the nearby motel, Suzie Cooper took him around the corner to the apartment complex where she lived. The apartment they entered was tiny, but still under furnished. The kitchen, off to the left, had two wooden chairs and a worn folding table. To the right sat a huge big-screen TV and an overstuffed couch that looked comfortable and well stained. Justice went into the kitchen and retrieved one of the wooden chairs.

She tossed her coat over the other chair and held out her hand. "Money first, baby."

He walked over and set the vodka on the counter. He then pulled out the tin, "How 'bout happy first?"

She didn't think about it long before smiling broadly, snatching the box from his hands and sauntering into the kitchen. Her eager fingers opened the tin and hungry eyes admired the contents.

"All this for me?"

"All of it." He answered.

"What are the pills for?"

"Speedballs, for us. They make for a killer after-high. Promise."

"Baby, you can come back anytime."

"Let's see how things work out tonight. Go easy with the pills, though."

He handed her the liquor bottle.

She eagerly shook four pills into her hand and closed to bottle. "I'll show you easy," and popped them into her mouth. She washed them down with the vodka while he retrieved his bag of needles and supplies. He set it on the counter in front of her.

She looked at the bag. "Your shit's almost exactly like mine."

"Really?" He smiled.

She nodded. "You want me to fix you up?"

"You first. I want you ready for later."

She opened her mouth and licked her lips suggestively. "I'll be ready."

Justice managed not to wince.

Suzie set his bag down and picked up a cheap plastic canister with "Sugar" written in chipped blue letters. She pulled out a rolled up cloth and laid it out on the counter. It was almost identical to the one he'd brought.

"Use mine," Justice urged.

She shrugged and set her kit to the side. Then she washed her hands with soap, under very hot water. She then put a drop of dish soap on her spoon and scrubbed it thoroughly before setting it on a paper towel.

She reached over to the gas stove and turned the nearest burner on high. She next reached up and turned on the overhead vent hood where the fan wobbled and squeaked to life. With the razor blade, she carefully trimmed a section of the black rock and pushed it onto the spoon.

Justice chided. "We're going to party harder than that!"

She smiled and trimmed an even larger section of rock into

the spoon. She opened a bottle of water on the counter and poured a small amount into the spoon, then held it anxiously over the burner.

Justice moved closer, curious. He'd never actually seen this done in person. This would be his last opportunity. The smell hit him quickly, powerfully, revoltingly. A smell that combined the absolute worst elements of a flaming fondue pot filled with old inner tubes and a smoldering outhouse, threatened to consume his nose and lungs. His stomach wanted to expel every bit of food that had ever passed through it, but he held on.

Barely.

Suzie smiled, oblivious to the olfactory assault, and took another drink of vodka while the spoon got hot. When the tar began to melt she pulled it off, grabbed a toothpick from a holder on the counter, and stirred the mixture in the spoon. She heated the mixture again, then stirred, then repeated that process three more times. Finally, she nodded at the liquid with anticipation.

Suzie then took a Q-tip and ripped a section off the puffy white end. This she rolled into a tight ball which she dropped into the liquid. Using one of the syringes from the kit, she eagerly but cautiously drew up the solution, being careful not to get any of the raw product inside.

She next poured water from the bottle into a small saucer. She then drew a small amount of water from the saucer into her partially full syringe. Justice knew that this would lower the temperature of the solution enough to be injected, and that any undissolved particles would be removed before injecting.

She continued processing her magic potion until she had a syringe containing a light-brown liquid that looked like the iced tea he'd had with his lunch. She removed her wrist watch, which had a thick leather band adorned with colorful beads and glass. The band managed to hide most of the evidence of recent injections on the inside of her wrist. She carefully washed her hands again, and then swabbed the injection site with alcohol. She slid the needle into her wrist, at a practiced right angle, preparing to deliver the imitation rapture into her vein.

She pushed the plunger hesitantly, injecting a small portion of the drug into the vein of her wrist. She waited to see how her body would react. An instant later, the beginnings of a smile curled at the corner of her mouth. She liberated the remaining contents of the needle into her body.

Her eyes rolled up, and her head lolled slowly back. After several seconds, she inhaled deeply then blew out a long, slow breath between her lips. Seconds more passed, and she turned her head toward her guest.

With a slurred drawl, she declared, "Yeah, baby! You can come back here any old time you want."

Justice watched, fascinated by the transformation. Time slowed down for Suzie. Eagerness had become an imitation of ecstasy. The hint of nervous desperation was gone, swallowed up by a surge of chemical oblivion. But, as educational as this was, he had a reason for being there. And, he had a schedule to keep. *Time to finish this.*

"It gets better. Much better."

She lowered her eyes to the box, and then smiled over at him. "How much better?"

Justice walked over to Suzie. He picked up the spoon and scooped up the rest of the rock, which he dropped into the plastic bag. Using the bottom of the spoon bowl, he crushed the Valium into a fine powder in the tin. He then opened drawers until he found the silverware and retrieved a dollar store steak knife, which he handed to Suzie.

She looked at the knife, then skeptically at the powder.

Justice tried to sound eager himself. "I just want to make our first time special."

He reached for the tin, but she pulled it back. She set the tin down, dipped the blade of the knife in the powder, and then lifted the heaping tip to her nose. Blocking her left nostril with her other hand, she carefully lifted the knife and snorted. She blinked a few times, wiped at her nose, then looked at Justice and shrugged.

He smiled, "You'll see. It won't take long."

Inside he wasn't smiling. This was taking too long.

She picked up the baggie with the remaining heroin. "Can you get more of this shit?"

He nodded.

She began to sway slightly, then walked over and pulled at the sleeve of his sweatshirt. "Why don't we get comfortable?"

He didn't move, and Suzie frowned. She looked at his face, still partially obscured by the hood, so he uncovered his face.

She stared briefly. "You look familiar."

"I've been in the news."

Her eyes narrowed suspiciously. She looked at his hands, still wearing the gloves, then back at his face.

"Yeah," he nodded. "Let's get comfortable."

He smiled, then removed the hoodie completely and laid it over the back of the chair. She started to relax until she saw him reach for the stun gun clipped to his belt.

Chapter 31

Wednesday Morning
Denton, Texas

Dawn hurried out of the Cyber Crimes man-cave, and went directly to the task force's work room. She slipped inside, and began a desperate search for her sanity.

What are you doing, Johnson?

She slumped down into a wobbly metal chair and looked incredulously up at the acoustic tile ceiling. She had just turned her back on the thing she'd been working tirelessly to attain for almost four years. She had not only failed to take the opportunity she wanted; she now found herself in danger of losing it forever. This was crazy; Dawn needed to go back in there, thank Pratt profusely, and get into the life of a real FBI agent.

Dawn leaned forward and put her face in her hands.

You can't quit.

The little voice in her head had just ambushed her good judgment.

You can't leave this undone.

No! She shook her head. This would not be one of those good angel/bad angel debates while she whipped her head back and forth from shoulder to shoulder.

And, exactly when did she become so indecisive?

When the situation got complicated.

"Shut up," Dawn commanded her good-self.

Dawn had two options.

One. Accept Pratt's offer and good will. Report back to the Field Office. Get full access to the resources of the Federal Bureau of Investigation to follow up on the leads she had in her father's murder. Not risk being reprimanded and failing on a promise she'd made to herself and her father's memory.

Two. Subject herself to two more days of Bubba Scates. Lose two days of work on her father's death, if she were lucky. If things worked out as expected, she could destroy everything. Lose the goodwill she'd achieved with her boss and possibly turn him into a greater enemy.

When she analyzed it like that, the choice was clear.

Right, nothing is ever that clear.

Dawn exited the work room and hurried to her car.

If she rejected Pratt's offer and continued with the investigation, she could be betraying her goal and fail in tracking down her father's killer. If she accepted Pratt's offer, she would be rejecting her father's legacy as an FBI Agent by not tracking down a serial killer. He would never have quit when he thought he could contribute.

And Dawn had a nagging, inescapable feeling that she could contribute. She just needed to figure out how. Fast.

At that moment the door burst open and Pratt's head appeared around the corner. "Looks like he's going to finish it tonight."

Chapter 32

Wednesday Morning
Gainesville, Texas

Justice finished the text message. Things were going exactly as planned. He turned off the phone and slipped it into his pocket, then looked at the body of Suzie Cooper, lying peacefully on the floor in front of him. The crack smell still battered his senses, but he managed to stay focused on his task. After a few seconds, he could clearly see the rise and fall of her chest, which was good. He wanted to get this over with, but he also wanted to make sure that everyone understood what had happened, and why.

He went to the old, dial thermostat near the front door and turned up the temperature as far as it would go. He then walked to the sink, turned on the hot water and let it run.

He checked on Suzie. She still lay there unconscious, but breathing, so he continued his preparations. He pulled the bag containing the empty nasal sprayer from his pocket, removed it from the bag, and then put the bag in his other pocket. He walked to the kitchen counter and dumped the black rock into the tin with the Valium. He sliced the rock into small pieces with the razor blade, and then dumped the contests of the tin into the nasal spray bottle.

The water from the tap was now hot, so he let a little of the water run into the bottle. He shook the bottle vigorously until the drugs had dissolved. He could feel that the mixture was more of a paste than a liquid, so he added more water and shook it up again.

He went to Suzie and knelt next to the unconscious girl. He examined her face. She looked peaceful, almost innocent. Justice again imagined the little girl she had once been, such a few short years ago.

It wasn't the years. It was the mileage. Suzie had driven her life too far, too fast, and over some very rough terrain. He couldn't help but feel sorry for the life she'd had to endure. He wished she'd given her grandmother a chance.

Then he pictured another little girl, just a baby. Carlie was truly innocent. Carlie never had a life to enjoy or destroy; her mother took that choice from her.

The pattern of her breathing had changed, coming at irregular intervals and levels now. The Valium he'd given her were 30 mg, the maximum he could get. He couldn't imagine how her heart kept beating, even with the coke. He'd been assured that no one could survive that dosage.

He believed it. Cooper would die, eventually, but there was an uncertainty to the time elements of tonight's plans and Justice felt a little extra pressure at the moment. All of the tweets had been pre-entered and pre-scheduled, and were now out of his control. He needed to finish so he could get out of there and stir things up.

Justice took the nasal spray bottle, shook it again, and then put the spray tip in her left nostril and squeezed. A long spray coated the inside of her nose, followed by a subtle shudder through her body. He repeated this in her other nostril, then sat in a chair to wait.

He did wait, impatiently, for another fifteen minutes as her breathing slowed further, but refused to stop entirely. He knelt again, and again sprayed the hopefully fatal mixture into her nose. He returned to his seat, and unzipped his sweatshirt. The temperature in the room became unbearably hot.

Ten minutes later she began to shudder, almost convulse. Stroke, heart attack, he had no idea. He could have smothered her earlier and sped up the process, but he wanted it to be the drugs that killed her. The same way she had killed her baby.

And at last they had. He saw now that her chest no longer rose and fell. Suzie Cooper was dead.

He watched carefully for a few minutes longer, and then sent two final streams from the bottle into her nose. He pinched her nostrils closed with one hand, and covered her mouth with the other. He waited a full five minutes before removing his hands.

Justice went to the stove and turned off the burners. He hurried to the thermostat and returned it to 72 degrees. Room temperature had reached 87 degrees. By the time they found her body, the room temperature would be back to normal. Hers would not. It wasn't critical, but he hoped that this would make it impossible to pinpoint the exact time of death. Keep her body temperature up and make it look like she'd died later than she actually had. But again, it wouldn't make much difference in the long run.

He returned to examine the lifeless form on the floor. She was dead, definitely. Any regret he had over killing a teenage girl was overwhelmed by the sense of relief that this was his final visit. Justice had been executed, time to execute Justice himself.

A final, bigger question remained. How and when would justice find him?

Chapter 33

Wednesday Morning
Denton, Texas

Guzman and Bird had returned to the Cyber Cave, and Walker had briefed the entire team. A team that now included Pratt and Tucker. The tweets came in slowly, irregularly. The delays caused by the anonymizer programs caused maddeningly long periods of uncertainty.

The first tweet had been cryptic, explaining why Justice had selected her:

Justice_4_theInnocent @mytweetrevenge
She was abused by her parents, and then abused herself. Just a baby when she murdered her own baby. Now she sells herself to buy escape.

It wasn't much, but it was enough to tell them it wouldn't help. Juvenile records are sealed, even if they had a name and place. The chances of them identifying a prostitute with a drug problem? Right—they'd never make it through the list.

The task force, sans Scates who'd returned to Montague County, had assembled and waited impatiently in the Computer center. The second tweet came soon after they'd all gathered.

Justice_4_theInnocent @mytweetrevenge
Booze and #Speedballs don't mix, especially this much.
Kill your baby with #Crack, and baby #Crack will kill you.

This gave them more to work with, which drove them crazy because it was simply a little more nothing. A crack head prostitute that killed her baby as a juvenile was all they had, so they sent a request to all of the law enforcement agencies in North Texas for anyone who might be able to identify a girl who fit that description. In the last six or seven years.

Sure, they'd have something any minute.

It took thirty-seven minutes, and it came from the killer.

Justice_4_theInnocent @mytweetrevenge
Suzie Cooper is dead in Gainesville. May baby Carlie RIP.

That would be enough to get them moving, to Gainesville. Unfortunately, it would be too late. They knew that Justice would be gone, but with the number of news departments that now followed Justice's every word, they would have to hurry. The Montana murder had been nice and tidy; the news people hadn't figured it out at all. It had been a press release from the Denton PD that finally tipped them off.

This time they had the name and the location at the same time the police did.

Let the race begin.

Dawn slipped immediately out of the Cyber Den and gathered her notes and equipment from their room. She then hurried down the hall toward the exit and her car, when a voice called her name.

Pratt, she had hoped to get out of there before he found her. He sounded excited.

Dawn turned to face him as he jogged up to her and stopped.

"We've got her. Suzie Cooper in Gainesville. Multiple arrests for prostitution, possession and distribution. Gainesville PD will be on scene in 5 minutes. Guzman and Bird are getting ready to move now, and I think I'm going to try and send Tucker with them. I have to go over important autopsy questions with you before you leave. I'll tell them Tucker will just fill in until you get there."

"When will that be, sir?"

"Unclear, but not soon."

Dawn felt the blow to her gut, knocking the air from her lungs. Or maybe she'd just stopped breathing. Either way, she felt like she was about to pass out.

No, that was not going to happen.

"That's not what you promised me."

"The situation has changed."

"Not that much! Sir."

He stared stubbornly back. "This will be our last crime scene. Tucker has worked hundreds of scenes."

Pratt didn't actually mention that she hadn't worked any, an unexpected act of courtesy. But then again, he didn't have to.

Dawn grasped at the few straws she could find. "Tucker is a computer specialist."

"He's still and experienced agent. You don't even know how to file a proper report. It's getting hard for me to follow the investigation without complete and accurate updates."

Pratt had complained about her reports. Frequently. About both the quantity and quality. He even apologized. If he'd thought that she was actually going to contribute to the investigation, she would have been pared with a senior agent who could have helped her file them properly. Now it was too late.

"I'm sorry, Johnson. I'll try and get you back with the task force as soon as possible. You've earned that, but right now I need you to . . ."

Guzman and Bird rounded the corner from the task force center and hurried toward them down the hall. Guzman stopped, stared at Pratt a moment then pushed Dawn toward the exit.

"Come on, Johnson, I need you to hurry. We've got an investigation to work."

Good news, Dawn was still on the case. Bad news, Pratt was not going to be happy about it.

Chapter 34

Wednesday Morning
Gainesville, TX

Dawn stood just inside the apartment door, taking pictures with the digital camera from her car. The task force had been there all day, conducting interviews in the apartment complex and the surrounding neighborhood. Now they were about to return to their lair. She wasn't sure the crime scene team would have their photos ready for examination tonight. She had these, and could send them to her tablet for immediate review.

She took a close-up of the little girl still lying on the floor; a pale, stick figure who would never abuse herself again. Suzie Cooper's body would normally have been transported by now, but inconsistencies in the estimated Time of Death had delayed that. The initial TOD had been placed at early tomorrow morning, give or take a day, when calculated by body temp. No one knew why, but her body temp first registered at fever levels. The coroner would have fun with this one, and they may never get an accurate time to match up the death with the tweets.

Dawn looked down the hall to where one of the crime scene techs emerged from the bedroom. That had been furnished much better than the living area. Suzie had an expensive water bed, though Dawn had thought them extinct. The bed had a heater, and a variety of wave motion settings. The other accessories included whips, handcuffs, blindfolds and a variety of turkey basters.

Dawn tried not to imagine what they were for.

The bedroom also sported an elaborate lighting system, which could be turned on to different colors and intensities. Suzie Cooper had managed to acquire an extensive collection of porn, and an equally extensive collection of individually decorated paddles. These, Dawn assumed, had been used to turn on her John's to different colors and intensities also.

The tech leaving the bedroom wheeled several suitcases, which were being taken in as evidence. The investigators had found drugs, which surprised no one. What shocked them all, was that the stash of pills and other chemicals had been so truly prodigious, enough to keep this whole apartment complex high for the next year. Suzie had a lockbox that proved to be a crack mine, with rocks of all sizes and shapes stacked inside. The pills had been in bags, and suitcases. The crime scene team had let Dawn examine the rolling case as they wheeled it out. It had been crammed to overflowing with zip locked bags of pills, many of which Dawn did not recognize at all.

While the forensics and chemical analysis of the scene would take a while, their interviews had provided immediate, though inconclusive results. The neighbors hadn't heard a thing. Almost everyone knew Suzie. Almost everyone knew Suzie was a hooker. Almost everyone knew Suzie was a drug user. Two of her neighbors answered the question "How did you know Suzie Cooper?" by stating that she sold them drugs. They were taken away for further questioning.

Two teenage boys had witnessed the meeting between Suzie and Justice. They were able to provide no description of the killer except that his shoes were cheap, and that he was taller than

Suzie. They were, however, able to give an exact description of the car, since they thought about breaking into it. They decided that anything they got from a shitty blue, ratty and busted, old Ford wouldn't be worth making Suzie mad.

The coroner finally arrived to claim the body, and forced Dawn back outside. Guzman and Bird were waiting, having just finished talking with the upstairs neighbors who had just returned home. A team of detectives from Gainesville had also arrived and were expanding and following up on what the task force had done. Scates had taken off to get some sleep, and ordered them to get a couple of hours before their meeting at seven back in Denton.

And they did need sleep. Almost as much as they needed a real lead.

Chapter 35

Wednesday Night
Denton, Texas

Back in Denton, the meeting had barely started before Scates kicked Agent Tucker out and began to abuse her and Guzman for letting *another useless fed in a suit*, into the investigation. Guzman hadn't known about Tucker, but had no intention of letting Scates push him around. They shouted back and forth, until she decided to leave the room before she told the Sheriff what she really thought about him.

After dousing her face with cold water a few times in the restroom, Dawn decided she couldn't avoid it any longer, and walked back to the bickering. She slipped into the temporary task force meeting room and sat at the back instead of in her regular seat. Things had obviously calmed down, but not moved any further along. The Bird man of Oklahoma had begun to update everyone on his part of the murder spree, giving a detailed report on all of new facts relating to the Ada murder. Dawn filed it in her mental case notes under, *Yeah, we don't know anything useful.*

That finished, Guzman decided to start brainstorming. The brainstorming brought such a flood of nothing that it threatened to wash Dawn back into the hallway. She understood the need to go over the facts, but after about an eternity of verbal Ping-Pong, they'd managed to cram almost ten minutes worth of information into their two-hour meeting.

So far!

She needed to get going.

A day had passed since Pratt put an expiration date on the can of worms this investigation had become. She was frustrated, and a little worried that she would not be able to complete her first real investigation. She had less than twenty-four hours now, less than twenty-one actually, to solve the case. Pratt would keep his word, to the letter, until he found an excuse to get rid of her. He would give everyone else some lame excuse to pull her off and slide Tucker, and maybe others, into her place. While she could see his reasoning, she knew he was wrong. She just had to prove it to him.

If the FBI took over, she would try to talk herself back onto the case. She actually thought that would happen, if only to do leg work.

Dawn turned her head and looked again at the white boards hanging on the far wall of the task force command center. One wall held the victim information. Guzman had put a picture of each victim at the top, with bio and case details underneath. To the right was another board labeled evidence, where the little bits of real evidence they had were listed. What they did have was a list of forensic details fresh in from the lab. The final white board listed what they knew about the twitter account and process the killer had used. Again, there wasn't much there. They had a list of forwarding and anonymizing servers, several Internet Addresses used by Justice – mostly in Russia and Romania, and a complete list of their killer's tweets.

There had to be a starting place, a next step, buried in there somewhere. Each of them knew that, so each of them felt frustrated by the lack of progress. At the front of the room,

Detective Guzman was brainstorming with the rest of the group. He used what he called a "free association" method, which he had been forcing on everyone for almost half an hour. He would point at one item on two of the different lists and ask, "What links these facts, what do they have in common?"

Sheriff Scates had had enough. "What links those facts is that they're bein' used in a worthless waste of time. I'm tired, and sleep would be a better use of my time at the moment. Let's pick this back up in the morning."

Guzman replied patiently. "We simply haven't tried the right combination of facts, and that means we need to try more combinations. That's how free association works."

Scates slumped back in his chair. "No, this is how free association *doesn't* work. Hell, I don't even agree on what your facts are."

"What do you mean?" Guzman seemed genuinely insulted.

Scates pointed at the middle board. "You've got the perp listed as a white male."

White Male was number four on the list, behind *Computer Expert, Dark-Blue Ford Taurus,* and *Disposable Phones.* After that came *Wildlife Refuge, Knows OK, Grey Shag Carpet,* and *Yellow Cat.* Forensics had found hair from the same cat at the last two murder scenes, enough to match it to a specific person, but not enough to find them. This was the meager list of facts they had to work with.

Guzman looked at the board, the indulgently back at Scates. "The kids from the Cooper site said she met a white male."

"But that doesn't mean it wasn't a woman dressed like a man. Look, I think it was a man, too. But you keep saying *we know,* when what you really need to be saying is *we can assume.* It's a subtle difference, but it's something we need to keep in mind. We know he drove a Ford Taurus, model year 1995 to 1999. We know it was dark blue, as well. But we're only assuming that he's the actual owner. And what if it has been painted, and that the color on the State's computerized vehicle information no longer matches the car. It could actually be registered as any color, which narrows the field down to about two hundred thousand vehicles in North Texas"

Guzman had been growing frustrated and angry with Scates for well over an hour – like four days over. In a sarcastic voice the Detective asked, "So you think we should call off our search for a dark-blue Taurus?"

"No, that's not what I'm saying." Scates sounded frustrated and angry now as well, which Dawn suspected had been going on since birth. "We need to search for things and people based on those details, but we can't let ourselves EXCLUDE anything or anybody because they don't match them."

Dawn had to agree with Scates on this one.

Should I worry about my mental state?

As if sensing her approval, Scates stood and walked to the board.

"We need to be careful in how we discuss this, because it will determine how we think about it. I have ordered a DMV search on all dark-blue Taurus' from that model year. But as soon as I have that I will ask for another search for every color. Same with the sex. I'm going to look for a man, but if we find a woman that pops up on our radar, I'm going to follow up."

Dawn realized that Scates was right, again. She had been thinking exclusively about a man, but maybe she needed to expand her thinking a little as well. She was learning from the angry old man. Angry, and getting angrier.

And tired. Every minute or so he would pause and take a deep breath, or wince like he was in pain. It was a Yin/Yang kind of thing – Scates is in pain/Scates is a pain. Scates is exhausted/Scates is exhausting. Truthfully, they were all tired.

Scates began to pace stiffly. "I want to catch this bastard. But to do that, we need to think outside the box. In fact, we need to realize that we may be looking in the wrong box to begin with. What we include in our thinking sometimes causes us to exclude other relevant facts."

Dawn chuckled to herself. Scates' bushy white moustache was bouncing and swaying as he continued his rant. She had never seen him so animated.

He ranted on. "Our killer has finished his list, so we won't be getting any more clues or evidence to work with. We have to wring every clue from the existing . . ."

And on and on. Dawn thought back to something Deputy Sharp had mentioned. In the county jail they called him "the walrus." She looked again and had to agree. He did look like a walrus.

Walrus. She repeated the word to herself slowly. *Walrus?*

"Walrus! That's right." She shouted.

Everyone turned to stare as she sprang to her feet with growing excitement. She hurried forward to where she'd left her notes, and paged through the list of tweets that Guzman had printed off. She found the reference she had been searching for and raised the paper like it was an Olympic gold medal.

"Walrus." She stated with conviction.

"What walrus?" Scates asked.

"You." Dawn declared emphatically.

The others looked to each other for some clue as to what she was talking about.

"I beg your pardon!" Scates seemed to be wondering if he should feel offended or go along with the joke.

Dawn waved the paper proudly over her head, then lowered it and began to read. "Say good-bye to my little friend. Dim R sum obvious clues I left, but cops and walrus R 2 stupid to figure it out." She looked up, "This is a tweet from the Montana murder."

Her revelation still brought only confusion from her teammates, so she pointed at Scates. "You, you are the walrus. That's what the prisoners call you in your county jail. The killer has been in the Montague County Jail, or at least we can assume that. At a minimum, he has a close association with a former guest of the county."

Scates still looked confused. "Who said they call me walrus?"

"Deputy Sharp mentioned it. She also mentioned that no one was going to tell you that to your face, though I honestly though you would know. I think we need to add that to our facts list."

It only took a second for Detective Guzman to nod, stand, and add *Once in Montague Co. Jail* to the list.

Scates corrected. "Or knows a former prisoner."

Guzman scowled and made the change.

It didn't take any free association for Dawn and Guzman to exchange triumphant smiles. Nathan "Skank" Phillips fit their profile perfectly. They looked at Sheriff Scates, who obviously didn't share their excitement.

Dawn stated confidently. "We need to look at Nathan Phillips."

Scates shook his head, staring intently at the floor. "I don't think it's Skank." He looked up. "I've had Kenny keeping an eye on Skank since this whole thing started. The Twitter connection was too obvious to ignore. As far as we can tell, he has no involvement whatsoever."

Damn!

Dawn had felt sure she'd broken the case. Maybe she still could. "We need to talk with him anyway. Even if he's not involved, it's very possible that he would know about other inmates with the computer expertise to pull this off."

Scates looked at Guzman, who glanced over at Bird. They all looked back at Dawn and smiled.

Scates nodded smugly. "I'm thinking that a visit to our little jailbird nerd is in order." He checked his watch. "We wouldn't get to Montague until almost midnight. Then we'll need to find out exactly where he is. It's been a long day, a long couple of days, so let's meet back here at seven thirty and head out. I should know where he is by then. Bird, I want you to go through the DMV records and see if Phillips, or anyone he's related to, owns a Taurus. Guzman, sit down with your nerd and get everything you can on him. See if there is anything to link him to the murders. Then go through and see if there is anything else in his pathetic existence that merits further investigation. Then get some more rest. We just may be making progress on this case."

Smiles and congratulations made their way around the room.

Dawn interrupted. "What about me?"

Scates stretched, rubbed his eyes, and then looked at her gravely. "I've got a tough one for you. I need you to convince your tight assed boss to wait before yankin' the rug out from under me. He's planning on taking over, isn't he?"

Dawn simply stared back.

Scates looked at the others. "Hear that, boys, we need to wrap this up or the feds are going to shove us out the door."

Guzman and Bird glared at Dawn just a second, then gathered up their papers and binders and got back to work. There would be no rest for them tonight.

As Dawn gathered her papers and notes and stuffed them into her garbage bag and started toward her car. She wondered about four people showing up at Skank's door, how would he react? Then she wondered at why the always impatient Sheriff would be willing to wait until morning to follow up on the best lead they'd had to date.

Dawn finally wondered where Sheriff Scates had parked his nice, big Suburban.

Chapter 36

Wednesday Night
Denton, Texas

Dawn leaned against the driver's side door of the Suburban, now tired of waiting, as Sheriff Scates approached. He did not look happy to see her. But, he did not look surprised either. He simply unlocked his car and motioned for her to go around and get in.

Before she could step up into his SUV, Scates reached across the seat and snatched a pair of prescription pill bottle out of a cup holder before she could get a good look at the labels. She didn't get a good look, but she knew what to look for. One bottle appeared to be 500mg Naprosyn. That was a high dosage, especially for a lower level pain management regimen. His back must have been giving him a lot of trouble.

As she settled in, Scates tucked the bottles into a little shelf in the dash. They both bucked in, and the Sheriff turned the key and brought the massive engine to life. He shifted his gaze to Dawn. "You got protection?"

Dawn wanted to say, *I thought the guy brought the protection.* But she didn't think Bubba would appreciate that, if he understood at all.

"In my car." She answered. Pulling out her keys she told him. "Handicapped parking."

He started to shoot her a reproving look, but then seemed to recall her history of getting shot. He stared at the keychain dangling from her index finger a moment, and finally slipped the remarkably comfortable vehicle into drive and eased to the front of the building.

Dawn hopped out, pulled her body armor from the trunk, and tossed it into the back seat of Scates' vehicle. She crawled back inside, and the Sheriff accelerated through the vacant visitor's lot toward the street. Scates did not say a word, he didn't even look over. Finally, Dawn broke the silence.

"What took you so long after the meeting? I almost thought I'd made a mistake and left."

"You were right, but that doesn't mean it's not a mistake." He shrugged, 'I'm an old man, Agent Johnson, with an old and murderous prostate. Things take a little longer these days."

"Do you know where we're going?"

Scates gave a wicked smile as he turned left onto a major, four-lane street that Dawn didn't recognize. "I will by the time we get there."

Scates took the smart phone from his belt and slipped it into a cradle on his dash. He pressed a button. Two beeps sounded through the car speakers, and he said clearly.

"Call, Kenny, mobile."

His car responded politely. "Calling, Kenny Fox, mobile." He glanced at Dawn, "I'm callin' his cell so his mamma doesn't find out I'm waking him up. She's a little over protective."

The phone rang four times, and a hushed voice answered. "Hello."

"Kenny, it's the Sheriff. I know it's late, but . . ."

"Damn right it's late!"

Dawn suspected that the angry, female voice did not belong

to Kenny.

Scates winced involuntarily, and then spoke in an unusually pleasant voice. "Good evening, Gracie, nice to talk to you."

"Then it won't be nice for very long, and it's not good evening; it's good morning. It is well after midnight. We've talked about this, Bubba."

"Yes we have, and I wouldn't be calling if it weren't important."

The woman, who was obviously Kenny's mom, sounded indignant. "What could be more important than his education?"

"This is a murder investigation, Grace."

After a brief silence, she answered. "That Twitter thing?"

"You know I can't talk about my cases."

"Right, you can talk to a teenage boy, but not his mother. Where's the sense in that?"

Dawn could hear the heavy sigh through the car speakers. "I'll get him."

Several seconds later a deep, unexpectedly mature voice echoed through the vehicle. "I'm here, Uncle Bubba."

Scates turned right and entered the access road for Interstate 35. "You on your computer?"

"Getting there." The sound of typing could be heard in the background.

They were now on the freeway, heading north toward Gainesville. Scates stayed in the right-hand lane, driving carefully and fidgeting slightly. He seemed to wince in pain. Significant pain, as Scates glanced at the pill bottles then over at Dawn.

Kenny's voice sounded again. "Ready."

Scates again glanced uncomfortably at Dawn, and then shrugged. "You're still keeping track of Skank, right?"

"Yes sir, I just updated my information this evening. In case . . . you know."

"I do know. That's why I'm calling. Think you can find him for me?"

"I'll try. Let me check his *secret* Email account to see if he's logged in." More typing, then, "He is logged in. Let me put a trap on the IP for main server at GMX Mail. This may take a while."

Scates nodded. "No problem, as long as you can tell me where he is in thirty minutes.

Kenny snorted. "Right, no problem."

Scates reached over to his phone and ended the call. He looked over, more serious than Dawn could remember. "Not all of this is strictly legal, so you're going to have to decide how much you're going to remember. Put your head back and close your eyes. You can say you were asleep and didn't hear a thing. Anyway, part of Skank's parole provisions state that he cannot touch a computer until his parole is over. It also states that I can monitor his parole, if he stays in my county. Anyway, it looks like he's been in violation of those terms, but it hasn't been serious-so far."

Dawn looked at Scates, and then stared straight ahead. Finally, she looked back. "Sorry, Sheriff, for an observer I guess I'm not very observant. I have no idea what you're talking about."

Scates smiled and nodded. "I guess key chains are making a comeback."

Dawn frowned, "Pardon?"

"Key chains." Scates tapped his keys. "Our killer seems to have a fixation with them, and now I see you have an interesting one, too."

Involuntarily, Dawn's hand went to her pocket.

"Yours looks a might shabby, how long you had it?"

None of your business. "Since my sixteenth birthday."

Scates nodded, thinking. "Raggedy old thing looks as old as your car."

It's exactly the same age, can we drop the subject?

Scates blinked thoughtfully then looked over. "What year is your car?"

Dawn didn't answer.

Scates smiled in understanding. "That old bucket you're driving is at least a dozen years old. That was your first car, wasn't it?"

Dawn nodded. *Shut up!*

"Damn, I though they paid you FBI prima donnas better than that. You still payin' off student loans?"

My loans are all paid off, you asshole. "I have another car. It's in the shop." She glared over. "If this is an interrogation, I'd like my attorney present."

He smiled amicably. "I just like to get to know the people I work with."

Now Dawn smiled, but there was nothing friendly about it. "Me too. So, how about you? Did you become such a prejudiced old SOB naturally, or do you work at it?"

Scates laughed, a positively robust roar that surprised her with its honesty. He quickly winced with pain and stopped. He glanced over with a truly strange look transforming his face. "Sweet cheeks, you have no idea how hard I work to look like something I'm not."

What does that mean? She thought about what he said. "What does that mean?"

He smiled back, one of those "I'll never tell" smiles.

His phone range before Dawn could press him about it. Scates pressed the answer button, and Kenny came back on. "Got him. The computer address of the modem he accessing through belongs to—good news, it belongs to NTCC CableComm. They're local, but it probably means he's not at home."

Scates took his phone off mute. "Why?"

"He wouldn't use a local company, so he's probably hijacked someone else's connection."

Scates looked over at Dawn and smiled. "We've worked with CableComm before." He leaned slightly toward the phone. "How we doing?"

"Calling their NOC now, from our land line."

Scates sped up, moved one lane to the left and passed a large truck full of cows.

Dawn shuddered; she really didn't like live cows. Except the dead ones, which tasted great.

He slid back into the right lane and explained. "NOC stands

for Network Operations Center."

Dawn nodded. She knew that, but didn't feel like pointing it out at the moment.

Kenny's voice echoed through the car, a little muted as he spoke into the receiver of his house phone. "This is Kenny Fox, working with the Montague County Sheriff. I have a . . ." after a brief pause, Kenny sounded relaxed. "Hey Paul, yeah, I got another one. I need a location." Kenny recited the offending Internet Address and waited.

Moments later, Kenny repeated the information he was getting for Scates and Dawn to hear. Dawn jumped when Scates glanced at her urgently, and then nodded down at the notepad next to her bucket seat. She snatched up the pad, but Kenny had finished.

"Again, please." Scates asked

Kenny repeated the information. "Michael and Victoria Edmonds, 7412 Catamont Drive, Gainesville." His voice changed as he spoke into the other phone. "Thanks Paul. No I can't tell you anything, but if you've watched the news, you can probably figure it out."

Kenny typed in the background. "Let me get you directions, Sheriff." More typing. "It's north east of Gainesville. A subdivision north of Highway 82."

Scates thought "East, off County 151?"

"That's it."

"Thanks Kenny, I think I can find it."

"Should I keep tracking him?"

The Sheriff thought about it, "I don't want to get Gracie mad at us."

Kenny laughed, "Way too late to worry about that."

"Okay then, keep tracking his signal – or whatever. I may call again."

Scates ended the call, hit the gas, and totally forgot about maintaining a safe and sane rate of speed.

Chapter 37

Wednesday Night
Denton, Texas

Ten minutes later, they turned right onto State Highway 82, and then made an immediately left onto a poorly maintained county road. They passed a trailer park and two small subdivisions, and finally turned right into an older, but clean looking little community. Scates took his time, inching down the street to orient himself.

"This looks familiar."

Two streets later, they turned left and stopped in front of 7412 Catamont. The house appeared annoyingly well kept. The front porch was framed by evergreen topiaries, and the white shutters on the windows looked freshly painted. A massive red Buick, at least thirty years old, sat in the drive. They both noticed the handicapped plates, and exchanged a glance.

Neither of them though they'd find Skank here, that would be too easy. Besides, this house must belong to an elderly couple who didn't bother, or couldn't figure out how, to secure their wireless network. Skank, however, could very well be close enough to hijack their Internet connection.

He called Kenny again. "He still there?"

"Still online, same IP. But I've been thinking. He could be somewhere else, anywhere else. If the old people left their computer on, he could be using firesheep and sidejacking their session. It's not likely, but . . ."

Scates waved his hand like Kenny was standing in front of him. "Can it! I've had enough nerd speak lately." Then he smiled, "Good work, boy. I'll take it from here."

The Sheriff ended the call, and then drove slowly around the block. He slowed even more as they passed a small, brick one-story house. He hesitated, and then stopped. He looked back, deep in thought, and muttered. "I've been to that house."

He backed up until the license of the compact four-door Toyota in the driveway became visible in the light of a nearby street lamp. Scates punched numbers into his dash-mounted computer. Seconds later, he smiled. "Registered to Tammy Phillips." A wolf's grin played across his face. "Skank boy is driving mama's car."

They examined the house. The lights in the front rooms were out, but there were several lights on in other rooms. Scates pulled forward and parked in front of the house next door. He looked over at Dawn and smiled.

"Let's go say hello to Paula."

They walked across the lawn to the front porch, where Sheriff Scates rapped gently on the door. He looked over, "She has two kids; don't want to wake 'em."

Nothing happened, so Scates knocked again, louder. It still took over a minute for a light above their head to come on, and the drapes to their left to part. Someone wanted to check them out. Almost immediately, the door opened slightly and an angry voice whispered to them.

"What are you doing here?"

"Sorry to bother you, Ms. Stone. It's Sheriff Bubba Scates. I took your complaint a few years ago in the Nathan Phillips case.

Do you remember?"

"Yes I remember, but that's over. Please go away, it's late. I want to go back to bed."

He spoke much louder. "Yes ma'am, I am sorry about the hour, but we really need to visit with you now."

"Quiet, you'll wake up the kids."

"Ma'am, I have to talk loud, since you're forcing me to communicate with you through the door and all."

"Then just go away."

"I can't do that Ms. Stone, but I can call for your local PD to come here and assist. But that would mean lights, and sirens, and a lot of attention." He paused to let her consider. "Is that what you want?"

She jerked the door open, stepped outside, and pulled it most of the way closed behind her. She had on a heavy white robe, but still wore makeup and her long black hair was neat and freshly brushed. She was tall, slender, and had not been asleep. "What do you want?"

Scates pointed at the car in her driveway. "Is that your car?"

"No. I, I borrowed it."

"From who?"

She looked flustered, and stammered to answer when a buzz came from the pocket of her robe. She pulled out a cell phone, read the screen, and spoke confidently. "From a nice lady at my church."

Scates smiled. "Did you know that nice lady was Skank Phillip's mother?"

She smiled indulgently. "Small world."

She looked at her phone when it buzzed again. "I need to go to bed. I'll be happy to talk with you tomorrow."

Scates smiled apologetically. "Tomorrow doesn't work for us."

The phone buzzed. She read the screen and pronounced triumphantly "We're not in Montague County. You don't have any jurisdiction here. Please leave or I'll call the Gainesville police."

Dawn didn't want to play this game any longer and pulled out here Fed Creds. She displayed her FBI badge to Paula Stone. "I'm Special Agent Dawn Johnson, FBI, and we're investigating a serial killer. I do have jurisdiction, and right now you are impeding that investigation. We need to talk with Mr. Phillips immediately."

She stammered, "He's not . . . I don't know where he is. Go away."

Dawn snatched the phone out of Paula's hands, spun her around and pushed her face first against the wall. Dawn pulled out her handcuffs, and dangled them in front of Paula Stone's face, as she craned her neck to look at them. Her eyes glowed wide with fear.

Dawn spoke slowly. "Besides interfering with a federal investigation, we have now added making a false statement to federal agents. Do I need to have Sheriff Scates call Child Protective Services to pick up your kids, while we drive you to the federal lockup in Dallas?"

The front door flew open.

"Wait!"

A short, dumpy little man in striped boxers rushed out. He looked to be in his late twenties, and his hairless chest looked white and pasty under the feeble porch lamp.

"What do you want?"

Scates smiled."For starts, we want to have a little chat with you. After that? Well, that kind of depends on how our chat goes. Let's step inside. And please make sure we can see you, both of you, at all times"

Scates walked past Dawn toward Skank. As he passed, he smiled and whispered. "Remind me never to piss you off."

He ushered Phillips inside, and Dawn followed with Paula Stone. Paula led them back to the kitchen, where a laptop computer sat open on the table. The two chairs, standing side by side, meant that they had both been using it.

Scates looked at Skank and shook his head. "You're still on probation, son."

The woman answered. "That's mine. He has never touched

it."

"Hope that's the case. And I hope you can answer a couple of simple questions, so we can be on our way."

Skank smiled maliciously. "Paula works for an important lawyer here in Gainesville. I texted him and said she was in trouble."

His phone buzzed. He looked at the screen, smiled, and held it out for them to read. It said simply "Be there in twenty."

Dawn looked at her watch, and then glared at their hosts. "Then you have fifteen to answer all of our questions here, or I take you to my office in Dallas. But it could take a day or two for us to get them all answered there."

Scates spoke to Phillips. "And I have enough here to at least have you pulled in on suspicion of violating your parole. You may be innocent, but it will definitely take a while to make sure."

Paula looked angry. "Let me check on my kids."

Dawn raised her voice. "Sorry. You don't seem to understand. We are investigating five brutal murders, and the more you obstruct our efforts, the more like suspects you appear to be. No one is leaving this room until we have answers, or we will take you in for questioning."

Dawn only had seventeen hours left, and there was definitely something going on - right here, right now. She had no intention of letting this opportunity disappear into a legal black hole.

Dawn stared directly at Skank. "Do I need to call down to the Federal Building and have them get a couple of interrogation rooms ready?"

He hesitated only a second, and then moved toward the chair to the left of the computer.

"Not there." Scates stopped him and pointed to a chair at the other end of the table. He turned to Paula Stone. "What is he doing here? You had him arrested for hacking your Facebook page, then your computer. He conned you into having sex with him. You testified against him twice. Skank almost ruined your life."

"He's not that Skank anymore. He's Nathan, and he's

reformed."

Dawn slid a chair back from the table and motioned for her to sit. In a slightly more sympathetic voice she demanded, "Convince us. What is he doing here in your house, if he took advantage of you before?"

Over the next few minutes, Paula gave a disgustingly romanticized account of Nathan's conversion to light and truth. From jail, he wrote and apologized sincerely. He promised to do anything he could to make it up to her. When the law firm where she worked got involved in an identity theft case, she called on the reformed and upright Mr. Phillips for help. He did help, consulting only, and never touching a computer. The new Nathan's help was good. The old Nathan's sex was great-even if no longer coerced, and they began a permanent relationship.

Nathan was there, with her, on the nights of the last two murders. One of those nights Nathan had been guiding Paula's nimble fingers in search of dirt on a cheating husband whose wife had retained her boss.

Scates called Kenny, who was able to confirm at least a part of the story.

Dawn looked at her watch. It had been fifteen minutes. She returned the phone to Paula. "It looks like you're not in any trouble, so you should tell you boss not to come. We're cool, but that may change once legal counsel arrives. And feel free to check on your children."

Paula still seemed a little angry but she nodded, took the phone, and left the room.

Dawn and Scates turned their attention to Skank, who met their gaze defiantly.

"I haven't done anything."

Scates spoke softly. "Technically, you have. You were forbidden from using a computer, and just because she was at the keyboard, it doesn't mean you weren't the one using it. It becomes worse if one of our clever and thoroughly vindictive prosecutors can convince a judge that what you were doing is hacking. You willing to take that chance?"

Nathan lowered his head, and then shook it slowly.

Scates continued. "I don't give a rat's ass about what you were doing, and unless you give me a reason to care, this will all go away. We have some questions. You want to take a stab at answering them?"

It was Nathan, not Skank, who looked up and nodded.

Without warning Dawn spoke sharply. "Walrus."

Nathan blinked twice. Then with nervous eyes looked over at Sheriff Scates.

The sheriff smiled, shaking his head. "Really?"

Nathan nodded. "The moustache."

Scates shrugged, "Guess I can see that."

Dawn leaned closer, and Nathan turned to face her. "So you've been following the Twitter killer case?"

He nodded.

Scates' turn. "We think that the killer was once a guest of Montague County."

He nodded again.

Dawn followed up. "Any names come to mind?"

Nathan stared at her, hesitated, and then looked back at Sheriff Scates.

"One, maybe two."

Dawn and Scates waited for him to continue, but he had no intention of making this easy for them.

Scates finally asked impatiently. "Who, and why."

Skank stared at the crayon art stuck to the fridge for several seconds, then whispered. "Oscar Fuentes, maybe Frank Halprin."

Chapter 38

Thursday Morning
Gainesville, Texas

They'd wrung every bit of information about their two new suspects from Skank, and Dawn felt the adrenaline surge of a big cat that has caught the scent of its prey. She stared impatiently as Sheriff Scates settled deliberately behind the wheel of his Suburban. Now that they had solid leads, the first really solid leads of the investigation, Scates seemed to have slowed down. Dawn wanted to shove him out the door and take off on her own. If she had any idea where to find Fuentes or Halprin she might have.

Scates retrieved the cell phone from his belt and carefully set it into the dash cradle. He put the keys in the ignition, and then turned sideways in his seat to face Dawn.

"Ya'll did OK in there, sweet cheeks. Scared the shit out of Skank's little friend, but it worked out just fine."

Dawn pretended to smile. "Thank you, but shouldn't we be moving? We have suspects now."

Scates shot her an indulgent smile. "Oh, we have more than that."

He touched the phone, and after the beeps he said clearly. "Call, Jail, office"

The phone rang twice, and then a raspy female voice filled the car. "Montague County Jail, Officer Williams speaking."

"Ginny, Scates here. I need you to pull the records for Oscar Fuentes, released two, two and a half years ago. Then do a DMV and records search. Get everything together and send it to Detective Arturo Guzman from the Denton PD. He's going to need to find Fuentes *muy pronto*, so be quick but be thorough."

"Yes, sir," came the reply. "Need me to send you a copy as well?"

Scates thought before answering. "No, but get a copy ready just in case."

"Will do, anything else?"

"Not right now, but give me a call before you punch out."

Dawn stared in disbelief as Scates ended the call. He then turned his head to smile at her. Dawn glared back, not at all happy with the way things were unfolding. Nathan Phillips had just given them a fairly detailed, and totally convincing explanation of why he thought that Oscar Fuentes should be our prime suspect in the murders. Fuentes was "one messed up dude," according to Phillips. He was vicious, but not very smart.

His little brother, however, was just the opposite physically. Ramon Fuentes was small and slight of build. His contribution to Oscar's tiny group of thugs and criminals was intellectual. Ramon had actually visited Skank once in jail to get more information on credit card theft. Skank hadn't told him everything, but there was no doubt that Ramon would fill in the missing details himself. Ramon was a clever one, the perfect complement to his brutal brother.

Dawn was about to ask why they weren't going after Fuentes when Scates touched his phone loudly.

"Call, Arturo Guzman, mobile."

Through the car's speakers, they heard Guzman picked up on

the first ring.

In an irritatingly casual voice, the sheriff began. "I got someone you may want to check out, name's Oscar Fuentes."

Guzman replied, "Hold on, let me get a pen."

"No need, my office will be sending you a file on him in a few minutes. His full name is Oscar Raymundo Fuentes, and he's in the system. Start by checking DPS records; see if they have a 'last known' for him. Then run a check on his brother Ramon, they'll probably be together. When you have something solid, let me know, but don't wait on me if you decide to track him down."

Guzman sounded eager. "Got it, Bird's pulling it up now. What will you be doing?""

"Me and my little FBI sweetheart have another name. We'll check it out and let you know what we find."

"How good is this?"

"As good as it gets, so be very careful. If he's not involved in this, he will be involved in something. Don't move on him without backup, and wear protection. He is not a nice person."

"Copy that. You don't want to run this?"

"I think we'll find our man first, so we can probably meet up with you before you move. If not, give us a heads up, but it's your show for now."

"We'll be in touch." Guzman hung up.

Scates hit a key on his dash mounted computer. It blazed to life as he typed commands. He actually began to whistle an irritating, monotone little song as he worked. A list of names and numbers flooded his screen, and he scrolled up and down, reading carefully. With a flourish, he hit the enter key and examined the record that appeared on his screen.

The happier Sheriff Scates seemed to become, the angrier Dawn grew inside. She tried not to let it show, but when he looked at her and winked, she blew up.

"What the hell was that all about?" she fumed. "Why did you give Fuentes to Detective Guzman?"

Scates shrugged. "Maybe I want him to get the credit, then he can share it with the FBI."

Dawn gave him a scathing look.

He smiled. "I'm being facetious – you probably know that it means I'm teasin' you. And did you know that . . ."

Dawn interrupted, "Yes, I know that facetious is one of only two words in the English Language that has all the vowels used in order."

Scates beamed at her. She scowled back at him.

Scates shook his head, "I must be mellowing out in my old age. I'm startin' to like you."

She asked, "What's your obsession with words. After studying medicine, I got really tired of long, difficult words."

"Too bad, words are about all we got to communicate with. And two reasons."

Dawn was getting tired of this. She was ready to bring down a killer. But, she had no choice but to play along.

"Two reasons for what?"

"You asked why I gave Fuentes to Guzman. The first reason is Es-pan-iol"

"What?"

"How's your Spanish, Agent Johnson?"

"Not very good."

"It's probably better than Fuentes' English. Guzman's got the language to find him faster than us."

"What's the other reason? Fuentes is perfect for this. He's violent and sadistic; the murders fit his profile exactly. His brother has all of the technical skills to pull it off, and he's originally from southern Oklahoma. He's a match, for all of it."

"Not exactly," Scates corrected. "We don't have a motive."

"We don't really have a motive for Halprin. Why are we going after him and not Fuentes?"

Scates started the car, and then studied the computer screen a moment longer. He smiled smugly and pulled carefully away from the curb. Only then did he look over at Dawn and explain.

"I can think of several reasons for going after Halprin. First, motive. Skank said that almost every day Halprin got mad about being locked up when other 'real criminals were out free, getting' high and getting' laid,' is how he put it. Maybe you don't agree, but that's pretty close to motive for me. What didn't come up is that Halprin worked on the fire crew at the Wildlife Refuge, and as I recall he helped out there a couple of times after that. It also turns out that Mr. Halprin drives a . . ." Scates glanced at the computer again. "1997 Ford Taurus. Blue in color."

Scates turned onto County Road 151 and stomped on the gas pedal of his cruiser.

"On a personal note, Frank Anthony Halprin is the son of a bitch that killed my wife. If he's going down, by god, I'm going to be the one to do it."

Dawn watched carefully as Sheriff Scates picked up his radio handset. "Dispatch, have Sharp, and anyone else in the vicinity meet me at the Montana scene as soon as they can get there."

"Ten-four," replied a young man that must have been the dispatcher.

Dawn recognized Deputy Sharp's voice, then two others who acknowledged their response.

Scates snapped the handset back into place, then glanced at Dawn.

"So, do you want to roll with me, or should I have Sharp take you to Guzman so you can help track down Fuentes?"

Dawn faced forward, made herself comfortable in the seat, and folded her arms across her chest. "Who's Fuentes?"

Chapter 39

Thursday Afternoon
Montague County

Dawn wanted a shower.

Desperately, quickly. Any shower, hot or cold. Lots of soap, maybe the industrial-strength antibacterial foam like they used for scrub-ins at her old surgical suites.

Better, the decontamination spray they had used at the Academy for bio-warfare drills. Perfect! Well, not exactly perfect, no moisturizer.

She looked around and nodded. This place actually looked like it had been developed for bio-hazard training. "This place" meant the dilapidated camper which the Montague County Sheriff's department used for its stakeouts. Dawn wasn't sure how old the camper was, but she suspected that in one of the drawers – most of which had been fused shut by the growing slime – she would find a newspaper clipping that reported the end of the Civil War.

The seat cushions had all been covered by freshly laundered

sheets, which was a welcome touch. But, unless this was the first camper Dawn had seen which came standard with dirt floors, the vehicle she currently inhabited was in desperate need of a cleaning – or a fire.

The "Montague County Mobile Surveillance Vehicle" sat in the parking lot of the Creek Bottom Apartments, one building over and across the parking lot from Apartment 207C, Frank Anthony Halprin's apartment. They arrived about an hour before dawn, and parked where spotters could see Halprin's apartment, but still maintain a discreet distance.

Sheriff Scates seemed to like his stakeout pad. He assured her that it had all the comforts a mobile stakeout vehicle needed, though he seemed to grow less comfortable there every minute. It had a bathroom, a fridge, and a couch. What else could she want?

Maybe a tetanus shot.

To accentuate its comforts, Scates had used the facilities four times now. During his last visit, Dawn thought she heard the subtle rattling of a pill bottle. Scates was still in pain.

Scates was a pain.

It seemed like his back was worse than she'd previously observed. Actually, it didn't seem like his back at all. She heard water run briefly in the sink. Scates exited, drying his hands on a worn brown towel that had once been white.

Gross, she would hold it as long as it took.

A radio resting on the faded counter crackled and reported softly. "Blue vehicle pulling in."

They both looked out the window on the right side. Indeed, a large blue car had turned into the parking lot.

Scates picked up the radio and keyed the handheld. "Sharp, you get a make on the vehicle entering from the east?"

Several seconds later, Sharp's muted voice echoed off the mold. "Chevy Impala, not him." Sharp pulled the envious task of watching from the vacant apartment directly across from Halprin's. Sharp's clothes wouldn't need to be burned at the end of the day.

They sat back, and Dawn returned to the secondary, though

critical task of not becoming infected. She looked again at her watch; she had been doing that a lot. It was after two in the afternoon, and before long she would have to pull out and go back to Frisco. Pratt had been specific, and Dawn had no intention of ignoring his instructions.

Scates gave her a reproving glance. "You got somewhere to be?"

"Actually, I do. I have been given a deadline. I have to break off and return to my office by eight tonight. I'll have to leave here by six in order to get back to my car in time."

"Just how are you planning on leavin' here? Was it that Pratt fellow that told you to come on home by eight?"

Dawn nodded.

Scates snatched his phone from the counter and began to scroll through his contacts list. Dawn suppressed the urge to give him a handy-wipe.

Scates pressed send with emphasis and put the phone to his ear. After just a few seconds, his face turned serious. "Yeah, Agent Pratt? You need to stop messing with my investigation." He paused, listening impatiently. "Johnson and I are on a stakeout, and all she can do is look at her watch and wonder if she's gonna make it back by bedtime. I need her full attention on what we got going out here."

The next pause lasted significantly longer, and Scates face took on an angry, then an incredulous look. "You're 'scheduling constraints and manpower anomalies' don't mean a rat's ass to me. I got a killer to catch."

Pause.

"Yes, I got her here, and no, I can't put her on. I will, however, put it on speaker so we can *both* participate."

Scates covered the phone with his hand as whispered to Dawn. "He always such a pecker head?"

Dawn managed to laugh and shrug at the same time.

Scates set his phone to speaker and set it on the table.

Pratt's voice boomed out. "Special Agent Johnson, are you there?"

"Yes, sir."

"I appreciate your dedication, and the fact that you are actively involved in this ongoing manhunt, but your participation in activities here at the Field Office is still quite essential. I need you back at our prearranged time."

"I understand that sir, but . . ."

Sheriff Scates cut her off. "Just how is she supposed to get back? Her car's in Denton, and I'm short staffed out here myself. I can't spare anyone to take her back."

"I'll have someone pick her up. In fact, I can bring extra agents to help alleviate your staffing difficulties."

"I can't be sure where we'll be when ya'll get out here."

"Hold on," Pratt demanded.

There was silence on the line for several minutes. Scates and Dawn finally exchanged confused glances, and the sheriff bent over and examined his phone to make sure the connection was still active.

Pratt's voice boomed out, and Scates jerked his head back. "You're in the southwest parking lot of the Creek Bottom Apartments. Is that correct Johnson?"

A little surprised, she replied. "Yes, sir."

"Don't sound shocked, we are the FBI. Finding people is a point of emphasis for us. We've become quite good at."

Scates face turned sour. "Why don't you point your emphasis somewhere else? Your girl here needs to stay."

"Less than forty-eight hours ago, you wanted *my girl* out of your hair. Look Sheriff, I empathize with you. It's very difficult having to rely on inexperienced personnel. As previously mentioned, I'll be glad to assign a team of experienced agents to augment your task force. A task force which you will continue to lead. Our only desire is to provide the best possible support at this critical point in such an important investigation."

"Son, don't piss on my boots, then try and tell me that it's just a little rain. I know you're just trying to get your hooks into this investigation, like with the computer geek you brought in the other night. And as far as experience, the two days Johnson's spent with me probably taught her more about real police work than two months at your Academy."

Pratt actually chuckled at that.

The Sheriff pressed his point. "I even gave her a real police radio, and if she's a good girl for the whole day, I'm gonna let her have her one of the toy Sheriff's Badges we give the kids when they tour the jail. I may even make her an official junior deputy."

Pratt replied, "How kind, I don't know what to say."

"Do us all a favor and don't say anything." Scates went on impatiently, "If you want to be involved, fine. Detective Guzman is having a hard time tracking down another suspect, a nasty little shit named Oscar Fuentes. Fuente's definitely dangerous. I'll call Guzman and tell him you're assisting us in the location and apprehension of Fuentes. You can even send some of your G-Men up here to help me babysit your agent if you've a mind, but I don't want the flow of my investigation interrupted. Things are moving. I don't intend to let that change."

Pratt spoke in a light, professional voice. "If your department is requesting help with this case, my office will be happy to respond. I'll contact Detective Guzman to determine how best to assist him. I may also want to send others to work with Agent Johnson. I'd love to have more of my agents benefit from your tutelage. I'll be in touch."

"And Pratt." Scates barked.

Pratt hesitated, and then answered, "Sheriff?"

"We wouldn't have gotten this far without your girl's help. She deserves to finish this out."

The line went dead.

Scates picked up the phone. "Prick!" His eyes narrowed with determination as he glared at Johnson. "No more sitting on our asses, let's go find our suspect."

Scates dialed another number. "Ginny, I need you to look through the file on Frank Anthony Halprin. Everything that happened while he was locked up, who he called, who visited him, who put money in his account, everything. Email me a summary, quick as you can."

Scates frowned. "Guzman won't be a happy camper, but like your Pratt said, the FBI can find people."

Dawn looked around. No happy campers here, either.

The Sheriff continued thoughtfully, "I don't think Halprin had any family, but there may have been a girl friend. I want to end this before your new babysitters arrive."

Chapter 40

Thursday Afternoon
Montague, Texas

Sheriff Scates' Suburban had a lot less room than the "Mobile Surveillance Vehicle" they'd just survived, but it sure smelled better. She also didn't have to worry about the slime and mold coming to life, engulfing her body in a pulsating green ooze, turning her into an alien zombie – or a Deputy.

Through jail records, they'd established that inmate Frank Anthony Halprin, during the last three months of his incarceration, received weekly visits from one Reba Fay Tolliver. Once a month she even put money into his prison account. On the last visit before his release, she had been forcibly removed from the visitation room and almost arrested. The braless Reba Fay had unbuttoned her blouse, rubbed her naked breasts against the window, and moaned loudly.

"We're waiting for you baby, me and the girls here miss you. One more week. We'll be ready."

Dawn instantly reached the same conclusion regarding Reba

Fay that everyone else had. As a result, she and Scates now waited in the parking lot of Lady Tolliver's apartment, just one building away from Halprin's. They left Sharp and another Deputy watching Halprin's place, and were now trying to decide how to proceed. Reba Fay, they discovered, lived in that very same complex. She had a third-floor apartment, making it impossible to see who was home, or what was going on. All they had was a view of anyone trying to enter or drive away.

Dawn chuckled, "After the Midnight Run audition, I'm surprised you didn't have her locked up."

"How come a nice girl like you saw that movie?"

Dawn shrugged, "Maybe I'm not that nice."

Scates smiled, then winced, then fidgeted in his seat. He winced again with the effort. He gave a disgusted frown as he replied. "If you get to meet Reba, you discover that even wearing latex gloves, no one wanted to search her. We did a background check, and she seems harmless. Just a stupid kid, living off her mom and rich doctor step-dad from Houston. The parents pay the bills so little Reba can live far enough away so as not to embarrass them."

Dawn asked, "She live alone?"

Scates laughed. "According to the landlord, it's just her and the girls."

The Sheriff's radio crackled. "Haley should be rolling through about now."

Scates pointed at a four or five year old, white Explorer that had just turned into the parking lot. "That's Haley's car there. Officer Haley Babbitt is one of our patrol officers. She actually lives here in this complex, two buildings over. Tolliver drives an Acura registered to her step-dad. We need to know if she's here. With luck, we'll find Halprin's Ford here too.

They watched the Explorer do a careful, but not suspiciously slow lap of the parking lot, then drive off toward the rear of the complex. The radio came to life.

A voice, presumably Babbitt's, declared, "Tolliver's vehicle is there, no sign of the suspect's Ford."

Scates snatched up his mike. "Ten-Four. Roll around to the rear of her building. Jess should be here in a few minutes and will find you."

"Already there," came a voice which probably belonged to Deputy Jess.

"Got him, we're in position," responded Babbitt

Scates continued. "Good. I've got Kate and Paul Marques coming too. They'll take up position where they can watch the front. Everyone be advised that this is our entire team, including me and a female FBI Agent named Dawn Johnson. She's about five-nine, African American, wearing the standard, tacky, Fed colored pant suit. Acknowledge."

Four deputies responded, so the team was set. Sheriff Scates had been forced to call in half a dozen deputies who had been off duty. He refused to pull people off their regular duties to find and apprehend Halprin. It was obvious that Sheriff Bubba Scates took the safety of Montague County very seriously, and very personally as well.

He pointed at a red and white Dodge pickup truck, Kate and Paul, as it turned into Tolliver's parking lot. It found a spot directly across from her apartment. The deputies backed in, giving them a clear view of her building, and hopefully her car.

Scates pulled binoculars from under his seat, and focused on the truck. He then looked carefully at Tolliver's apartment, and finally scanned the rest of the scene.

He grabbed the mike and announced. "That'll work. Sit tight until you see movement, or until I give the word."

Four voices again acknowledged their instructions, and Scates settled back in his seat. "Now we wait."

"How long?" Dawn asked.

"Long as it takes," Scates looked at the clock on the dash, which gave the time as 3:42. "Or four-thirty, whichever comes first. We don't have a fix on Halprin by then; I'll have Haley do the 'lost dog' thing."

Dawn frowned and shook her head.

Scates elaborated. "Babbitt, in plain clothes, goes to the

apartments near Tolliver's and knocks, asking if anyone's seen her lost dog. She finally goes to our target's door, and asks them too. Haley'll find out if she's alone."

"Why not do that now?" Dawn felt a growing impatience. When her fellow FBI Agents arrived, she would become a spectator. She didn't want that, she wanted to stay on the playing field.

"Right now the adrenaline's pumping. I like to give my people a little time to settle in, calm down. Fewer mistakes that way. We'll give it half hour, how's that sound?"

Sounds like a half hour too long, but Dawn would have to wait.

She didn't have to wait. Twelve minutes later, the radio clicked to life. "Door opening, appears to be Tolliver. She's carrying something. A cat."

Scates snatched up his mike. "What kind of cat?"

"Yellow, fat, long hair, I don't know. A cat, how many kinds are there? She's going to her car."

The sheriff spoke, "Hold your positions. We're moving."

Scates struggled stiffly out of the car. Dawn hopped out as well, and she and the Sheriff hurried over. Dawn sprinted to stand behind the Acura, and managed to stop Reba Fay before she could back out. Tolliver hopped angrily out of the car. In her arms was a cat that looked like a perfect match for the hair found at the Oltman murder scene.

Dawn and Scates exchanged a smile as they walked over to meet their first, real, "person of interest."

Scates looked over to Dawn and said . . . something unrecognizable.

Dawn scowled, "What?"

He spoke slowly, glancing at Tolliver, who glared over at them. "Hippopoto-monstrosesquipe-daliophobia."

Dawn could only shake her head. "What does that mean?"

"From Skank's, you don't like big words. That means a fear of big words. You want me to say it . . ."

"No!" Dawn growled.

They approached, and got a better look at their target. Reba

Fay Tolliver had what she may have intended as blonde hair, though that was certainly not its original or actual color. It almost looked yellow. Her "girls" were an impressive pair, bouncing merrily and unrestrained under a white, "Love Pink" t-shirt. Her jeans were expensive and tight, though she wore cheap flip-flops on her pedicured feet. Dawn had no idea where she could be going dressed like that. Scates was in uniform, and Reba looked worried as they approached.

Sheriff Scates smiled pleasantly. "Sorry to bother you, ma'am, but there's something we'd like you to help us with."

Dawn was going to introduce herself, but the look on Tolliver's face clearly indicated that Scates' presence was enough.

She huffed impatiently, "Sorry, I've got to meet my boyfriend."

"Frank Halprin?" Scates asked.

"He's not my boyfriend."

Dawn followed up. "So you're not still seeing Frank Halprin?"

Reba cocked her head indulgently, "A'course I'm still seeing him, but that doesn't mean he's still my boyfriend."

The sheriff smiled indulgently. "This sounds a little complicated, can we talk about it inside?"

"I'll be late." Reba Fay pouted.

"You'll be later if we take you all the way to Montague for our little chat."

Ms. Tolliver spun, and bounced her way back to the stairs, then up to the apartment. She juggled the cat in her left arm as she fumbled with the keys. She reached toward the dead bolt, but then froze and then turned to face them. A look of understanding preceded a look of dread. She clutched the keys.

"I would rather talk out here."

There was something inside, something she didn't want them to see. They had leverage.

Dawn said seriously, "You'll answer all of our questions?"

Reba nodded.

Dawn smiled, "Maybe I should hold your cat."

Reba spun away, shielding the cat protectively.

Dawn shrugged, but reached over to pet the cat, making sure to collect enough fur so they could test for a DNA match.

Tolliver scowled defensively. "You lookin' for Frank?"

Scates asked innocently. "Is there a reason why we should be?"

She shrugged

Dawn's turn. "He's not your boyfriend, but you still see him?"

Reba tossed her hair indifferently. She tried to sound a little bored as she answered. "He comes over a couple of times a week, but just for sex." She glanced nervously back at her apartment."We party, watch basketball, no big deal."

Dawn wondered if the partying involved what Reba had hidden inside the apartment. Scates took his turn. "Sex, parties, TV, sounds like you're still his girlfriend to me."

"It's not like that, it's the NBA playoffs. I got an awesome big screen and Frank, he's a huge Dallas Mavericks fan. He brings the . . ." She stopped herself just in time, ". . . refreshments, and we just kind of hang out. Besides, he's got a new girlfriend."

Dawn picked up the interview. "And him coming here to party doesn't bother his new girlfriend? Or your new boyfriend?"

"I don't actually have a boyfriend, I just said that. And I guess Karen doesn't mind. She came over with him a few times." Reba frowned as she thought. "Maybe it does bother his new one; he stopped coming over a few weeks ago."

"When was the last time you saw him?" Dawn followed up.

"Like I said, a couple of weeks. The Mavs played the Rockets. I like the Rockets."

Scates looked at his watch impatiently. "Do you have any idea where Frank Halprin is right now?"

"He's probably at work. He works at the dweeb. He does . . ."

"The dweeb?" Dawn needed help with this one.

"Stands for Dallas, Water," Reba hesitated "boats, and?" She looked at Scates for help.

He shook his head in disgust, and then turned to face Dawn. "Dallas Wilderness Equipment and Boats. DWEAB. They're one of the largest RV and Boat dealers in the state. They also run most of the local marinas."

"Yeah, he's got a nice office at their new building by the marina, he does their computer work. He's pretty smart with computers. If he's not there, he's probably at his girlfriend's. Karen Allen's her name. She lives north of Nacona."

Dawn and Scates exchanged a smile. They had enough. Scates stared menacingly at Reba Fay Tolliver. "Ms Tolliver, if you tell Frank we were here, or warn him in any way, we will come back. We will find whatever it is you're hiding inside there. You and the girls won't like it where I'm going to stick ya'."

She nodded earnestly as Dawn and the sheriff turned and made their way down to his car.

Scates looked over as they walked. "I say we visit the girlfriend. I don't think we can make it to Nacona before he gets off work."

Dawn nodded. "Don't care, whichever's quicker." Dawn was getting impatient. She could be demoted, or removed entirely at any time now. She asked, "The new girlfriend. Think she'll be as smart as the old one?"

The Suburban beeped as Scates pressed the remote. "If she was smart, she wouldn't be his girlfriend." He opened Dawn's door, reached into the glove box, and pulled out a roll of tape and a ziplock evidence bag. "Get the cat hair off with the tape and put it in the bag. I'll label it."

He walked to his side of the car, and they both got in. He reached for his radio, "I'll have someone cruise by his work, see if his car's there. We're closin' in, sweet cheeks!"

Chapter 41

Thursday Afternoon
Nacona, Texas

Even with a long, and undeniably welcome potty break, they'd made good time to Nacona. Both Dawn and the Sheriff approved of the rest stop, but they hadn't agreed on much else. Dawn wanted the sheriff to organize a dynamic entry team and break into the suspect's girlfriend's place if they though he was there. Scates wanted to . . . well Scates didn't seem to want to do anything for a while. Scates seemed impaired and Dawn almost asked him to pull over so she could drive.

The sheriff also stopped complaining about his back, which had caused him such serious discomfort earlier in the stakeout. Dawn recognized the effects; Sheriff Scates had taken a painkiller at their stop, a strong one, very possibly stronger than the Naprosyn she'd seen in his truck. That explained some of the behavior she'd noticed before. The fact that he returned to normal so quickly seemed to indicate he was used to it, and had acquired some tolerance. She would have to watch to see how

quickly the back pain returned. The symptoms of Bubba Scates'
affliction were in possible conflict with the medical explanation
he'd given her.

She was in shock that he may have lied to her. NOT!

They reached downtown Nacona, and met up with a plain
clothes deputy driving an old yellow Ford Crown Victoria. Scates
identified him as Deputy Travis. The Deputy had parked in the
alley between a one-story brick restaurant and a three-story office
building. Scates pulled beside him, driver's side doors almost
touching.

Through lowered windows, Deputy Travis explained that
Halprin's car had not been in the parking lot of his office.
Subsequently, the Deputy had driven to the little frame house
outside of Nacona where Ms. Allen resided. There he'd found
what appeared to be the suspect's car in the driveway. No other
vehicles visible. The house had a chain-link fence around the
entire property, and three massive, nasty looking dogs running
free in the yard.

He thought they were dogs, but could have been wolves. He
was afraid to get close enough to find out.

Sheriff Scates nodded, congratulated his Deputy on a
thorough job, and told him to return to the girlfriend's
neighborhood. He needed to locate a couple of places where they
could set up surveillance, front and rear. The sheriff then called in
three of the deputies from their other stakeout to assist. This
would give them enough manpower to watch and apprehend
Frank Halprin, but Scates did not look happy.

"What's wrong?" Dawn finally asked.

"Dogs. That complicates things."

"Why?"

"I'm not hurtin' somebody's dogs, especially when we don't
even know if he's there. Hell, we're not one hundred percent sure
he's our killer."

Dawn didn't want to hurt any innocent animals either, but
time was slipping away, and she had no intention of letting
Halprin slip away with it. She looked around, considering her

options. She noticed a grocery store down the street. Drugged food slipped under the fence could work on the dogs. She would have no problem calculating an effective dosage of over the counter sleep aids once she saw the dogs and calculated their weight.

That would work, but that would also take a while. Dawn needed to get things moving now.

"Maybe we can wait him out," Scates concluded. He obviously did not share her urgency. "I bet he'll come on home tonight, if he doesn't go visit his old, old lady that is. Mavs play tonight. Either way, we'll get him. Better still, I can get someone here from the wildlife preserve with a tranquilizer gun in a couple of hours, that'll take care of the dogs."

Dawn agreed, since that would remove the dogs as a problem. Dawn also disagreed, since waiting that long would probably remove her from the investigation when the other agents arrived. There had to be something they could do now.

A car honked behind them. Scates ignored it, but it honked again with some urgency. They both turned to see a small truck. The pimple faced driver, a boy with long hair and a ball cap on backward, pointed emphatically toward the office building to their right. The sheriff had blocked the rear entrance to an office supply store on the bottom floor. Scates pulled forward, and the boy hopped out of the truck carrying a clipboard. He snatched a package from the rear of the truck and bounded through the now unobstructed door.

Dawn turned and stared at the truck, then glanced at Scates. "Is there a UPS Store in Nacona?"

He shook his head, and then gestured to the truck behind them with his thumb. "Just a local courier service. FedEx and UPS both deliver here though."

Dawn shook her head. Too far, they wouldn't work for the plan now forming in her mind. Behind her, she saw the boy burst from the doorway and jog toward his truck. She tried to get out, but the wall was too close to the truck. She spun toward Scates.

"Stop him, stop that delivery boy."

Chapter 42

Thursday Afternoon
Nacona, Texas

Dawn stood at the gate, yelling toward the house. Shouting was both unnecessary and useless, since her voice could not be heard over the barking and growling of the dogs trying desperately to dig their fangs into her throat through the fence.

Dawn HATED this. Big animals had always scared her, and big animals with fangs, claws or sharp horns terrified her to the core. She stood three panicked feet from the aforementioned angry fangs and claws, refusing to withdraw. She reprimanded herself angrily, again, for suggesting this. How could she not have anticipated that it would be her delivering the package? All the local deputies would be recognized.

"Quiet!" a small, redheaded woman shouted from the porch.

The dogs responded by barking louder and lunging even more desperately at the fence. Dawn felt sweat running down her armpits, reactivating the already ripe smells of the shirt she'd taken from the delivery boy.

Damn, she though. *He didn't have one deputy from another city who could do this?*

The plan was to go to Karen Allen's residence with a package for Frank Halprin. The delivery person would refuse to go inside because of the dogs – which anyone could believe. Assuming Halprin was there, and then he would have to come out to sign. Then the delivery person, Desperate Dawn, would ask him to step outside the gate to sign. Said delivery person would grab and hold the suspect while other deputies converged and subdued him.

But according to her original version of the plan, the delivery person was supposed to be one of the sheriff's deputies. Scates had insisted that Halprin would recognize most of his deputies, especially after spending over half a year in the county jail. Dawn had refused, explaining her fear of big animals. With obvious pleasure, the sheriff had explained that it was her plan, and that her making the delivery was the only way it would work.

No good deed goes unpunished.

The red-haired woman, matching the driver's license photo for Karen Allen that Scates had pulled up on his computer, stalked toward the gate. She stopped about six feet short. "What do you want?"

Dawn held up the large, cardboard envelop she had put together for her ploy. "Delivery for Frank Halprin."

The woman stopped, cocking her head and squinting suspiciously. "We ain't expecting no deliveries."

Dawn read from the clipboard she carried. "It's from the Dallas Mavericks Promotions Department." She read slowly, "The fan for life ticket giveaway."

Karen stared blankly at Dawn. No, she was not very smart.

Dawn continued, "Did he enter a contest or something?"

Karen continued to stare blankly, and Dawn wondered if this was actually her normal expression.

Dawn asked impatiently. 'Is he a Mavericks fan?"

Allen managed to nod without showing a hint of understanding.

"Then he did enter some contest, register for free tickets, or something?" Dawn persisted.

Finally, she blinked and stammered. "Maybe. I guess."

Dawn held up the clipboard. "I need him to sign for this."

Karen continued to stare.

Yep, that's her normal expression.

She walked to the gate. "I can sign."

Dawn shook her head. "Sorry ma'am, I can only deliver it to the addressee. And, I'll need to see a government approved ID, such as a driver's license, and he will have to be the one to sign for it." Dawn looked at the dogs, then back at Allen. "And he will have to come out here to do it. I am *not* going in there."

The woman frowned, and looked back down the street to where Scates was parked. "He ain't here, but he'll be here any minute."

Dawn glanced at the faded blue Ford in the drive. They had hoped he would be here as well. Dawn noticed the dust-covered windows, and the dirt and leaves that had accumulated in the rear bumper and underneath the wheels. They had guessed wrong. She shook her head and looked back at the woman.

"Sorry, I can't wait. If you tell me where he is, though, I may be able to swing by and get it to him it if it's close to another delivery."

They had considered this possibility, and decided that she shouldn't wait. There was no telling how long it would take for him to arrive, and a delivery driver waiting would be suspicious. They did have a backup plan to accommodate this.

"I will take this back to our office. He can pick it up there; we'll have someone on duty until eight."

Taking him into custody at the store would work, since the store would be staffed by deputies. There wouldn't be any bystanders, not even his girlfriend or her dogs. Dawn turned to leave.

"No, wait. He'll be really pissed if he misses this. Let me give him a call."

Dawn turned back impatiently. "Hurry."

Karen Allen fumbled in her back pockets, pulling out a small blue cell phone. She hit one button, probably redial, put the phone to her ear, and turned away to talk. Dawn couldn't hear what she said, until her voice grew louder in frustration.

"I don't know, Dallas Mavericks, playoff tickets or something. No, it wasn't me, maybe that bitch Reba Fay. Like I said, I don't know."

At that point, Karen lowered the phone from her ear, turned, and looked back down the street. A small, light green two-door had turned the corner and was driving deliberately up the street. A male driver appeared to be alone in the vehicle. He slowed as he passed the house, staring at Karen, then at Dawn, then at the delivery truck she had hijacked for their ruse.

The car slowed further. Allen made a little half wave at the car, and then disconnected the call. She smiled as the car stopped at the street. Dawn and Karen both watched as the man, now recognizable as Frank Anthony Halprin, looked around the neighborhood. He did a double take in the rear-view mirror, and then spun in his seat to stare.

Dawn followed his gaze, to where a large grey sedan full of kids made a u-turn and drove away, leaving the black Suburban driven by Sheriff Scates clearly visible. Halprin spun back to Dawn, eyes narrowing with suspicion, then fear. Halprin threw his car into gear and sped off. Dawn chased briefly on foot, but he was gone.

She stepped aside when Scates roared past, with full lights and siren. Seconds later, Deputy Travis in his yellow Ford skidded to a halt next to her. She threw open the door and managed to dive inside before the car lurched into motion.

The rumble of the engine, and the acceleration forcing her into the seat told her immediately that the car was only a mess on the outside. This was a police interceptor, and she hurried to get herself strapped in.

Travis was already on his radio. "This is Unit 27. Montague One and Units 27 and 18, 10-80, subject vehicle is a light green, two-door," he thought a moment then continued. "Mini Cooper, possibly registered to Karen Allen. Vehicle driven by Frank Anthony Halprin, person of interest in ongoing murder investigation. Request backup."

"Ten-four, Unit 27, I have your 20 as — seventeen hundred block of Carson Road, Nacona. Backup on the way, estimated arrival twenty minutes soonest."

Dawn heard a siren and turned to see a marked Sheriff's Department vehicle behind them, red and blue lights flashing urgently. That would be Unit 18. She could see two deputies inside.

She turned to face forward again, but Halprin and the Sheriff had both disappeared. At that moment, the sheriff's voice boomed calmly from the speakers.

"Now heading north on Mathews, subject turning west on 1191."

"Copy!" Dawn was pressed deeper into the seat as Travis demanded every rpm his engine could generate.

Travis glanced at Dawn, grinning wickedly. "No one gets away from the sheriff."

Chapter 43

Thursday Evening
Nacona, Texas

Dawn grabbed the armrest of her door as Deputy Travis executed a right turn and almost lost control. The chase had taken them to a residential area. The large and heavy police vehicles barely managed to maintain visual contact with the small and very quick little vehicle they chased. Several times they had to slow down because the large, top-heavy Suburban had an even harder time negotiating the streets than the police cruisers which followed.

"East, Macon Drive," Travis shouted and then glanced at Dawn. "Send it."

Dawn grabbed the mike and keyed the send button, speaking loud enough to be heard clearly over the siren. "Suspect traveling east on Macon Drive."

As a passenger, Dawn's hands were free, and she took over the responsibility of keeping the other units and departments appraised of the chase.

"Nacona PD five now in pursuit," blasted from the radio. Soon this would look like a parade.

"Roger, Nacona five," she responded. They had notified the Nacona Police Department immediately, and now two of their vehicles had joined in.

"Hold on!"

Dawn's head snapped right as Travis made an extreme left turn and skidded sideways, slamming into a parked minivan that had stopped part way into the intersection. Travis started to speak, but Dawn was already on it.

"Nacona five, Sheriff's twenty-seven in minor accident at Mason and," she looked around.

"Twenty-First Street." Travis barked.

"Twenty-first, looks minor but someone should check for injuries. Now headed north on Twenty First."

Ahead they saw the end of the houses, and what looked like main road. Travis smiled wickedly and glanced at Dawn.

"County Sixty-Two, bastard's finally making a mistake."

About time, since he had managed to open up a significant lead among the houses, residents and dogs. Scates had almost come to a complete stop twice to avoid hitting dogs that had started chasing Halprin.

They watched Scates' Suburban execute a high-speed right turn after the Mini Cooper. Seconds later they skidded onto the well-kept road and accelerated violently.

"Now heading," Dawn oriented herself, "East on County Sixty-Two."

Ahead they saw the black Suburban flying towards its prey, but the little green car was moving much faster than Dawn would have thought, this was still a chase. They drove past several small roads, running perpendicular to Highway 62, and with each one Travis' smile grew.

In a blur, they passed a sign that informed them they had entered the Nacona Lake Recreational Area. Travis had glanced at the sign and chuckled.

"Dead ends at the lake."

Sheriff Scates' voice buzzed through their car. "Nacona PD, this is Montague One. Suggest establishing a road block on Sixty-Two, in case he manages to double back."

"Roger, this is Nacona Eleven, now on Sixty-Two about two miles behind."

For the first time since they had begun this investigation, Dawn felt like they were in control. The surge of adrenaline cleared her head and burned through her veins. She fidgeted slightly in her seat and leaned forward. This was her first high-speed pursuit, and they were going to nail the SOB they were chasing.

Ahead Dawn saw a massive sign with boats, fish, and a large arrow pointing left. It announced that the Nacona Marina was half a mile away. Halprin had passed the turn, and Deputy Travis glanced at her.

"He's going to the golf course; club house is straight ahead. This course is new. He may not know about it." He sneered. "I doubt he's a golfer."

At that moment, two rows of trees appeared on either side of the road, with a white rail fence behind them. The brush disappeared, and to her left she could make out the manicured green of a golf course. Halprin may be trapped, but Dawn realized that at this time the course could be occupied, maybe even busy. If he wanted hostages, he would find plenty.

She could clearly see the Sheriff ahead, and he had almost caught up with the little green blur they hunted. The Mini swung left into the parking lot, and didn't slow down. The Sheriff, followed by Dawn and Deputy Travis, followed mere seconds behind.

Dawn spoke clearly into the radio. "Entering the . . .' she looked around for a sign. "Nacona Municipal Golf Course."

Dawn glanced around; the lights and sirens had brought the golfing to a halt. Groups of men and women all turned to watch as the caravan headed straight for the club house. The faint sound of honking could be heard in front of them. The Mini honked madly, and barely slowed down as it passed to the left of a brick building that Dawn assumed was the club house.

The adrenaline burned even stronger inside her as Dawn realized that this was it. They had him. He was out of road. She reached down and pulled the safety strap off her .40 caliber Glock automatic.

Dawn replaced the safety strap, as the Ford bounded madly over the curb and onto the cart path. Halprin had entered the course. Specifically, he now traveled the paved path to the tee boxes, driving a foursome madly onto a putting green. The Sheriff was right after him, still closing, ignoring everything but his prey. Travis, grinning wildly, took up a position behind. Travis grinned so hard that Dawn though it must hurt, he was completely into the pursuit.

She informed the other units. "Now entering the course itself, left of the club house."

They were right behind the Mini now, but the going became tenuous. The Mini barely managed to keep its wheels on the path, but the wider vehicles chasing it were forced to drive on the grass itself, straddling the cart path. Halprin slowed as he passed a foursome that had just managed to get out of the way. He lowered his window, and threw a bag into the back of one of the carts, then sped up again.

Travis' eyes narrowed in thought, but then popped open in understanding. Dawn figured it out at the same time, and they glanced at each other quickly. "Drugs."

Halprin had drugs in his car, and had figured out a clever way of getting rid of them. The golfers would surely pick up the bags, which meant that their fingerprints would be on them. And if the police managed to find the drugs at all, they would be in their possession of someone else. It was a thin defense, but much better than if they'd been found in their suspect's possession.

But, why would a serial killer be worried about being caught with drugs? Dawn would worry about that later.

They had managed to close even further on Halprin. The Sheriff's siren went silent. Dawn understood why when the squeal of a loud speaker took its place.

"Stop now. You . . ."

The Mini slowed, and the Suburban slammed on its brakes in response. They all watched as two more bags flew from the car, one landing in the lap of a terrified, blonde, teenage girl with braces and braids. The other struck a woman who looked like the girl's mother, in the chest. The drug evidence was disappearing, but that would be the least of Halprin's problems.

The Sheriff's loud speaker sounded again. "You have nowhere to go." The gruff voice boomed through the golf course, drowning out what were clearly obscenities from an elderly couple who had crashed into a tree to the right of the path.

"Stop now! You cannot -- SHIT!"

Brake lights blazed bright red as the Suburban fishtailed and skidded along the path. Neither Dawn nor Travis could see ahead of Scates, until the Deputy hit his brakes as well. Their Ford slowed, but still skidded precariously to the left. They missed the Sheriff's Suburban by the width of a golf tee and shuddered slowly past. Their Ford now spun unsteady, and continued sideways further onto the rough. Dawn glanced out her window at a rapidly approaching drop and the not so inviting rocky creek below. Dawn's eyes went wide as the car slowed further, then stopped. She now stared out her window, but could not see the ground below. She saw only a portion of the stream, and the vertical wall on the opposite side. They had barely avoided what was easily a twenty-five foot drop into a stone strewn creek below.

She looked back toward the cart path. Scates had crashed into a pair of heavy wooden posts. Those massive wood pillars marked the entrance to a bridge which spanned the creek. The bridge appeared undamaged, but Scates' SUV smoked threateningly.

On the bridge, the Mini Cooper still progressed slowly, forcing its way along the bridge. It ricocheted forward, sides scraping the railings as it inched along its path to freedom, wheels barely staying on the wooden planks that floored the bridge. Dawn hoped he'd get stuck. If he did, there was no way he could get out of his car.

Unfortunately, Halprin scraped his way forward. He could still get away.

Travis responded to her unspoken fears. "There's nowhere he can go. We still got him."

Dawn didn't agree. "Unless he gets out of here on foot."

Dawn opened her door, looked down, and then slammed it closed. She couldn't fly, so she turned and pushed Travis out of his door. She crawled over the console, and followed the Deputy onto solid ground. She reached over and snatched the handheld radio from Deputy Travis' belt and ran back toward the bridge.

She yelled back at Travis. "Back your car away from the edge, *carefully!*" she shouted as she hurried toward the Sheriff, who had managed to dismount.

Sheriff Scates stepped away from his vehicle and examined himself carefully. Everything was there, in the right place, and still seemed to be working. He heard her approaching and turned to walk toward Dawn. Travis pulled up beside her.

Scates pointed at the Ford, "Get in. We'll go back to the club house and lock everything down."

Dawn shook her head, looking around. She just didn't believe that the mastermind of the killings, the man who had just managed to elude a convoy of cops, would be that easy to track down.

"Are you positive there is no way he can get out of here? How about on foot?" She asked the Sheriff.

He thought. "Maybe, what do we do?"

Dawn took two steps toward the bridge. "You go with Travis and secure the course," she pointed at a golf cart that had stopped at the other end of the bridge. "I'm going after him."

Scates turned to Travis, who had stepped out of his vehicle. "Get the area secure, I'm going with her."

They approached the bridge, but the entrance was blocked by the SUV. Scates shook his head dejectedly and turned to Travis. He pointed to the back bumper of his truck. "Push the back end off the path; give us some room to get by."

Travis looked, and understood. He backed his car about twenty feet, and angled toward Scates SUV. He moved carefully forward until he hit Scates' Suburban, which shuddered slightly on impact. Travis accelerated until Scates' bumper began to buckle. The Deputy kept his wheels spinning until the rear end of the SUV shuddered to the side. This cleared a two-foot space for Dawn and the Sheriff to squeeze onto the bridge.

Ahead of them, Halprin was having his own problems. The Mini Cooper was scraping forward, loudly but slowly, along the bridge. The smoking tires barely kept him moving away from them.

Together Dawn and the sheriff jogged after their quarry. Unfortunately, the Mini had reached the other end of the bridge first, and shot out onto the freedom of the cart path. Halprin skidded to a halt, reached out his window, and handed several baggies to a pair of teenage boys in a cart by the path. Then, in a cloud of squealing smoke, their suspect lurched down the path.

Dawn and Scates still followed, but she had to slow slightly to allow the Sheriff to stay with her. Seconds later, however, they'd made it across the bridge as well. Their posse of two hurried toward the twosome of teenagers and their cart, parked to the side of the path. As they approached the youths, the sheriff shouted. "Out, hurry, we're taking your cart."

The kids threw their baggies into the back of the cart and jumped swiftly out. Dawn hopped behind the wheel. Scates, panting heavily, crawled onto the other seat. Dawn spun the cart around and hurried down the path. Scates reached behind the seat and retrieved a clear plastic baggie, full of what they both recognized as marijuana.

Dawn raced down the path, both of them examining the course for any sight of the Mini or Halprin. They had passed three tee boxes when Scates held up his hand.

"Stop," he panted and looked around carefully. "We're almost back to the club house. We missed something. Turn around and go back."

Dawn obeyed, and carefully retraced their trail. At the twelfth tee box, Scates pointed down a side path. "That way."

They hurried down the smaller path, passing the tee box for the eleventh green and reaching a fence. They found a sign with '10th Hole" in big red letters, next to an arrow pointing ahead. They also found a metal gate with a heavy green paint scrape on the left post. Outside the gate was a road.

Scates face showed obvious frustration. "That's the Marina Road." He pointed through the gate. "Let's go. To the right, it's only a couple hundred yards. Hurry."

The cart lurched forward as Dawn stomped the pedal. Scates snatched the radio from his belt with one hand, as he kept his Stetson from blowing off with the other.

"He got out of the golf course. Looks like he's headed toward the Marina. I need a unit to back us up there; the rest of you keep the roads and golf course secure. Radio if you have contact."

Dawn flew through the gate, and almost fell out of the cart as she turned. Scates held on, face grim. Without looking at her, he growled.

"This boy is really startin' to piss me off, but we're close now. Real close."

Chapter 44

Thursday Evening
Nacona, Texas

Dawn's dislike for the game of golf grew stronger, as the battery of their golf cart grew weaker and began to die. Finally, the cart they had commandeered crept weakly onto the marina's main drive and stopped. It wouldn't even roll downhill to the water. They jumped out and began to run. Dawn quickly left Scates behind. He had seemed to be in good shape for an old guy, but he was still and old guy.

Without the whine from the electric motor in her ears, they could now hear angry shouts coming from the large dock ahead. As Dawn approached the marina store at the dock's entrance, she noticed a cluster of people near the rear. They stared over the rail at the water, watching a tall man in black sweats shout angrily as he struggled out of the water and onto the rail. Now within range, several of the spectators reached down and hauled him the rest of the way over.

Shaking off water, he immediately turned to scan the lake.

His search must have been a failure, since seconds later he stomped his feet and began to shout again. He noticed a teenage boy talking into a cell phone. The man rushed over, grabbed the phone, and began to dial.

At that point, a woman in the crowd noticed Dawn and the Sheriff approaching and pointed. She grabbed the man's sleeve, turned him to face the approaching duo, then grabbed the phone and handed it back to the boy. The still dripping man, ignoring Dawn, rushed past her toward the sheriff.

"He stole my boat! He pointed a gun at me and took my boat. Go get him." However, the man found himself shouting at the top of Scates' hat.

A breathless Sheriff Scates leaned forward, his hands on his thighs, and said . . . nothing. He gasped, huffed, tried to speak, and then pointed to Dawn.

Dawn pulled her credentials, "I'm Special Agent Johnson, FBI. This the man?" She pulled up Halprin's DMV photo on her phone.

The man nodded. "That's him."

Dawn looked around; Halprin's car should be here somewhere. It took a few seconds, but she noticed the Mini parked behind a trash dumpster near the boat launch. Dawn grabbed Scates by the arm and dragged him to Halprin's car.

"You secure the vehicle. I'm going after him."

Scates shook his head weakly then leaned on the car. "No way, you . . . stay with . . . the car."

"Look Sheriff," Dawn started but Scates staggered off toward the dock, pushing the man in sweats ahead of him.

He shouted back "Don't leave the car."

She faced a dilemma. She couldn't leave the car; there could be evidence, drugs, or even weapons inside. On the other hand, she was a trained doctor and could begin treatment immediately when Scates had a heart attack from the exertion.

At that moment, the Nacona PD solved that dilemma. A patrol car skidded into the entrance and flew down the drive toward them. Dawn held her creds high and waved as the car fishtailed to a halt. Two officers sprinted toward her.

"Johnson, FBI. This is the suspect's vehicle," she pointed at the larger officer. "You secure the vehicle until a crime scene team gets here."

She looked at the second officer. "He's taken a boat; we need to patrol the perimeter of the lake. Pass that along to the local PD's and Deputies."

Dawn pointed toward the dock, "I'm going with the sheriff."

Before they could respond, Dawn turned and sprinted toward the water. She managed a quick inspection of the dock, then the marina, as she closed the distance. Suddenly, she veered to her left, running straight toward the sign that said, "Jet Ski Rentals."

In less than three minutes, Dawn had donned a life vest, acquired the key, and mounted the most powerful Jet Ski the rental company had. It was a large, red, two-seater with the marina's name and logo on each side. She liked it. Dawn had been a co-ed at the University of Nevada, Las Vegas for three years. During her undergraduate years, she had spent hundreds of hours boating on Lake Mead. The little craft she had hijacked was top of the line, but the boat they chased had a huge head start. She didn't like her chances.

She roared around the marina to the boat slips, where everyone searched frantically for a boat with keys. Dawn jerked the handlebars left and let off the throttle as the Jet Ski settled in next to the dock, where Sheriff Scates and the boat-napping victim stood.

Dawn shouted. "Which way did he go?"

"I'll show you." Scates hobbled toward her.

"No you'll only slow me . . ." Her protest did no good.

The sheriff hopped stiffly into the boat next to Dawn, and made his way across the bow to where Dawn and her jet ski waited. He stopped and felt his chest, then smiled. Dawn realized after a moment that he was checking for body armor, not a bad heart. She remembered that her vest was still in her car, she took it off for her delivery ruse. She smiled also. Drowning was more of a danger than bullets at the moment. It's hard to swim in body armor. He unbuttoned his shirt to check, no body armor. Why wasn't he wearing?

That makes no sense.

"Life jacket!" She shouted to Scates and pointed into the boat. He grabbed a yellow vest and climbed precariously over the rail.

The man in the sweats shouted to Dawn as Scates settled stiffly onto the seat behind her.

"If he didn't go straight across, he'll be adrift. I came in to get gas."

Scates put his hands on her hips. Dawn grabbed them and wrapped his arms around her waist. "Hang on!"

She opened the throttle, and the little craft launched itself toward the deep waters. Dawn caught a glimpse of Scates' life vest fluttering away behind them.

"Great, he's got a death wish," She mumbled to herself.

Scates pointed over her shoulder, directing her toward a thin finger of land to the right. He shouted in her ear, "Around there."

She nodded, and the powerful little craft had them around the thin ribbon of land and into the main body of the lake in seconds. Once there, they spotted a boat, three boats, a lot of boats. A quick inspection revealed about a dozen boats, of all sizes, moving in all directions.

Dawn throttled back, and the Jet Ski settled patiently in the water. She shouted over her shoulder, "Where?"

Scates looked around, and then pointed at a finger of land extending directly toward them from across the lake, probably no more than a mile away. "Head straight across, we'll search the shore for where he landed."

Dawn reached for the throttle, but stopped herself as a large yellow cigar boat glided to rest in front of them. A very fit looking man in his early twenties stood and pointed to their right, south. "He's over there, almost to Shady Grove Road."

"Who?" Scates shouted back.

The man looked at the side of the Jet Ski, frowned, and

asked. "You're not marina services? Some guy's out of gas, I assumed he'd called."

Dawn smiled. "That's right, thanks." She reached for the throttle, and then asked. "What kind of boat?"

"Looks like an old Skeeter!" He shouted helpfully.

What the heck is a Skeeter?

She cranked back on the throttle, throwing up a wall of water as the Jet Ski flew to the right.

She called over her shoulder, "What's a Skeeter?"

She felt Scates' mouth move close to her ear, "Fishing boat. I'll recognize it."

She tried again, "You know where Shady Grove Road is?"

He nodded and pointed about ten degrees to the left of their current course. Dawn adjusted their line and opened the throttle.

Scates had no problem grabbing Dawn's waist at this point; it was Dawn that now had a problem - a problem breathing. She felt his head buried in her back, eyes down. As the little craft skipped along the top of the small chop on the water. It spent as much time in the air as on the water. To his credit, Scates didn't say a word. He simply matched the movements of her body with his. They were making much better speed than Dawn had anticipated.

Several minutes passed, and the southern shoreline of the lake came into view. Dawn slowed to look for their quarry. Scates head came up and he looked over her shoulder, examining the trees and houses ahead. The entire lake front was dotted with houses, most of them on large tracts of land. All had private docks with boats tied up. If he'd made it to shore, they would have to search every one of those boats and houses, and still couldn't be sure if they had the right ones.

But, if he had run out of gas, he should still be in the water. Dawn started her inspection to her right and scanned the water in a circle around them. Scates found him first.

"There!"

He pointed to their left. A nice-looking boat, with high seats used for fishing, was headed away from them and directly toward a stand of trees on the shore. In fact, it was almost there. In the stern of the boat hunched a man, holding something in the water.

Scates recognized what had happened. "He ran out of gas, but he's using the electric trolling motor." He analyzed a second longer. "He's going to beat us."

Dawn opened the throttle, but Scates was right. About thirty seconds before they caught up with Halprin, he beached his fishing boat, hopped off the bow, and disappeared into the trees.

Dawn pulled up a few feet from the shore. She steadied the Jet Ski while Scates hopped off. She was about to hop off as well when he stopped her. She looked down at him in the knee-deep water. He'd lost his shades and squinted desperately in the light.

And Dawn heard alarm bells go off in the doctor side of her brain.

"No," he shouted. "Follow the shore line to the north." He pointed left. "When you get to the other side of this finger dismount. There's a road about thirty yards from the water, he may try and get a car. Go to the road, work your way back but don't let him slip through."

Dawn nodded and looked him in the eyes. Scates looked away quickly, but not quickly enough.

The Sheriff waded quickly away. He pulled his gun, then his radio as he reached the shore. Dawn heard the sheriff radio an update to all the other units, which was drown out by engine noise as she moved her little watercraft into deeper water where she could open it up.

She thought of Scates' eyes, no wonder he wore those glasses all the time. She then remembered Halprin's blue Ford, that they'd found in Karen Allen's yard. And the pill bottle in the Sheriff's car

She needed to sit down and put this all together, but later. Right now, she only had time to catch her suspect.

Chapter 45

Thursday Evening
Nacona, Texas

Minutes later, Dawn had rounded the bare finger of sand and rock pointing into the lake, and beached the Jet Ski on the other side. She quickly began her movement back toward the suspect. She radioed her position to Scates and the other units, and got news in return. Bad news, all the Sheriff's and Police vehicles on this side of the lake had headed to the other side when the madness had begun. Good news, several Sheriff's Department and Nacona PD units were on their way. Kind of bad news, they were at least a half hour out.

The excellent news was that a TV station in Dallas had been monitoring the police frequencies, and had sent a news chopper from Dallas to cover the story. Dawn could see and hear it hovering nearby. The dispatcher at the Sheriff's department informed them that she could relay updates to everyone from the helicopter overhead.

Then came the really bad news. Her phone vibrated with an

incoming text. Dawn wanted to ignore it, but knew she couldn't. She grabbed her phone and read. It was from Pratt, and said simply: "There in 20. WAIT!"

She would wait, as instructed. However, he never said where she should wait. So, Dawn decided to find a place closer to the action to *wait* from. She circled further to her left, into the stand of trees. The trees and brush stood only about ten or fifteen feet tall, but it was thick enough to make visibility almost impossible. If she could reach the road, she could wait there for Halprin to break into the open. She could also turn back any unsuspecting vehicles from approaching the search area and becoming hostages – or targets.

Dawn heard Scates' voice from the radio now back on her belt. "Can they see Halprin?"

After a slight delay for the messages to be relayed, dispatch replied. "Negative, they see you and Agent Johnson. No sign of him."

Dawn hurried, hoping to beat Halprin to the road.

"Movement!" came the dispatcher's voice. "Ahead of you sheriff, to your right. He's heading toward the road."

Dawn ran as fast as possible through the brush and fallen trees and limbs. At first, she tried to move quietly. When that became impossible, she decided that speed was her best option. She listened as she ran, but could not detect any other sounds of evasion or pursuit.

The dispatcher radioed again, "He's just ahead of you!" Dawn assumed the directions were for Scates and not her, but she slowed slightly and gave more attention to the path ahead of her anyway. The brush and trees grew thicker the further she went. Dawn was forced to move with more caution, and even go around obstacles at several locations where the vegetation was too thick to penetrate. Her frustration grew as her pace diminished.

"Suspect's out of the trees. He's in the field along Casino Road." Dispatch was now providing a play by play account. "He's looking around, moving slowly toward the road. He sees the helicopter and is running back toward the trees. Sheriff's out of the trees, there on top of each other. Sheriff's reaching for his . . . "

The air went dead for a few seconds. When the dispatcher came back on her voice was different, frightened, "What do you mean he's down? Who's down, the Sheriff? Get closer, find out."

The faint sound of the helicopter overhead grew louder as it approached. Dawn wondered whether the pilot and photographer realized the danger. What did they think they could do?

Crack!

Gunfire sounded from ahead and the right. She heard the engine of the helicopter roar and looked up. The helicopter flared left and rose several hundred feet higher. The shot was probably a warning for them; at least they'd take it that way.

Dawn ran forward as her phone buzzed again. She read the message from Pratt, "Make for the road, still 15 away." She was way ahead of him.

Seconds later she broke through a line of low bushes and stumbled into the open. Her eyes adjusted to the brighter light as she looked around. To her right, she saw two men. Halprin pointed a gun at Scates, who stood about fifteen feet away from him. Dawn recognized the gun; it was Scates' .44 magnum. Scates had his hands raised high over his head, and was talking intently to Halprin.

The Sheriff moved, and Halprin took aim. Scates bent slowly and pulled something from his right ankle.

Stop! What are you doing? Dawn couldn't believe what she saw. Scates had just pulled his backup weapon. She expected gunfire any second.

Dawn blinked to clear her head, and then examined the scene. She was in clear view of the pair, and would be spotted immediately if Halprin decided to look around. She knew she needed to help Scates, but couldn't afford to startle Halprin while he held a gun on the Sheriff. Halprin had already fired at the news chopper, no telling what he would do to the sheriff if he felt threatened.

Dawn drew her weapon, crept back into the trees, and made way back around to where the standoff awaited her. She forced herself to move carefully, which meant slowly. It took several seconds for her to get close enough to hear their conversation.

Scates said, "We have all the evidence we need, Frankie, they are going to put a needle in your arm and you're going to shudder, shrivel up, and die. I've made sure of it."

"No! For what? They can't, they won't. Drop that gun, Sheriff."

Dawn slowed even more, moving silently forward.

"No. I'm going to grab you, beat the living shit out of your sorry ass, then gloat all the way to your execution. Better still, I may just shoot you dead right here."

Dawn shouted in her mind. *Order him to drop his gun!* Why wasn't the Sheriff trying to get him to surrender?

Scates almost whispered. "I've wanted to shoot you for years."

It was Halprin that screamed, in panic. "Drop that gun. Not another step closer!"

Dawn looked through the trees; Scates had actually started to move forward.

"What are you going to do about it?" Scates mocked.

Does Scates have a death wish? Maybe he wants an excuse to kill Halprin. Dawn thought that was the only thing that made sense. Halprin had killed Scates' wife, and now that he had the chance, the sheriff wanted revenge.

Dawn stood only a few feet from the sheriff, who inexplicably took another, menacing step forward, gun pointed into the air.

The sheriff growled, "There, what are you going to do about it, you little coward?"

Panic on his face, Halprin looked around then raised the gun and pointed it directly at Scates' chest. At that range, and without a vest for protection, it may work out. The magnum rounds would make a big hole, but from that close they wouldn't have time to expand and make a massive hole. Plus if they hit only flesh, they would pass through without doing major damage.

If they hit bone? Yeah, that would be a problem. Scates would be killed.

Dawn moved closer and stepped to the edge of the brush, as Scates took another step toward Halprin. Halprin tensed, clearly about to fire.

Dawn took two quick steps forward and shouted, "FBI. Drop it, now!"

Halprin spun toward her and fired, two shots, from reflex, toward the sound of her voice. The first shot hit, she felt her left arm twist back and her balance shift. But her arm was still there, flesh wound. The second shot from a double-action pistol is never accurate, and she had no idea where the second round went.

She kept her focus on the suspect and saw that her first shot was true, and fatal. A fountain of red erupted from his chest. A heart shot. Dawn waited and watched.

But he didn't go down. His brain hadn't stopped yet. From reflex, he pulled back the hammer and fired once more.

Now Scates fired, but Halprin had collapsed.

Dawn felt it, another round, in her abdomen. It hurt like hell. Her whole lower body felt the insult of trauma and pain as she realized she was staggering backward. Impossible to project the bullet's path through her organs.

Inferno and abuse everywhere. Breath gone, vision going.

Dawn doubled over at the waist, struggled to take in just one more pathetic breath, and then slumped to her knees. Finally, she fell face-first into the brush; she had stumbled back into the trees. Halprin was probably dead. She wondered if her wound would make them hell mates.

＊ ＊ ＊ ＊ ＊

Light!

Dawn didn't exactly wake up, but she was able to turn her mind inward and take inventory of her condition.

She was alive.

She was bleeding, but not an arterial flow.

And it hurt. It really hurt. Again!

Dawn blinked as the world grew darker again. It took several seconds to realize that it was Scates leaning over her, blocking the sun.

"How bad?" he said mostly to himself.

He looked her over quickly, and then his eyes met hers. She could clearly see the yellow coloration. Even semi-conscious she knew it. She had been right.

"You heard it all, didn't you Johnson?"

Dawn felt herself blacking out. Real darkness now, not just a shadow.

Scates shook his head. "I want you to know I'm sorry."

Dawn passed out as Scates reached for her throat.

Chapter 46

Thursday Evening
Nacona, Texas

Dawn became aware of the brush grating against the side of her face. She must have passed out briefly from the shock; her mind was now a fog of confusion. She had been shot, but she could already tell it wasn't as bad as last time.

Scates!

He knelt beside her, speaking urgently into his radio.

What just happened, what is this all about?

He noticed her open eyes, and stopped transmitting. He reached again for her throat, his fingers pressing gently over her carotid artery.

He's not going to kill me?

Without smiling, he spoke. "You're the doc, but the pulse is still strong. I think you'll make it."

The roar and bluster of a landing helicopter made it impossible for her to hear anything. She felt herself slipping into shock, so she lay still and attempted to give herself a quick mental exam.

Fingers and toes, all there, all still working. No spine damage. Right arm, check. Left arm, damn! That hurts. But it's still there, so no bone impact.

Problem on the left side, but both her legs seemed to be okay. She tried to move, but stopped when the waves of pain from her abdomen reminded her she'd been shot. The blinding pain convinced her that staying quiet and still constituted her best option. The roar of the helicopter grew thunderous, stayed constant, then diminished as a dark blur rose in the road in front of her and disappeared. It had taken off, and she could hear again.

Scates looked toward the road. "Your boss just arrived. Life Flight's right behind."

Dawn nodded.

Scates jaundiced eyes met hers. "You figured it out, didn't you?"

Dawn winced with the building pain, but stared silently back. *No, but I will.*

"Over here!" Scates shouted and raised his hand.

Seconds later, she heard the sound of running feet. Scates stood, and SAC Pratt rushed into view, stopping in front of her. He knelt urgently and inspected her body, quickly and expertly. He held a cloth of some type over her abdomen, the second but more critical wound.

"Hang in there, Johnson." Pratt ordered.

The pain continued to build, and she found it difficult to focus. She did hear a second chopper landing, which she hoped was good.

Pratt stood and pointed back toward the road. "Get a stretcher over here."

Dawn realized -- what? What should she tell him, what did she know? She realized her head was getting light and thinking became almost impossible.

"Halprin?" she asked.

"Dead." Scates answered. She hadn't wanted to kill Halprin,

but she hadn't been trying to just wound him either.

Two men ran toward her, carrying a basket or board between them. Pratt bent down, smiled and shouted. "You'll make it."

The wounds hurt more with each breath, and her own thoughts became more difficult to follow. The two men set a board down next to her. One examined her back while the other attached a cuff to her arm. They talked, but Dawn couldn't understand what they were saying, she couldn't really hear anything at all now.

She felt hands grasp her shoulders and legs. They began to roll her toward the stretcher.

Pratt's face hovered close, "It's going to be okay."

PAIN!

Chapter 47

Saturday Morning
Gainesville, Texas

Her mind had rebooted. That, or she had been dropped into the thick, inky void of a thousand foot well. The only feature in this world of enveloping darkness became a single point of light. A hint of being in the black.

She spoke. Probably. Maybe. Dawn, her name was Dawn. Maybe she had just tried to speak, but found no recollection of any words forming on her lips, or even on her mind.

A voice echoed in the dark, a voice she felt she should know. The voice disappeared. The darkness reclaimed her.

*****

The voice came back, but the darkness never left. But it was a different darkness. She lay in the darkness of night—or sleep, not the darkness of a black hole, lost in some distant corner of the universe. She wondered if she would die, if they would get her to the hospital in time.

The voice came yet again, closer, reassuring. He, a he voice, was still here. Still promising her she would be alright.

Not her father's voice, so maybe she wasn't dead.

Pratt said encouragingly, "The initial surgery went well. You are going to be fine."

Dawn fought to open her eyes. The field where she'd been shot was gone. The helicopter had vanished; the beating no longer assaulted her ears. Her eyes opened, and light seared burning stakes of flame into her brain. She winced them shut, but the after image of a face still loomed close, tilting to the side as it examined hers.

The voice cried out. "Nurse!"

Pratt was there.

Dawn blinked several times, and began to embrace the wakefulness. She blinked again, and her eyes stayed open. She turned her head.

She lay in a bed, a hospital bed. The piercing light made her look away again, and Pratt strode over and turned out the lamp.

Dawn tried to speak. She had a thousand questions, none of which she could remember at the moment.

Thankfully, Pratt began. "It's Monday. You were shot twice, neither striking a major artery or organ, though they are still assessing some possible damage caused by the round passing through your lower abdomen. They completed a second surgery last night, and feel very confident you will enjoy a full and speedy recovery."

Her mind still operated, barely, through the post-anesthetic fog, but a fog that had begun to lift. "Scates?"

"Fine, no significant wounds or injuries." He stood and thrust his hands into his pockets. "You lucked out, Agent Johnson. Again."

Luck had nothing to . . . She stopped herself. "Yes, sir."

Maybe luck had a great deal to do with it.

He sat near the right side of her bed. "The only thing you need to concern yourself with at the moment is recovering. The sheriff and the others in the task force have continued with the investigation, and believe that Halprin acted alone. From their perspective, the case will soon be closed. However, there are a couple of things that don't make sense to me; I would like to get your opinions when you're able."

Dawn looked at Pratt, whose face remained slightly out of focus, and far away.

She thought carefully, and with difficulty, to form the question properly. "When will I return to duty? And where?"

"The doctors don't anticipate a lengthy hospitalization, a few weeks. There will probably follow six weeks to two months of convalescence at home—and yes, you can remain at Balzac's apartment for the time being. After that, you'll report for duty at the Frisco Regional Office."

He smiled, but Dawn could not decide whether he looked happy or simply reconciled to the inevitable. "You did an admirable job. Sheriff Scates assures me you made a significant contribution to the timely and successful resolution of this case. He even sent a formal, and very eloquent letter of commendation to the Director in Washington. I now have no reason to keep you out of the field."

Dawn smiled, "Thank you, sir."

He furrowed his brow, "Let me rephrase that, I still feel I have excellent reason for wanting you out of the field, but your performance to date gives me no justification for doing that. I hope you understand the difference, and that I will still try to have you assigned to a posting that will make full use of all of your talents and training."

Dawn's faculties had returned enough for her to recognize that this was progress, and constituted a major concession for Pratt. It was enough for the moment.

"You won't regret it."

Now he frowned. "You told me that before, and I did. I already regret it this time, also. The only question is, how long will it take me to find out why?"

His phone rang; He looked at the display and spoke to her

quickly. "Get well, Johnson. I'll check in as often as I can."

He put the phone to his ear. "Yes, sir. Everything is fine, and . . ."

The door closed behind him. Yes indeed, everything was fine. *No, it wasn't.*

Pratt may have questions, but Dawn had bigger ones! She just couldn't remember what they were. If they both had the same questions, then she needed to have answered before he showed up. She fought to clear her mind, but realized the pain control regimen and fatigue would make that difficult for now.

What am I missing?

Chapter 48

Tuesday Morning
Gainesville, Texas

Dawn felt the throbbing grow, dancing flames burning into her side. She enjoyed the lucidity of being out of post-surgery "pain management," and very shortly she would be totally free from the temporary refuge of opiate induced relief.

It had only been two days since the doctors at North Texas Med Center patched her up. She'd inspected their work, and then appreciated their work. She also appreciated other good news from her brush with death, news which almost outweighed the bad.

She had only been shot twice, less than last time. Progress.

One bullet was a "through-and-through," meaning it passed completely through her body leaving no bullet or bullet droppings which needed to be cleaned out. More progress.

Go to the head of the class progress! No important body parts had been harmed in the making of her brush with death. She would be up in a couple of weeks and ready to go back to work a few weeks after.

Some bad news. The second bullet had barely chipped her pelvis. While there was nothing life threatening, it would be a while before they would know of any long-term effects of the bone fragments.

More bad news. Despite Pratt's assurances, she wasn't absolutely sure she had a job to go back to.

SAC Pratt had sent flowers and a card. The flowers cheered her up -- the card, not so much. Pratt wrote simply. "Most Agents go their entire careers without being shot. You can't even fully recover from one set of bullet wounds before being almost killed by the next. The message should be clear, even to you. I've secured tentative approval for your transfer to Quantico. The official request needs only your signature."

Well, more of a note than just a card. And she knew he was right.

She also knew she wouldn't sign the papers. Besides her desire to stay and find out what happened to her father, there was this Justice thing. She did not like what came into view as her mind cleared. She needed to find out more before she talked with anyone about it.

The door opened and a new, tough looking nurse pushed a wheelchair to her bed. Dawn wasn't happy to see the wheelchair, because that meant she wasn't getting a painkiller. The nurse hefted Dawn out of bed and into the chair.

Nurse Attila rolled the shiny metal IV tree to Dawn's side and growled. "Grab it."

Dawn grabbed it, and they accelerated out the door. Instead of turning right to the x-ray room and labs, they turned left toward the elevators. The nurse swung the chair around so they could back in when the door opened and pressed the up arrow.

Dawn looked over her shoulder at the Nurse. "Where are we going?"

Evil eyes glared silently down. When the doors opened, they backed roughly inside. Dawn saw her press the top button, "R." They were going to the roof.

They ascended the two floors. When the door opened, the nurse pushed Dawn forward, through the swinging metal door at the end of the short hallway in front of them. She found the helipad in front of her now.

The sun blinded Dawn. By the time she could see again, she realized her caretaker had disappeared. Something was wrong, but the sunlight and fresher breeze made it impossible for her to worry too much.

"You are one tough young woman." The unmistakable voice came from behind her.

The tranquil moment evaporated. The time to worry had officially arrived.

Sheriff Scates moved forward and stopped at the low wall to her left. He stared at a small herd of longhorn cattle grazing in a field behind the parking area. After a moment, he dropped the overnight bag in his right hand, and without turning asked, "Did you know there's only one word in the English language whose plural form doesn't have one single letter in common with the singular form?"

He seemed to be waiting for a reply, so Dawn pushed on the wheels and forced the chair forward. She spun to face him. "You brought me up here to play Scrabble?"

Without looking down he said, "And you are feisty one, and remarkably smart as well. I actually thought you might know this one. Kine, it's an old word for cows. Nobody believes it at first, and most of the time you have a hard time convincing people it's true. Even after they read it in the dictionary." Scates looked down and smiled sympathetically. "You may have that problem, too. About people believing you."

He smiled amicably. "I need to find out how much you know. One can never be too careful, you know."

Know? How about barely suspect? She thought.

Then came the final burst of understanding, clarity, confirmation – images and facts swirling like a vortex in her mind. Scates was never available when the murders were actually happening. Scates knew too much, right from the start, though he tried to hide it. All the little doubts, questions and inconsistencies confirmed themselves into one brilliant image.

And there is something else about Scates, something obvious that she was still missing.

With unexpected disappointment, she looked up at Sheriff Bubba Scates. "You're right; I would have a hard time convincing people it's true."

"Well I'll be, you didn't know for sure, did you? But, you would have figured out the details eventually. That's why I wanted you to know now, so we could have this little chat before you talked with anyone else."

Dawn couldn't disguise the betrayal in her voice. "You killed them. You killed them all."

"Not exactly true. You killed the one I wanted most. I feel just a little cheated, actually, but I can live with the way it all ended up." He shrugged, "Except for you getting shot, of course. I never wanted that, but you move too dang quick. I didn't have time to resolve things on my own. I am sorry you got hurt."

Dawn stared, and then shook her head in astonishment. "How? Why?"

Scates shifted his weight and winced in pain. He smiled at Dawn again and explained.

"The *why* is easier, so let's start there. He killed my wife, my Becky girl, and she was actually his third victim. His truck crushed her little car like it was an old empty beer can. Frank Anthony Halprin's family is big in state politics. When Halprin got off with pleadin' guilty to only leaving the scene of an accident and drunk driving, and then only got six months for it, I realized my whole career had been a sham – a lie. I spent decades working to enforce the law, never givin' a thought about justice."

He paused and looked away, blinking rapidly from tears and not the sun. Pained eyes looked back down at Dawn.

"Becky. My dear, dear Becky girl. We were sweethearts since the seventh grade. Becky was the only girl I ever dated, ever kissed – ever wanted."

He kept his gaze on Dawn, but had to wipe a swelling river

of tears from his eyes before going on.

"Ya' know? It's not that she died, so much as that she suffered. She sat there in her car for hours, crushed and broken. In pain and alone, before she finally . . ."

He stopped and turned away. Dawn felt bad, but his next words were devastating.

"I never got to say good-bye."

The pain searing through Dawn's heart made the bullet wounds a forgotten irritation.

"Daddy!" It escaped her lips in a plaintive whisper. She couldn't hold it back the ache.

I never got to say good-bye, either.

Her greatest regret. Her greatest pain. She wanted to tell her father how much she loved him, just one more time. But somebody took that from her. She could never say *I'm sorry* for doing that to him.

She regained her composure and looked up, only to find Sheriff Scates watching her with intense interest. She forced herself to meet his gaze.

The Sheriff nodded, staring intently into her eyes. "I thought as much."

Dawn couldn't speak, so Scates continued. "I'm not going to go into detail on the how, for a number of reasons."

"But in a nutshell, Halprin's slap on the wrist sentence had one benefit. Instead of being sent to a state prison, he stayed in the county lockup. He was so damn smug, braggin' about getting a six month paid vacation. One night at dinner, me eating alone at what had been our favorite restaurant, I realized that he had to die. I came up with the perfect plan, too."

Sheriff Scates smiled, obviously pleased with his strategy.

"We had a mess of wild fires last year, and my solution became obvious. I sent work details to the Red River Wildlife Refuge, supposedly to help build fire breaks. My initial plan was to have Mr. Halprin perish in a failed escape attempt and be burned to death. Get him ready for the fires of hell, you see."

Sheriff Scates stood emotionless now. He continued to

explain the process with an almost bored expression on his face, like he was telling a rookie deputy how to change the batteries in his flashlight.

"Then I thought about stickin' him in the lion enclosure, let him die helpless and slow. Then I found out about the African Painted Dogs. Dogs seemed more appropriate."

He stopped and looked away, lost in thought as he pictured the event. Then he blinked twice and turned back to Dawn.

"I was about to do it when poor Suri Kenneman got killed, and that bastard Oltman got off scot free. I almost felt worse about Suri than I did about my wife. I realized there were other families who deserved justice. Right then I decided to *be* Justice. Execute some of the local scum that the justice system failed to punish. I could frame Frank Halprin for the murders, and have him make his long-overdue appointment with the executioner's needle."

Dawn realized that Sheriff Scates had probably manipulated every part of Halprin's life to make this happen.

"You set it up? All of it?"

"Yes, ma'am. I got him a cell mate who could teach him enough to manage all the technical stuff, and then be willing to testify against him later. I got him his job, so he could build his technical skills and there would always be gaps in his schedule and not give him a regular alibi. I did it all. The wildlife preserve, the cat hair, the forensics, everything. I think I did a damn fine job."

An amazing job, actually, Dawn realized. She also realized she was alone with a killer, vulnerable, with nothing but a thin blue hospital robe and shower shoes for protection.

Sheriff Scates had it all worked out. He'd had six months to plan and prepare, so Dawn shouldn't be surprised he was now ready for her. She still wondered how a man who'd spent half a century upholding the law could turn so completely away from it.

"I'm impressed. You almost got away with it."

"I did get away with it."

"I know the truth."

He smiled, this time with more than a hint of cynicism. "Agent Johnson, I believe you'll find that truth has no more importance in a court of law than justice does. What you can ultimately make twelve people believe is all that matters. There is absolutely no physical evidence linking me with the crimes, and quite a bit that proves our boy Halprin's the killer."

Dawn remembered Halprin's car. It didn't look like it had been driven in weeks. Yet, that car fit the description from the Cooper murder.

"How did you get his car to Gainesville?"

"Wasn't his car. I found an old Ford with the exact same body style, painted it myself to match."

Dawn wondered if there was a record of the license plate numbers of the different vehicles.

Scates seemed to follow the same line of reasoning. "I never registered my copy-car. The plates it had came off an old hearse out of Collin County. It's already been junked, crushed into a little cube of metal, and shipped for recycling. Hell, it may already be on its way back as a can of hot dog chili by now. I had plenty of time to prepare. It was all I lived for since I decided to do it."

"What are you going to do with me? I killed him, and not you. Do you feel cheated?"

"No! I was never going to kill him. You still don't see it, do you?" He wearily shook his head. "The plan was for him to kill me in, front of witnesses."

Dawn opened her mouth in shock. This didn't make sense. She looked up at Scates in total confusion. "No, I don't understand."

"I couldn't risk his connections getting him off, like before. Him gunnin' me down like a dog, in living color on the five o'clock news, would make sure justice was done. With a slam-dunk case of killing a cop, Halprin's part in the other murders would have just been glazed over. I wanted him to kill me, not for me to kill him. I wanted him strapped to a gurney and juiced up like the animal he is. Was."

"But you'd be dead."

"I'm already dead, just workin' out the painful details. I'm not just here to visit you. I'm checking in."

Scates has cancer.

He announced matter-of-factly. "Pancreatic cancer."

Of course! Two-stage painkillers, sudden weight loss, jaundice, and more. Dawn recognized the indicators now, but hadn't seen any of the treatment side effects. She found this curious. Pancreatic cancer treatment would have unmistakable consequences.

The sheriff saw her confusion. "No real treatment up 'till now, had to stay on the job. That's one of the reasons I hurried to finish, I didn't think I could pretend any longer, and I really wanted the pain to be over. I only took something for the pain. Actually had Halprin getting' it for me. I start chemo tomorrow, but I'm at Stage 4. So, even if someone believes you and starts to investigate, I'd be dead before the trial. Him killing me would have spared me a lot of pain and unpleasantness."

Dawn tried to process a sudden flood of facts and emotion. She discovered that the federal agent and the doctor inside of her had very different opinions on how to proceed. Both, however, did agree on one thing.

"But you murdered those people. You used your position of authority to pursue a personal vendetta."

"Executed," he cocked his head slightly and smirked. "And I'm not sure you should be lecturing me on pursuing a personal agenda."

Dawn hesitated; made sure she had her mind and emotions under control, and then asked. "What are you talking about?"

"I heard about your papa."

"Be careful what you say about my father, you redneck . . ." With great effort, she controlled herself and simply glared.

"Why?" Scates laughed, but there was no humor in it. "There is nothing you can do to me that's worse than what my body is doing to itself. I met your daddy; I think I mentioned that. Didn't particularly care for him. I knew your grandpa better, and I actually hated him. You, I almost like. I must going soft in my old age. The FBI can be a royal pain, ya' know."

He grimaced and bent over in pain, breathing in short, shallow gasps. After a moment, he straightened up slightly and whispered.

"Know what, sweet cheeks, you really complicated things for this redneck, country fried, old Texas Sheriff. I'm supposed to be dead at this point. Now that I'm not, and I may want to take my time joining Becky. So why don't we make us a deal, you and I."

Dawn wondered what he could possibly offer, so decided not to answer.

The Sheriff continued on. "We keep the fact I'm not such a backwoods Neanderthal as I want ya'll city folk to believe, and a serial killer of course, between just us. In return, I'll try and help you find out what happened to your daddy while he was undercover. That is why you joined the feds, ain't it?"

Dawn felt the blood rush to her head, a rising volcano of anger burning at her mind. What could this liar, this murderer, possibly know about her father?

Scates saw the fire in her eyes. "You need to think about this, seriously consider what I'm offering. The FBI doesn't live in a vacuum; though that's the way they act most of the time. They have to coordinate with other agencies, federal and local. The FBI has this locked down tighter than a virgin's . . . anyway, you won't get a scrap of information from within your own agency. But there were others involved in your father's last assignment. The little I know came from a former DEA guy. I can find out who, what, and how to ask."

She was still angry, but now curious as well. She'd wondered where to go next in her search.

"You will help me find out what happened to my father?"

"That's not what I said. I can't promise a damned thing. I may die tomorrow. I may be too sick to do anything but puke my blood and guts out, and then die the day-after tomorrow. But, I found my justice; I'm willing to spend some of my remaining time helping you find yours."

Dawn examined Sheriff Bubba Scates again. She realized that

the stooped, fragile man before her was no longer the take-charge law enforcement icon she'd met only days before. She also realized that he was indeed dying. She knew he was right. He would never be investigated, much less charged and tried.

She also understood that he had access to important people, from every law enforcement agency operating in the State of Texas. Dawn had a choice. She could make a case against the sheriff, though he would probably be dead before even being charged. Or use him until he died.

Justice versus law? Truth versus legal? She'd sworn an oath to uphold the law, but that oath was based on a lie. Dawn lived for her father now, for justice.

She wheeled closer and examined Scates, and then realized she could be examining her future-self if she continued with her sham of a career.

Finally, she whispered, almost to herself. "You're a murderer. I just don't know."

"You'll need to decide, and I'll accept whatever decision you make." He wasn't going to beg, or even ask her to lie for him. "In fact, if you think I'm still a danger, you have to turn me in."

And even if I don't think you're a danger, will that be the reason I don't turn you in?

Things were not supposed to be that complicated, and she really needed a pain pill. "Did you know Frank Anthony hadn't driven his car in weeks? It probably doesn't even run."

Scates pursed his lips and nodded. "I'll get it towed. A month in my impound should eliminate any questions."

Dawn wheeled herself to the door back into the hospital, yanked it open, and then paused to call over her shoulder. "I would have made a pretty good doctor. Maybe I'll follow your case?"

"I'd appreciate that." He continued in an unusually subdued voice. "What are you going to do about me?"

"Sheriff, I just don't know." Dawn moved forward and let the door close behind her.

Chapter 49

Thursday Morning
Gainesville, Texas

Dawn knew what was about to happen, she'd endured this dream almost every night since – she found out. She also knew, to the depths of her being, that she could do nothing to stop it.

She watched, a petrified observer, as her dream self put the phone to her ear. It rang; she had called him, again. The throbbing of her panicked pulse pounded a frantic counter beat to that beckoning ring. She wanted to make it stop, to hang up her phone. She struggled against her trance to break free, but the dream held her.

Like it did almost every night.

At some deeper, darker level Dawn realized that she hated sleep, now more than ever. She almost missed the industrial-strength, post-surgery pain drugs. They messed with her mind, but they also put her so far under that the ghosts couldn't haunt her.

The dream-phone rang again, and then he answered in his

dream voice. "Is that you, baby?"

"Yes, Daddy, I need to cancel our vacation." Her voice seemed clear, and cold, like the other times.

"I'm sorry to hear that. Maybe I will take an assignment back in Dallas, then."

No! The real Dawn shouted to the dream Dawn. *Don't let him go.*

But dream Dawn nodded, oblivious. This was where his voice began to fade, and the dream became darker. "I'll be gone for a while, out of touch. You can't call, so . . ."

The line went dead, she never said good-bye.

And he never says good-bye, either.

Dawn felt the pain and panic grow. She knew what came next. The other call, the new voice telling her . . .

"Dawn, you need to wake up."

That's not right.

"You have a visitor." That voice seemed familiar, from the real place.

"Agent Johnson, I need you to wake up." A new voice.

Her mind flared. Pratt! No question about where that voice came from.

From Hell.

"Yes, sir." She managed to open her eyes. One of them at least.

"That will be all for now," Pratt commanded the nurse softly.

Eyes now open, and mind toying with consciousness, Dawn watched as her nurse started to mumble in protest. The coalescing female figure in blue scrubs looked at Pratt and stopped. She closed her mouth angrily, spun toward the door, and walked out.

Dawn turned her attention to Pratt. His black face blended mysteriously into the darkness of the room, like camouflage on a night patrol. She noticed he carried a thick manila folder under one arm, and held a vase of flowers in the other. He set the flowers on the end table and dropped the folder on the bed next to her leg.

He leaned closer. "We need to talk. Do you want the light on, or should I open the drapes?"

Dawn needed to wake up, immediately. "Both, sir."

Pratt walked to the window. He threw open the curtains and drew the blinds up, opening the window to a green carpet of tree tops and clouds. He crossed to the door and turned on the overhead lights, which flickered to life faster than she did. She fumbled for the bed's remote, and painfully raised the back. Now sitting almost straight in bed she blinked rapidly, hoping the exertion of her eyelids would also pump thought-giving blood to her brain.

He crossed back and examined her eyes, as if he were reading her thoughts. "How are you feeling, Johnson?"

"I . . ."

What am I wearing? Dawn had no idea as to what she had on.

She shifted her position slightly in bed and gave herself a quick scan. Damn, she wore her inanely flowered hospital gown. But, excellent! She had on her underwear. Modesty over fashion, every time.

She went on, "I'm feeling fine, though my surgeon is concerned about possible bone and bullet fragments, which may have been dispersed through my lower abdominal cavity. They think they've located all of the lacerations, but they are monitoring it. Nothing critical, though."

Pratt nodded. "I've talked to your surgeon. He's not as upbeat about that as you seem to be. Are you awake and alert? Can we go over a few things?"

She adjusted her position again, wincing in spite of her efforts to fight the pain. She also resisted the impulse to pull her blanket up to her neck. Pratt, however, kept his eyes fixed on hers. A gentleman.

"Yes sir, I'm fine."

"First some administrative details." He gestured to her computer bag, which she now noticed resting on a side chair near the door. "I brought your computer. In the inside pocket is an envelope containing the information you'll need for remote access to Sentinel."

Yes! Her mind celebrated while her face remained impassive. The FBI's new case and intelligence management system, Sentinel, was only a couple of years old, and it seemed to work. Now she could start doing her own research. Relief and excitement worked on her pain better than Darvon used to.

Not really.

Strange, she thought she'd be more excited about Sentinel access than this. Now she could investigate her father's case directly, if discreetly.

Pratt went on. "It looks like Agent Balzac will be back before you're released. I have a couple of agents dropping by to pick up mail and check on things."

"Thank you."

"No problem. And we got a call from Classic Replicas of Richardson. They've finished unpacking it from storage. It appears that your other car really is a Ferrari. It's ready for you to pick up."

The car may be ready for me, but am I ready for it?

Dawn simply nodded back at her boss.

Pratt picked up the folder. "And now for this." He opened the folder and leafed brusquely through the pages.

Dawn panicked. Maybe she was becoming psychic too, but she did not want to go through what was coming. She looked at the flowers.

"Are those for me? Thank you sir."

He looked at the end table. "I had them prepared, especially for you."

Dawn frowned. Carnations. Red and white carnations. It looked like they were arranged in rows. She knew about red carnations, so why did he pick them?

She frowned, "An interesting arrangement."

Pratt smiled, "I think so. Take a look." He picked up the flowers and held them low, tilted toward her. She now saw the flowers from above. She saw the red center, changing to alternating white and red rings toward the edge. The flowers were arranged to look like a target. He'd brought her bulls-eye flower arrangement.

She didn't allow the smile to escape her lips, but it tried. *That's actually clever, and funny.*

Pratt continued. "The flowers are blood-red carnations. The reason for that should be self-explanatory. White carnations symbolize luck. I made sure the white carnations are much older than the red ones. As they wither, you need to remember that you luck can fade as well, at any time, leaving nothing but . . ."

Not funny after all.

Dawn needed to change the conversation, and the mood. She could see that Pratt had a copy of the report she'd finished and transmitted last night. She'd worked very hard, and included as much information and detail as possible, and only as much of the truth as was essential.

"I see you got my report."

Pratt nodded and continued to read. He stopped at one page, read a few lines, and then looked up. "Are you a Lewis Carroll fan?"

Dawn paused, "Sir?"

"Have you ever read *Jabberwocky*?"

"What? Yes, I think so. Why?"

"Jabberwocky is a work of fiction; it's called a nonsense story, never meant to be understood. I have to assume that was your goal with this report."

"No, sir. Why would you say that?"

"Because, Johnson, you submitted a fifty-two page report, an impressive if not heroic amount of typing for barely four days of work, chucked full of facts that lead nowhere and say nothing. It's like a medical journal in places. You spent twice as much time explaining the yellow tint in Scates' eyes as you did describing the details of his confrontation with Halprin."

Think fast, Johnson.

"Sir. Video of the confrontation between Halprin and Sheriff Scates was recorded by a news crew, and . . ."

"Video only, you and Scates are the only ones who know

what was actually said."

"I didn't hear most of it, either, and the lack of clear context makes it impossible for me to speculate as to the complete nature of their interchange."

Pratt stared incredulously, and then shook his head. "Heaven spare me from a doctor with a law degree. I'll never get a straight answer. Let me ask a simple question. Please give me a simple answer. There's something about Scates' involvement that bothers me. Do you have any questions or doubts regarding the nature of the Sheriff's involvement in, or investigation of this case?"

You have to decide, Johnson. Now or never. Turn him in, or let a serial killer — die a horrible death of natural causes.

"Absolutely, sir," Whatever she told him, it had to be the truth. "For a number of reasons. Scates is absolutely guilty." *The truth, Johnson.* "Of, flagrant civil rights violations in the Halprin case. Illegal wiretaps and surveillance. For long periods of time, he was derelict in his duties, which I believe was a result of the on-duty use, if not abuse, of prescription painkillers. These drugs may have impaired his performance of duty. He violated ethics and proprietary norms in his treatment of myself and others."

She caught her breath. "He can be a truly unpleasant man to deal with, and an incredibly unprofessional law enforcement officer at times."

Pratt waited, and finally asked. "That's it? Nothing else?"

You're not going to turn him in, are you Dawn?

"Nothing that you don't already know or suspect, sir?"

Pratt's eyes narrowed to slits. His gaze bore into her mind, and heart.

What does he know?

He finally relaxed, a little. "What am I going to do with you, Johnson?"

"I'm sure you'll think of something."

"I already have. I just can't get it approved, and you won't sign the transfer request. However, I'm sure I can come up with something to keep you busy while you recuperate."

"That would be nice."

He smiled, warmly. It took her by complete surprise. "Nice will not be my goal." He pointed at the folder. "I've included copies of a couple of dozen reports that have been properly completed and submitted. Read through them, all of them, and then rewrite yours correctly.

He started to leave, but turned at the door. "How is Scates?"

"He's dying. His Gleason Score is eight, and in Stage . . ."

"Quantico, Johnson, you belong in Quantico." Pratt slipped silently out the door.

I can live with that, sir, as soon as I find out what happened to my dad. And kill the SOB's that did it.

Other books by
Rickard B DeMille

HELLFIRE

A Debut Dagger Award Finalist.

"Packed with action, emotion and suspense." --Crime Writers Association

US Marine Travis Deacon must interrupt his vacation to Wales to stop an International Terrorist from devastating life in Britain forever.